NW

Emily Hendrickson lives in Reno, Nevada, with her husband. In addition to her many Regency romances, such as *The Dashing Miss Fairchild* and *Lady Sara's Scheme*, she has also written a Regency reference book. She is the recipient of the Colorado Romance Writer's 1997 Award of Excellence for this novel.

THE DEBONAIR DUKE

Lady Pamela Taylor's dull existence ceases when she receives a sapphire necklace with a mysterious note, initialled J.R. Who sent the fabulous gems and what is required from her in return? She turns to the Duke of Wexford, whose reputation for solving mysteries is impressive. A romantic Russian prince, a seductive French *comte* and an English lord, all with the same initials, suddenly form an attentive and flattering court. Had one of these sent the mysterious gems? As Pamela and the Duke plunge into their dangerous hunt, she discovers her heart longs for him . . . but does Wexford care for her?

EMILY HENDRICKSON

THE DEBONAIR DUKE

Complete and Unabridged

ULVERSCROFT
Leicester

First published in Great Britain in 2009 by
Robert Hale Limited
London

First Large Print Edition
published 2010
by arrangement with
Robert Hale Limited
London

British Library CIP Data

Hendrickson, Emily.
The debonair duke.
1. Love stories.
2. Large type books.
I. Title
813.5'4–dc22

ISBN 978–1–44480–442–3

Published by
F. A. Thorpe (Publishing)
Anstey, Leicestershire
Set by Words & Graphics Ltd.
Anstey, Leicestershire
Printed and bound in Great Britain by
T. J. International Ltd., Padstow, Cornwall

This book is printed on acid-free paper

Fondly dedicated to Elane Osborn
for help with things mysterious
and to Patricia Wing
for a pair of discerning eyes

1

'What is this world coming to, I ask you!' his lordship, the Earl of Gresham, muttered to the room in general.

His wife, Sophia, quite accustomed to these outbursts while her husband perused the morning papers, said nothing in reply.

'What is the trouble today, Papa?' Lady Pamela Taylor, his slightly indulged only daughter, inquired. Her pretty blue eyes grew troubled at his words.

That she truly wished to know her father's thoughts on contemporary happenings was dismissed by him as utter nonsense. Everyone knew that women had smaller brains, hence one did not bother their little minds with facts and unnecessary information.

' 'Tis a matter of another robbery here in London. There have been a great number as of late. I'm pleased your jewels are safe, m'dear,' he added to his wife. 'No thief shall ever find the way into our strongbox. Clever idea, that chap had.' He raised his paper again, cutting off additional comments.

'Who had what idea, Papa?' Pamela persisted. She was rather tired of being treated as though she hadn't two thoughts to rub together in her brain.

'Happened to discuss the problem of all these robberies with the young duke — the Duke of Wexford, you know. He gave me a capital idea for safeguarding our valuables. No outsider knows a thing because he helped me install the box himself. Clever chap.' Her father gave every evidence of being enormously pleased with himself and the duke.

Pamela suspected the box — whatever it might look like — had been put into place while she and her mother were in the country on a visit to her grandmother, the Dowager Countess of Gresham. Her father's mother was as shrewd as may be and would give lie to any notion that females do not have brains, had anyone bothered to pay attention to her.

'In regard to crime, well . . . ' her mother intoned, 'as someone once said, wickedness is always easier than virtue.'

Her father bestowed a sharp glance on her mother, then resumed his reading. Pamela resigned herself to another day just like yesterday and most likely like tomorrow. Dull.

Her father began muttering again as he continued to study the article in the paper. Pamela resolved to read that article once he had left the house for his daily routine. First he would go to Tattersall's, then meet a few friends at his club, perhaps lunching there. He might pause at the House of Lords to see what topic would be in debate. Most often he returned for dinner, though sometimes not.

Her mother would supervise the housekeeper and cook, planning meals and that sort of thing. And then dearest Mama would be off to confer with Lady de Clifford regarding the education of the Princess Charlotte. The young girl must have the finest of educations, what with little likelihood of another child for the prince. From what Pamela had heard, the girl was willful and spoiled and not much given to take advantage of that education.

Odd, that. Amazing how the Princess Charlotte was considered to have a mind fit to educate, yet not other girls, namely Pamela. They were only a few years apart in age, but a world apart otherwise.

At last the morning meal was concluded; the earl rose, bid farewell to his family, then left. Shortly after, Pamela could hear her mother informing the cook what was desired for dinner. Once they went out, Pamela was alone.

However, Pamela had work to do. There was to be no novel reading, no frivolous pastime. Mama firmly believed that one must not have idle hands, so Pamela worked a set of chair seat covers. She had now reached the eighth of a set of twelve. Each depicted clusters of flowers from a month of the year. At least that way she had a bit of variety.

She was about to seek out the morning paper before commencing her 'work' when the family butler entered the room, a puzzled look on his usually placid face.

'What is it, Grimes?' She glanced at the stout, graying, middle-aged man, obviously perturbed, yet too conscious of his position to say why.

'There is a parcel for you, Lady Pamela.' He stood stiffly at her side, proffering the package as though it contained something of which he did not approve.

She accepted the white paper-wrapped parcel, frowning at the thing, quite puzzled as to who might send her something that would set Grimes on edge. The parcel was about twelve inches long and ten inches wide, flat, and it did not rattle in the least when she gently shook it. Wrapped in plain white paper, there was no name on the outside. Indeed, there was no address, nothing to offer a clue as to the sender.

'That will be all, Grimes.' She received so few packages, she wished to keep this to herself, savor the unexpected. When he had left the room, she eagerly tore at the wrapping

4

to find a box — the sort that usually held jewelry — within. The day suddenly promised to be different.

Feeling a bit like a Pandora seeking untold mysteries, she undid the clasp of the brown leather box. Lifting the lid, she gasped at what she saw within. A magnificent necklace of exquisite sapphires surrounded with brilliant diamonds rested on a bed of cream velvet.

At first, Pamela could only stare at the lovely creation. Then her sensible nature asserted itself. Examining the wrapping and box more carefully, she discovered a card that had been tucked into the box but had fallen aside when she opened it.

With trembling fingers, she held the card to the light. 'Keep this safe for me — for us — until I come for both my treasures, my dearest.' It was signed with the initials, 'J.R.'

'J.R.?' she said, her voice sounding frightfully loud in the silence of the room. Across from her, placed adjacent to the door, the longcase clock ticked away, the hour nearing eleven. What could she possibly learn of the mysterious package at this time of day, or from whom?

Arising from her chair, she brought the little case over to the window that she might study the perfectly splendid jewels again.

Shafts of sunlight threw hundreds of glittering sparks from the facets of the sapphires and diamonds throughout the room, creating shards of brilliant color. My, how she wished this belonged to her.

Naturally, whoever sent the package here had made a mistake! But if not hers, then to whom did the jewels belong? What other Lady Pamela knew a man with the initials J.R. who would bestow this necklace upon her with the admonition to keep it safe until he could take it and the lady far away? Until Pamela could solve the mystery, she must keep the necklace secret, for if society knew, what a scandal would befall her.

Closing the lid with a snap, Pamela pondered on the proper course of action with such an intriguing item. That it was risqué, she had no doubt. She did not think a man would send such a lavish gift accompanied by a note of such a highly personal nature to a mere acquaintance. She was quite sure the jewels held a much deeper secret.

Good heavens! Might she be holding stolen goods? She clutched the box more tightly in her hands. She was not so protected that she wasn't aware of women who lived on the fringe of respectability and needed financial help. The way wills and property settlements were arranged, it was far too common a predicament. Lady Pamela had often heard her grandmother rage on about the wretched manner with which women were treated in modern England; she was not unaware of destitute gentlewomen, cut out of an inheritance by a clever lawyer or by purpose left out of a will entirely.

'My dearest,' the note had concluded. Fancy being someone's dearest, inspiring a gift of such magnitude. Concealing the box in the folds of her shawl, she ventured into the hallway to find Grimes.

'Did you perchance take note of the livery worn by the person who delivered this package?'

'No livery, milady. Just ordinary clothing and an ordinary face that I cannot remember in the least.'

'No matter, Grimes. 'Twas merely a jest of sorts. Ah, a friend has sent me a book . . . a lovely book of poetry and included naught but a cryptic message. I am to guess who it is and I must be a ninny, for I cannot think who might do such a charming thing,' she finished in a rush.

Unaccustomed to deceit of any sort, Pamela had floundered for a moment until she had caught the notion of the package containing a book. It *could* have been a book, for she actually possessed a book of poetry roughly this size if a trifle smaller.

The leather box enclosed in the folds of her shawl seemed to burn into her hands. Yet she would not reveal the contents to anyone just yet. It was a mystery — her very own mystery. She intended to solve it if she could. Of course, she might need a bit of help, come to think on it. A young unmarried woman of the *ton* could do little on her own. But should she consult her parents, they would be horrified and ask all manner of questions. Her innocence in the matter might not be believed, for although she sought to please them, she always felt as though she fell short of their standard.

She left the entryway and marched back to the breakfast room, searching for the newspaper that had put her father to muttering this morning. Finally, she found it, precisely folded, its neatly ironed pages looking just as though it had come from the press.

'Ah, here it is, the article about the robberies.' A chill began to creep within her bones. She strongly suspected the necklace was a piece of stolen goods.

If the lady was not J.R.'s wife, she must have had a clandestine relationship with him, for no true lady accepted jewels from a gentleman who was not her husband. If he could not give the sapphire-and-diamond creation to the woman in person, it must be because it was simply too dangerous to do so.

Placing the case carefully in her lap, then draping her pretty Norwich shawl over it so as to conceal it from accidental discovery, Pamela began to read more of the account in the newspaper.

'Goodness, I had no idea there was such a wealth of jewelry lying about the city, badly protected and subject to thievery,' she murmured when she finished the article. 'There are a great many foolish people in town.' The latest theft had been foiled by the same man who had assisted her father — the Duke of Wexford.

Robert William James Musgrave, the eighth Duke of Wexford, was described as tall and dark and very clever. She wondered if he was handsome as well. Probably not. It had been her experience that a title rarely went with excellent looks. He most likely had a weak chin, a beaky nose, and a lean face topped by thinning brown locks.

But . . . he did appear to possess an excellent mind.

'I must think about this,' she murmured to the pot of geraniums sitting on the table in front of the only window in the room. Rising from her chair, she tucked the folded paper under her arm, then hurried up the stairs holding the box as though it actually contained the book she had claimed it did. If anyone knew the truth . . .

★   ★   ★

When her father came home for dinner that evening, Pamela could barely contain her impatience. She wished to quiz him ever so gently on the matter of gifts from gentlemen to ladies. Could there be an exception that her governess, Miss Osborn, had not told her about?

'Papa,' she began during their soup course, 'is it *ever* proper for a gentleman to present a lady with jewelry?'

'Whatever brought that subject to mind?' he queried with a gleam of suspicion in his pale blue eyes.

'I merely wondered about it,' she said, adopting as innocent an expression as she might manage.

'Well, no gentleman would offend a lady by offering her such a gift. It is only proper for a husband to do so,' he concluded with a snap.

'Or a relative,' the countess added calmly. 'Your grandmother presented you with your pearls, if you recall.'

'True,' Pamela replied, hoping that she did

not display any uneasiness.

'And there are other relatives who possess family jewels that might come to you on a special occasion as well,' her mother said with a reflective wrinkle of her brow.

'Like marriage, I suppose,' Pamela said before she carefully thought about her words.

'No chap has dared to approach you without consulting me first, has he?' her father demanded, his spoon in midair. 'I'll not suffer any improprieties.'

'Never, Papa,' Pamela gently replied. 'I feel certain you are too well-known for a gentleman to trespass in such a manner.'

'A book of poetry is acceptable from a gentleman, or a posy, something small and not too valuable,' her mother concluded scrupulously before concentrating on her coming evening entertainment.

Pamela ate her way through a well-planned and well-cooked meal, scarcely tasting a bite. She was utterly absorbed in her problem. Since it was now plain that the Lady Pamela of the sapphires was not a real lady and that the man who had sent them was not a true gentleman, she was in a bind. She had no acquaintance with such people. At least, she amended, she didn't think she knew any like them.

How to discover the identity of the

unknown J.R. occupied her thoughts during the concert of antique music she attended with her mother that evening.

'If you look far to your left, you will see the Duke of Wexford,' her mother whispered during an intermission. 'It was most kind of him to assist your father in the matter of my jewelry, you know.' The countess bestowed a wistful look in his direction that most likely was prompted by a wish that she might align her daughter with such a peer.

Determined not to stare, Pamela turned her gaze in the direction mentioned and almost gasped. The duke, for he was the only man who was tall and dark in that part of the room, did not possess a beaky nose, nor thinning hair, and there was not the least sign of weakness about his chin. Furthermore, he was as handsome as could be. At least Pamela thought him to be excessively good-looking in an elegant, restrained manner. There was nothing flashy or dashing about him, just elegance and perfect grooming.

Her heart sank. The notion she had begun to nurture — that of calling upon His Grace to assist her in unraveling the mystery of the necklace — was simply out of the question. The man she had first thought him to be would be approachable. The reality was not. As the music began again, he tilted his head back and closed his eyes, listening with obvious pleasure to the delicate strains that floated through the room.

Impossible. Utterly hopeless. Pamela sighed and began to consider how else she might solve her mystery. Nothing grand came to mind.

Since a proper lady did not bring herself to the attention of a gentleman, especially one as splendid as the duke, neither Lady Gresham nor Pamela so much as cast a glance in his direction when it came time to leave.

Pamela brooded all the way home.

'The music puts one into a reflective mood, does it not?' her mother pronounced.

'Indeed, Mama,' Pamela dutifully replied.

'I believe I shall discuss the matter of music with the Lady de Clifford when next I meet with her.' The countess sat a trifle straighter — if possible — and appeared to mull over what she intended to say regarding the study of music.

Pamela wondered what her life might have been like had her mother been as concerned with her learning as Lady de Clifford was with the Princess Charlotte. Tedious, most likely. Pamela had viewed a list of reading material intended for the princess and did not envy her. Sacred works dominated the list, with history and biographies next, followed by drama, poetry, and literature, quite often in French. Not that Pamela would have minded reading geography texts, for she loved to read about foreign places. She enjoyed botany as well, but would have objected to learning the subject by rote. Since women had smaller brains, they could scarcely be taught to think, hence they had to memorize texts. And reading for the sheer joy of learning was unthinkable.

Putting aside such seditious thoughts, Pamela went up to her bed to dream about the remote and elegant duke who had obviously enjoyed the music as much as she had.

By the following day she had not reached any conclusions regarding the magnificent jewels that reposed on her bookshelf, tucked between a book of poetry and one of arithmetic. She had purchased *that* one on the sly, wanting to learn her sums that she might not be cheated at the shops. She thought it a good thing to know for overseeing a house as well. Could a housekeeper not cheat as well as a shop-keeper?

What was she to do? Pulling forth the newspaper from where she had concealed it, she again read the account she had almost memorized by this point. How shrewd the duke had been, outsmarting the thief with cleverness and daring. What would it be like, to know a man with such intelligence? Pamela sighed. This was not helping her to discover the truth of the jewels.

Admitting she needed some assistance — for there was little she might accomplish on her own — Pamela studied the article once again and the germ of an idea took root. Actually, who *better* to consult than the duke? He had successfully outsmarted a number of jewel thieves. At least the article implied that he had. There was no real reason she could not consult him, was there?

Of course, there would be no romantic involvement to be concerned about. She was such an ordinary girl, and he had the world at his feet and thus could choose any woman he pleased for a wife. Mama had told her that the duke was single, hence the fawning attention from all the lovely young ladies making their come-outs. She would avoid that nonsense and keep any association strictly correct and proper.

Pacing back and forth in her pretty blue-and-white bedchamber, she mulled over how best to approach the matter. One could scarcely march up to the gentleman and announce that she possessed some jewels that she suspected someone had stolen and had delivered to her by mistake. He would never believe that it had happened, never mind that it had.

There were things she could not do and needed the help of a wise and clever man. For example, how could she go to Bow Street to inquire about any missing jewelry? The very idea was shocking. Unthinkable!

What a pity she had led such an exceedingly proper life. She wryly doubted that there was another young woman in all of London who was more proper than she. This was in large part the result of her mother's preoccupation with the education of the Princess Charlotte. How better to convince Lady de Clifford that the suggestions put forth by the Countess of Gresham were excellent than to display a perfect daughter. Pamela wondered if she were held up as a paragon of virtue to the princess. She hoped not.

Nibbling at her lower lip while reflecting on the matter, she breathed a sigh of resolution and crossed to the dainty desk placed before one of the two windows in her room. As she sharpened a quill, she considered how best to phrase her request for help.

'Please, Your Grace, I have had a wealth of sapphires and diamonds dumped in my lap, and I do not know what to do with them,' she murmured, then chuckled at the absurdity of her words. She then began to write. 'My Lord Duke, I would be pleased if you might meet with me to discuss a particular problem. 'Tis a mystery, a rather unusual one, I think. A package has been misdelivered, and I have no clue as to the sender and little help as to the intended recipient. As I suspect the contents are enormously valuable, I should like your assistance in solving the puzzle. Yours, sincerely' — and she signed her name with a modest flourish, for she had a very good hand. In an afterthought, she added her direction, for she had no illusion that he knew who she was or that Lady Pamela Taylor was the daughter of the Earl of Gresham.

After sanding the letter, she studied it as a stranger might. Would it capture his interest, pique his curiosity? Above all, would he be inclined to arrange a meeting with her to discuss her little riddle?

The mere thought of a meeting with such a debonair gentleman made her shiver with delicious anticipation. However, she thought ruefully, while she might have the proper credentials to be a duchess, she was such an *ordinary* creature. How could such a man as he be attracted to a quiet, proper girl such as she with plain blue eyes and common brown curls? While her figure was pleasing and her bosom quite respectable, she was yet *ordinary*.

Then the thought occurred to her that having a possibly stolen necklace in her possession was scarcely proper, was it? And it certainly was not ordinary in the least. Perhaps she might learn to be a trifle out of the common in this way? With that little hope tucked in the back of her mind, she sallied forth, dressed for a walk in the park — chaperoned, naturally.

'Oh, Rose,' she exclaimed to her maid when they had reached a spot close to where the duke resided, 'I have forgotten my handkerchief, and I fear my nose threatens to require one. Would you be so kind? I shall wait right here, for this seems a highly respectable neighborhood.'

Once the maid had scurried off to the Gresham home, Pamela beckoned a lad to her side. Offering a sizable coin and the note in one hand and clutching her reticule and parasol in her other, she said, 'Please deliver this note for me to the house across the street, Number 56.'

Looking at her as though she was daft, the lad eagerly accepted the coin and the note, and dashed off to pound on the door of Number 56 with the enthusiasm of one who has been overpaid.

Pamela watched from behind the protection of her parasol as the door opened and an exceedingly proper butler accepted the note, glanced about the area, then firmly shut the door behind him.

She had done it. The note had been written as best she knew how, then delivered under her watchful eyes. All she might do now is wait. It would be a suspenseful, almost intolerable period until she knew whether or not the duke would assist her.

Where could she begin if he refused her his aid?

For one thing, she might hunt for a Lady Pamela, although the very notion of how such a search could be conducted daunted her. And if she found the woman, what then? Could she march up to her and offer a queen's ransom in jewels just like that? Or even worse, might a constable have to be summoned?

Deciding such speculation was fruitless, Pamela welcomed Rose, accepted the handkerchief, and daintily blew her nose after offering fervent thanks to the maid.

'We had best continue on if we are to enjoy the flowers before it is time for me to go to Lady Cotterell's Venetian breakfast.' Privately, Pamela thought it rather silly to have a breakfast in the middle of the afternoon, but that was when the social event occurred. She wondered if the debonair duke would attend the breakfast. While Pamela would not be so bold as to approach him, she might study the man and see if he would be the sort to accept a blind request such as she had made.

Since she had accomplished her true reason for her outing, she made a cursory inspection of the few beds of flowers to be seen, then announced she had best return to dress for the party.

On the way to the breakfast, Pamela relished the trip along the Thames. It wasn't often she had the pleasure of gliding along the river, with time to view the splendid gardens on the banks along the way.

She examined the faces of those of her fellow passengers on the barge, realizing a sense of disappointment when she found the duke was not among them. But then, what had she actually expected?

'Come along, Pamela, dear,' her mother ordered when the barge gently nudged the landing. 'We must make ourselves known to Lady Cotterell before we may enjoy the tranquility of the day.'

'Yes, Mama,' Pamela said dutifully while casting her gaze about the area, unconsciously searching for the duke.

They strolled along the well-scythed lawn

past beds of flowers of every hue until they discovered their hostess. Pamela did the proper, then drifted away from her mother, still in conversation with Lady Cotterell. Pamela watched several young girls at archery and beyond them she viewed two young things swatting a shuttlecock back and forth with their battledores.

There was a hammock made of netting that hung rather limply between two trees. Were she not among company, she would love to relax there, fasten her gaze on the puffy clouds, let her mind wander as she swung gently to and fro.

One didn't do such a thing in a setting like this, she decided. At least if one were a proper miss with the most proper mother in the world a few feet away.

And then she spied him. The duke was in the midst of a cluster of fashionable young men and women on the far side of the grounds. There was no mistaking him, for he stood out from the others. She had been correct when she dubbed him debonair, for he was all that and more.

Rather than seek an introduction, she decided to simply watch him from afar. As a highly eligible peer, he must be besieged with young women making their come-outs. Pamela had never liked being one of a crowd.

Perhaps that was why she failed to flirt at Almack's. Not that her Mama wished her to bat her lashes or lure a gentleman on with her wiles — of which Pamela suspected she had none.

He chatted amiably with the group clustered about him, then the gathering slowly began to disperse, drifting off to the various entertainments offered.

The duke chatted with a couple she had seen often in society but did not know, the Radcliffes. They glanced in her direction, and she was careful to look away, off to the river where some ducks swam noisily about.

When she peeked again, it was to see the duke strolling toward the river, hailing a gentleman along the way.

He had a good friend, it seemed, for the thin fellow left the admiration of some girls with a jaunty step. Pamela watched as they discussed something, then in short order climbed into one of the flat-bottomed boats tied to a post near the landing. The duke took the oars and began to row along the shore. She rather envied them their freedom to do as they pleased. Who was going to deny a young, handsome, and eligible duke what he wished? Not Lady Cotterell.

Pamela hoped that the duke would help her. He looked enormously capable now that she had actually seen him and observed him herself. If he failed her, it didn't bear thinking about. She'd feel uneasy keeping the jewels, knowing they belonged to someone else and were possibly stolen property.

In her room, serenely reposing between a couple of rather ordinary books, a necklace worth a small fortune waited. What the future held for it, and Pamela as well, was in the hands of the handsome gentleman rowing a boat along the Thames. Would he reply to her note?

And then she had a most worrisome thought. Where could they meet and how, should he accept?

2

Early that afternoon, the Duke of Wexford, known more familiarly as Robert to his closest friends, was seated at his superb mahogany desk in his book-lined study going over some reports. He did not seem to notice the pleasing aroma of leather, old books, and a hint of apple wood from the low fire burning quietly in the grate. It was not a pleasant occupation, but he had neglected his affairs a bit, what with the recent investigations he had conducted. His agent had sent accounts from one of his country estates that required prompt action.

There was also a stack of invitations that had grown considerably since the news of his successful find of the missing jewelry. Most likely these were from people who hoped to obtain his advice on foiling thieves. He didn't mind, actually. It was a challenge to thwart criminals, using his brains and nothing more. The Earl of Gresham was a case in point. Fellow had owned a safe a child could break into hidden behind an oil painting in the study. Robert smiled to himself; no thief would be likely to locate the new concealment, or easily figure out how to gain entry should he be so lucky to find it.

Robert had enjoyed that challenge, but also felt it well worth the present efforts of bringing paperwork up-to-date. He sighed and applied himself to checking the report of estimated crop yields, the list of repairs needing attention, and the problem of poachers.

There was a faint sound of footsteps in the hall. His butler rapped gently, then entered with a missive on a silver salver. 'This was just delivered, Your Grace. Boy said it was most urgent.'

The note was not scented, nor was it written on florid pink paper. Rather, crisp white paper of respectable quality was sealed with a modest brown wafer. Robert broke the seal, then unfolded the brief letter, frowning as he read the carefully written words. The black letters flowed over the paper, quite legible and sensible, only he could scarce believe them. He read the words again.

He glanced at Bently, asking, 'Did you say a boy delivered this? No livery?'

'Correct, Your Grace. Handed me the letter and said it was urgent. I looked across the street, but all I could see was a young lady holding a parasol.'

'A young lady, you say?' Robert considered

the message again, then dismissed his butler with a wave of his hand.

He noted that she had addressed him most properly, then pleaded for him to meet with her to discuss a particular problem. A case of a misdelivered package? Now, why would a misdelivered package create such an enormous predicament? Surely, the contents would not be so reprehensible that she could not seek help from her parents? Or . . . perhaps it was? 'Valuable contents' to him spelled jewelry, or something of that nature. If that were the case, he could understand why a proper young lady might be hesitant to ask help from her parents. Parents had a way of assuming the worst, or at the very least asking strange and bothersome questions.

And, he admitted, he had acquired a reputation for solving seemingly impossible problems. The chit did not give him a clue as to how they might meet. But she did sign her name and give her direction. That, more than anything, convinced him that the note was genuine.

He would investigate the young woman, inquire around to see what it might be that troubled her so before he stuck his head in a noose. He hadn't met the girl, at least he didn't think he had. Pamela was a common enough name, and no face came to mind when he considered it. Fashionable address, however, and it was familiar to him. It was where Gresham lived. However, he hadn't seen any daughter around at that time.

Opening a desk drawer, he consulted his calendar to note his acceptance of an invitation to the Cotterell Venetian breakfast this afternoon. Perhaps he might discover something of interest while there? The party would be a huge gathering of the *ton*, for Lady Cotterell was much liked and her parties always a *succés fou*.

He returned to his work for the time being, setting aside the intriguing letter and its contents.

★   ★   ★

Upon arrival at the Cotterell's party, the duke joined a group of fashionable young people he saw frequently while in London. About half were single, the remainder were young married couples whose company he enjoyed. In particular, the Radcliffes were there and he hoped to ask Lady Anne, the daughter of the Earl of Winterton, if she had heard of Lady Pamela Taylor.

When members of the group began to wander off in various directions, he found the opportunity he sought.

Lady Anne proved a fount of information concerning Lady Pamela. 'I cannot see what there might be of interest about a young girl who is finally making her come-out. Should have last year, I believe, but there was a delay of some sort. She is the only child of the Earl and Countess of Gresham. Attended her court presentation the last time the queen held a drawing room and behaved quite beautifully, so I thought. You know how exquisitely dull those affairs are, and she gave not the slightest indication she was bored to flinders. She is a modest little thing, certainly not the sort to attract *your* notice, Your Grace.'

'Her parents?' Robert remembered assisting the earl, but actually knew little about the man — other than he was a member of White's and had no scandal linked to his family name that could be recalled.

'Both incredibly stuffy and proper, particularly the mother. Lady Gresham is one of those who offer advice to Lady de Clifford regarding the education of Her Royal Highness, the Princess Charlotte.' Lady Anne wrinkled her nose at the thought of education of any sort.

'*Good* advice, as far as you know?' Robert asked lazily, while scanning the throng of people who drifted across the great lawn of the Cotterell country house. The weather was pleasant. People tall and short wearing a mélange of color and summer styles wandered here and there, admiring the gardens while gossiping. The fluttering of multicolored parasols were as so many giant butterflies hovering over the guests. Games were offered around to the side of the home, and he could hear the thunk of an arrow as it hit its target.

'Quite proper. Although in my humble opinion, Lady Gresham would be better off tending to her own lamb instead of poking her nose into the Princess Charlotte's education. It seems to me that there is quite enough of that already.' Lady Anne wafted her pretty ruffled fan back and forth while eyeing her good friend, the Duke of Wexford. 'If you are seeking a proper connection, you could scarcely find one more qualified — daughter of an earl with an enormous dowry, so I've heard, and passable in looks.'

'Only passable?' The duke shook his head, giving the wife of his old friend an amused look. 'Cecil ought to curb your tongue. You give voice to far too many opinions.'

'I heard that, my good friend,' Sir Cecil piped up from Anne's side after quietly joining the pair. 'She voices what I think as well; that it is high time you find yourself a proper wife and settle down. There is more to a good wife than looks. I'm fortunate to have it all.'

'That is the only thing that annoys me about you two — you are so blissfully happy that I believe it impossible to duplicate. Is Lady Pamela here?' he asked abruptly, quickly changing the topic.

'I believe I saw her trailing her mother awhile ago. There she is . . . over by that net hammock and looking as though she would rather be elsewhere.'

The duke stared across the great lawn, trying to make something of a graceful figure in a simple jonquil yellow gown. On her head she wore a deep bonnet that had but a neat cluster of ribands to one side for decoration, and in her hands she carried a parasol that matched her gown. She was quite the harmonious blend of yellows. Evidently, the mother did not believe in over-ornamentation of her one lamb. He could see nothing of the girl's face. Before he sought an introduction, he believed he would do a little more investigation.

He did agree with Lady Anne that Lady Pamela did not look at ease. That might be because she had no friends in attendance. And why did she not? Surely, her mother would have introduced her to other girls her age. Curious, he decided to mull it over while engaging in a pleasant activity. He sauntered down the lawn toward the river, catching Algernon Thynne by the elbow as he walked.

'Shall we take one of those boats, Algie? I would avoid people for the nonce.'

'By all means,' the obliging Algie responded.

'Good. I believe this one will do well enough.' The duke set about removing the rope from the mooring, then climbed to the seat where the oars rested in their locks. Within minutes, they had shoved off and were moving upstream at a desultory pace.

'Any woman in particular, or just women in general?' Algie inquired with a knowing look at his childhood chum.

'Ever meet a young woman named Lady Pamela Taylor?'

'Know who she is — an heiress.' Algie made a face at his friend. 'Deuced difficult to meet her. Mama is a dragon, you know. I tried to 'accidentally' cross her path on her morning ride in the park, but her groom is most zealous. Her mama must have picked him out. Couldn't exchange so much as a hello with her.' Algie tilted his head and gave the duke a shrewd look. 'Why? If I may ask.'

'Curious. Something came up and she is involved. Nothing improper, mind you.' The duke smiled at his old friend's reaction to his words.

'I believe you there. *Most* proper girl,' Algie said with a shake of his head. 'Heiresses tend to be that way, or so I have found.'

'Dun territory creeping up on you again?'

'I'll find my way out of the River Tic on my own, one way or another.' Algie had never been one to borrow or beg from his friends, no matter how deeply in debt he might be.

'You are never thinking of succumbing to one of the heiresses! I notice you were quite aware of Lady Pamela's status. There must be another way out of your dilemma?' Robert leaned on the oars a moment, allowing the little boat to drift back downstream.

'Come to think it ain't all bad, being leg-shackled. Look at Cecil and Anne. Ain't a nicer pair around.' Algie leaned forward, resting his chin on his arms, which he had crossed atop his bony knees. His gaze was direct. 'I could like that.'

'And how many women exist who have Anne's sense of humor or her loyalty to Cecil?'

Algie murmured something that might have been assent. 'Must be another around somewhere.'

'Look, over there. Lady Pamela wanders along the river, twirling her parasol. Pretty as a picture, is she?'

'Nothing out of the ordinary,' Algie admitted.

'Has a squint and mousy hair, then?'

'Not so,' Algie declared in affront. 'Fact is, she has pretty blue eyes — very open and trusting-like. Might have plain brown hair, but there's bouncy little curls all over her head. Don't think *she'd* have to use curl-papers at night like my sisters. Of course, she does have a determined little chin, which might indicate an obstinate person beneath all those curls. Still, she looks right pretty, if you ask me.'

'I just did, I believe,' Robert said mildly. 'So the lady is pretty. Scarcely a diamond of the first water.'

'Been my experience that most of those so-called diamonds are a trifle too hard for my taste. Seems like they all are missing common sense in the brain box. And spoiled? Never seen anything beat the pampering most of these darlings receive. Not for me, thank you very much.'

'No need to take umbrage. Do you think I care who you marry . . . within reason, of course.' The duke's grin took any sting from his words to his good friend.

Algie flushed a shade of pink that clashed with his gingery brown hair. Light blue eyes flashed a rueful acknowledgment that Robert teased with good cause.

Pamela glanced at the little boat that

carried His Grace and his friend. Suddenly, she heard her name called. But it was not her mother, as she had expected. A pleasant young woman of the group that had been clustered around the Duke of Wexford approached, seeming to skim across the lawn in an effortless glide.

'Lovely day, is it not?' the woman demanded with a smile and a charming chuckle. 'I suppose you have heard nothing but that comment since you arrived.'

'Indeed,' Pamela responded with a smile to match. 'I believe everyone is so glad to have a day of sunshine after that long and dull spring we've had that they cannot help but remark on it.'

'I am Lady Anne Radcliffe,' the woman announced, holding out an exquisitely gloved hand. 'You are Lady Pamela Taylor, are you not? I was at the queen's drawing room when you were presented. I am so pleased to meet you. Your mother is around, isn't she?'

'Yes,' Pamela said with a sigh. 'I believe she is in conversation with Lady Brock regarding the music that ought to be taught to the princess.'

'Poor girl. What a pity the prince was not permitted to marry where he pleased. It would have saved a great deal of trouble. We can but hope his daughter will be allowed to marry where she pleases. So much depends upon her.'

Lady Anne tucked her arm into Pamela's and proceeded to guide her over to a bed of early-blooming roses, admiring the riot of colors to be seen.

'You must enjoy flowers, for you seem to know far more about them than I do,' Lady Anne concluded after a few minutes of conversation.

'When one lives in the country, it is easy to become familiar with roses, particularly if one's gardener is fond of them.' Pamela bent over to sniff a rose she knew to be extremely fragrant.

'Ah, yes, gardeners . . . what would one do without them?' Lady Anne responded lightly. 'You are enjoying your Season?'

'So far, it has been lovely.'

'And Almack's?' Lady Anne gently quizzed.

Not about to criticize that temple of society where young aspirants to *le beau monde* worshiped, Pamela made a vague murmur that could have meant anything one wished.

'Quite proper,' Lady Anne said with a delighted grin. 'You shall do admirably,' she concluded with an air of satisfaction that totally mystified Pamela.

Just then a squawking was heard along the riverbank, and the two young women whirled around in time to see the ducks literally attacking the boat in which the duke and his friend now sat most uneasily.

'Oh, dear, the duke is going to endure a thorough soaking unless someone does something, and quickly,' Lady Anne exclaimed as she pulled Pamela along with her to the river's edge.

'They have dropped one of the oars trying to fend off the birds. Those ducks are impossible! What is the matter with them?' Pamela cried.

'I suspect they've become pests what with people feeding them. The boat drifts close to shore. See if you can extend your parasol to Algernon or the duke,' Lady Anne commanded.

Pamela saw immediately what she meant for her to do. Quickly, Pamela thrust the long handle of her parasol toward the boat. The duke grabbed it and levered the boat closer to shore while his friend shooed the aggravating ducks away by flapping his hands at them. Within seconds the boat bottom scraped the shoreline.

'Well done, dear lady,' the duke said most heartily. 'I thought for a moment we were to be buried in a flurry of feathers.' He smiled at Pamela, an endearing sort of smile that lit his eyes and made him seem less formidable.

She had thought him handsome at a distance; close up he was quite awesome. His eyes held the most engaging twinkle in their gray depths, while his dark hair was tousled about his head in a manner his valet would likely deplore and Pamela thought charming. There was something of the freshness and brisk quality of a summer wind about him. He quite took her breath away. She spared little notice for his impeccable garb of biscuit pantaloons and claret coat over a most elegant waistcoat of embroidered cream linen.

'Those ducks thought you ought to feed them,' Lady Anne said, a hint of laughter in her voice.

'It quite escapes me how — no scraps. May I know the identity of the lady who so gallantly came to our rescue?' He glanced at Lady Anne, then at Pamela with a speculative look in his eyes.

'Your Grace, I thought you would know; you are usually so clever,' Lady Anne said with a coy lift of her brows. 'Lady Pamela Taylor, may I present His Grace, the Duke of Wexford. The gentleman at his side is Algernon Thynne.' Without waiting for acknowledgment from any of them, other than polite bows, Lady Anne bubbled on, 'Lady Pamela and I have spent a delightful time becoming acquainted. She knows a good deal more about roses than I do,' Lady Anne said fervently. Then she exclaimed with alarm, 'My dear duke, your boat is about to sail away without you.'

At these words, Algie nimbly caught the trailing ropes and expertly turned the boat around so as to go downstream again. 'Would you care for a ride, Lady Pamela?' The expression of hope on his face was rather flattering.

Allowing herself another swift look at the duke's handsome face, Pamela nodded shyly and walked to the edge of the river, wondering how she would manage to enter the boat without disgracing herself by lifting her skirts too high or falling into the water.

Instead of disgrace, she found herself picked up in strong arms and gently plunked down on the rear seat of the boat with great dispatch.

'Oh,' she exclaimed, tossing a startled look into those rich gray eyes. 'Thank you, Your Grace. Most kind,' she murmured. Algernon Thynne shoved off from the bank, and they more or less drifted down the river with an occasional assist of the remaining oar.

'Nice chap, really,' Mr Thynne said by way of explanation regarding his friend's behavior in picking up a young lady he had just met. 'Actually, he was recently of great help to my father. I have read about his exploits in the papers,' Pamela dared to say. 'Does he actually solve so many mysteries?'

'Indeed he does. Has his pick, I expect.'

Pamela would have inquired more closely as to what was meant by that remark, but they had arrived at the landing and Mr Thynne was absorbed in securing the boat and reporting the loss of an oar because of the plaguey ducks upriver.

Pamela climbed from the boat without any assistance — Algernon Thynne being occupied with his explanations and directions to the man who tended the boats — then shook out her skirts. First checking to see if she might discover her mother's whereabouts, she darted a glance in the direction from whence she had come. Pamela did not wish to have Lady Anne think that she had expected to rejoin her, for that would be pushing. But, Pamela thought wistfully, Lady Anne was quite the nicest person she had met here so far, and she had enjoyed her company enormously. Most of the girls were rather silly and foolish, and Pamela had little desire to spend time with such wigeons.

Some distance away, strolling along the bank of the river, the duke bent his head to better hear Anne speak. 'What is your opinion of the girl?'

'I must say, I found her well-spoken, intelligent in her conversation, and not the least silly. I wish you would tell me why you want to know, but you will not, I suspect.'

'You would say that she does not appear as one given to flights of fancy?'

Clearly startled at this odd question, Anne frowned, looking up at the duke with puzzled eyes. 'She seems a sensible girl, quite proper in her manners, and as I said, not the least silly as one would be who is given to fits and starts.'

Robert raised his head to see Lady Pamela clamber from the boat unassisted. Apparently, she was not one given to sitting around until someone remembered to help her. Her determined little chin would account for that trait, he expected. All of which fell in with the message she had sent him regarding the strange parcel misdirected to her. She was not one to sit and wait. He'd have to remember that characteristic, when he became involved in solving the mystery. If he became involved, he corrected himself. Yet something told him that Lady Pamela and her mystery offered a diversion he would greatly relish.

She glanced in toward him, or more correctly, to Lady Anne. A girl that proper would not be casting out lures, even if he had a dukedom. A rare and rather pleasant change, he decided.

'She seems a nice girl. I trust you will not disappoint her or us?' Lady Anne said quietly.

The duke laughed at Anne's carefully innocent expression. 'You know I am always circumspect when around young women making their come-outs. When and if I ever marry, it will be to one of *my* choosing. But, my dear Anne, this particular interest has nothing to do with anything so mundane as marriage. Nothing at all,' he added in an undertone as he took another searching look at the figure in jonquil yellow.

The breeze tugged at her gown, shaping it to a very lovely and slender body. She possessed a delightful, if fuller than average, bosom that she didn't try to hide beneath a loose-fitting spencer. He approved of her appearance. It reflected a charming person — or was he influenced by Anne's evaluation? Time would reveal all, he suspected.

Algernon hailed him as he and Lady Anne drew near. 'Fixed the matter of the missing oar. Chap said it happens now and again. Not to worry.'

Perhaps she suspected he wished a word with Lady Pamela, for Anne began questioning Algernon about the boat and the nasty ducks. They drew slightly ahead, just enough so that Robert might have a word in private

— if one could call being in the middle of a huge party of people private.

'You ride in the morning?'

'Indeed, it is one of my pleasures,' Lady Pamela replied with a demure drop of her lashes.

'Bring whatever it is that you wish me to see along with you. I shall meet you along Rotten Row around nine of the clock, if that meets with your approval,' he added for politeness. If she were intent upon obtaining his help, she would make it a point to be on time.

Her face suddenly bloomed into a smile of purest joy, lighting her eyes into the cerulean blue of a summer's day.

'Thank you, Your Grace. I shall not disappoint you.'

At this juncture Anne turned to look at them and said, 'They are serving the collation over in that tent, I believe. I do not know about you two, but I am starved.'

'A lady should not admit to being so hungry,' Sir Cecil admonished, appearing at his wife's side with unhurried calm.

'Well, I have an excuse,' she said softly, laughing at his expression. 'It is all this fresh air.'

His look of knowing amused Pamela, causing her to wonder if Lady Anne might be in an interesting condition. While a city girl might not be so aware, Pamela had spent most of her life in the country, close to nature and folks who were more outspoken.

She decided to edge away from the group of friends, for she did not wish to intrude on the closeness she sensed within them. Pretending to have seen her mother, she excused herself and walked purposefully toward the far end of the tent.

'Very nice manners,' Anne observed lightly.

'If you are matchmaking, you are far and away off the path, dear lady,' the duke said, looking his most formidable.

'I have given up such an occupation as hopeless,' Anne replied with a chuckle, an engaging dimple peeping out in her cheek. 'You will find someone in your own good time. However, it does not do any harm to make a comment now and again, does it?'

'That depends,' he growled back before excusing himself to speak with another of his friends.

From the shadows of the tent, Pamela watched the little group of friends break up. Algernon Thynne went off with a chap he seemed to know well. The duke fell into conversation with an older gentleman, while Sir Cecil and Lady Anne were totally absorbed in each other.

The duke had agreed to meet her come morning! He urged her to be prompt, as though she would risk losing his help by being late or missing the appointment altogether. Rotten Row would be thin of company at that hour, which was good.

Somehow she must manage to persuade her faithful and overly conscientious groom to fall behind. Surely, he knew her well enough by this point that he would understand she was not the sort of girl to go dashing off with a gentleman. But then, he had been ordered by her mother to protect Pamela from everything harmful. It was true that she would surely cook her goose should she accept the attentions of some unprincipled rake.

Perhaps the duke would think of something. She had seen a very firm expression cross his face just before he took leave of the Radcliffes. The duke was not a man to cross, it seemed.

★   ★   ★

Later that evening Robert relaxed in his room before taking himself off to the theater. He hoped he had not committed himself to a foolish path in agreeing to meet with Lady Pamela, although she appeared disarmingly straightforward. It was not his habit to deal with young women, let alone one like her. It should prove interesting.

He finished inserting a tasteful diamond stickpin in his artfully tied cravat, then went off to gather up his guests for the evening, one of whom was the lushly beautiful Lady Smythe.

The vivacious redheaded widow would entertain him with charming tales and promised a great deal with her flashing green eyes. He hadn't made up his mind if he would accept what she offered so generously. Perhaps not so generously, at that. His investigation had revealed that her purse was shockingly to let. Did she think to bleed him for the ready with which to repair her fortunes? She would catch cold if she depended on that.

Pamela and her redoubtable mother occupied the theater box belonging to the earl's mother. Although the old woman rarely attended, she liked to hold the box, just in case she took a notion to view a new offering.

The ladies seated within the box viewed those who also attended the new production of an old Shakespeare favorite. Pamela dutifully listened as her mother made known the various luminaries of society, in case Pamela had forgotten any of them.

'There he is now,' the countess pointed out with a most discreet wave of her fan in the direction of the duke, who had just entered an opposite box with a staggeringly lovely woman on his arm. 'Did you see him this afternoon? The Duke of Wexford is the cream of the *ton*, my dear. Your father was most impressed with him. Pity you might not aspire to such heights, but you are a commonsensical sort of girl and will not repine, I feel sure. Be content if you find someone close to his caliber. Use him as your measure, if you will; you would not go wrong.'

Then her ladyship settled back to study the performance, most likely wondering if the royal princess would benefit from a dose of Shakespeare.

Pamela pretended to pay attention to the stage, but she was far too aware of the duke seated across from her. His companion was quite, quite beautiful, her flaming locks a charming contrast to his own dark hair. They looked to be comfortable with one another, revealing an ease of familiarity.

Conventional girls did not stand a chance with someone like him, she reminded herself. Then she took another peep from behind her fan and sighed. If only he weren't so handsome, well-mannered, and charming.

She had her hands full in dealing with him, but she promised herself that she would not reveal by the flicker of an eyelash that she found him fascinating. It would be strictly business.

And pigs might fly, too.

3

Early the following morning Pamela slipped from her bed, sure that her maid would not come at this hour unless called, and removed the leather case from its hiding place.

Breathing a sigh of relief when she checked the jewelry inside and found it safe, she considered how best to conceal it on her person when she went to the park to meet His Grace. No pockets, no reticule when riding, and one scarcely carried packages as a rule. This was one time she would have to do what no one else did and hope that no one in the park paid the least attention to her.

Mama would expire from serious palpitations should she discover that Pamela was off to the park to meet a gentleman, never mind it was the duke and that in addition, it was merely business — of sorts. Mama, however, need never know.

The leather case, now concealed in the original wrapping — so uninteresting and unimportant-looking — was finally placed with Pamela's crop and gloves. It was the best she could think of. After all, she owed no one in this house any explanations — other than her parents, and they were never around at this hour of the day.

Rose slipped into the room and nearly dropped the tray holding Pamela's hot chocolate and rolls upon seeing her mistress up and out of bed. No explanations would be offered, she reminded herself, that could only bring problems.

'You are up betimes this morn, Lady Pamela,' the girl said, her gentle, country-bred voice revealing her surprise and her curiosity.

'It is a glorious day, and I wish to ride in the park after I finish my chocolate. I shall want my blue habit today, please,' Pamela requested with her usual courtesy. She had observed that those who were rude to servants generally received very poor service. She did not approve of uncivil treatment of those who worked for another; her tender heart would not tolerate such when she was around.

'Yes, milady,' Rose softly replied, promptly going about her business, opening the blue-and-white chintz draperies, seeing to it that Pamela had all she needed before straightening the bedcovers and bringing forth the desired riding habit.

Pamela, ensconced on a plump-cushioned chair with a fat ottoman for her feet, thought it very much nicer than her bed and resolved to be up for chocolate from now on.

Once dressed, the image reflected in her mirror almost satisfied. The habit's rich blue contrasted nicely with the crisp white of her habit shirt, the collar of which peeped over the top of her one-piece habit. The skirt completely concealed her pink drawers; she trusted it would remain so. She had escaped disgrace yesterday. Today she might not be so lucky. One did not wish to have one's pink drawers exposed, no matter what! Not that she expected to have her habit reveal more than a glimpse of stocking above her half boots, but . . . accidents did happen.

The jaunty little beaver hat trimmed with a stiff little plume called an esprit sat neatly on her curls. She studied the effect while drawing on her York tan gloves. She would do. She would have to do, not that His Grace would pay much attention to her. It was the necklace that would attract his eyes, and she had better remember that!

She almost forgot to take the note from J.R. and hastily tucked it up inside of her cuff while Rose's back was turned. She hoped the fit was sufficiently snug that the important note would not fall out. It appeared to be adequate and she would be careful.

When she picked up the paper-wrapped

leather case, Rose gave her a questioning look. Pamela returned it with what she hoped was a confident nod, then left her room. Her half boots most thankfully made little sound on the stairs as she made her way to the front door. Grimes was elsewhere on his morning duties, and she was able to slip from the house with only Rose being the wiser.

Timson was in front with her pretty little mare, Star, alerted by a note sent down last evening that his mistress would ride out a trifle earlier this morning. Deciding it was useless to attempt to mount her horse while clutching both crop and box in hand, she gave the box to her groom, then mounted. After accepting the crop and the leather case, she rode off ahead of him. He fell in easily behind her.

Still undecided how best to order the groom to keep his distance, she mulled over the matter all the way to the park. A glance at the little watch pinned to her habit — another point of departure from her norm — she noted that she was properly on schedule. She respected time. She also expected others to be punctual as well. She had a hunch that the duke would be there promptly — and be surprised that she joined him right on the dot of nine.

A delighted chuckle escaped when she saw

the duke — unmistakable, even at a distance — riding across the park in her direction. She'd been correct.

He was no less awesome this morning than the previous day. In riding garb, he possessed that casual magnificence so desired by gentlemen and so rarely obtained. His dark gray coat over a pale gray waistcoat of pure simplicity was above dark leather riding breeches and, by their shine, his Hessians indicated a devoted polishing. Indeed, she thought, the entire man was flawless as was his gray stallion.

The matter of Timson was neatly solved. Apparently, there was not a groom in London who did not know the duke's identity. When the duke approached, Timson doffed his hat, then respectfully kept his distance when he saw the eminent gentleman intended to have a word with his mistress. By the smug expression on Timson's face, Pamela guessed he would be desirous of sharing this delicious news with the staff — something she must prevent at all costs.

'Good morning, Your Grace,' Pamela said with her pleasant manners firmly in place.

'It is, isn't it? You are quite on time, Lady Pamela. You are to be commended on your promptness. Would that my sisters might learn that lesson from you.'

He smiled at her in shared amusement, and Pamela thought his smile the sort that could positively melt your insides to a puddle.

'Your Grace,' Pamela said quietly. 'I am pleased that you decided to accept my request for a meeting. How clever of you to think we might meet here with so little difficulty.'

'Most logical, I believe,' he replied. 'Now, tell me about your mystery.'

'Of course.' She held up the parcel, wrapped much as it had been when delivered. 'This package was delivered to me the day before yesterday. It was morning, just after my parents had left for the day.' She moved Star closer to where the duke sat on his impressive gray and handed the case to him, then continued, 'That is precisely how it was wrapped. As you can see, there is no writing on it. The man who delivered it said it was for Lady Pamela. When I opened it, I saw what you will see now.'

He pulled the case from the wrapping and flipped open the leather case after undoing the catch. She could hear his indrawn breath in spite of their distance, the creaking of leather, and the distant sounds of the city.

'Good heavens!'

'Scarcely the thing for a young unmarried lady, is it?'

'Undoubtedly intended for a not-so-young lady who is less than proper, more likely,' he said quietly, studying the jewels. Casting a glance at Timson and seeing that he was watching some dogs playing tag, the duke lifted the necklace from its bed of velvet and held it up to the morning sun. Squinting, he commented, 'Outstanding quality, from what I can tell. The setting is exquisite.'

'The problem is that I can't imagine why they were sent to me. Note there is no direction on the wrapping, which you must admit is rather curious. They *must* have been misdelivered, although my name is indeed Pamela. But I do not know anyone whose initials are J.R.'

'J.R.? What is this?' he said in confusion.

'I forgot, there was a note as well.' She pulled the note from where she had tucked it up her sleeve and handed it across to him.

He read it aloud. When he reached the final words, he glanced up at her and repeated them. 'My dearest? That implies intimacy with the gentleman.'

Pamela could feel the heat burn in her cheeks and knew she must be blushing. 'That is quite impossible for me, as you might guess.'

'Undoubtedly.' Robert watched the proper young woman who so bravely sought this clandestine meeting with a stranger. She blushed a delicate wild rose. The extra bloom in her cheeks made her rather pretty — perhaps more than pretty, he decided. As observed yesterday, she had lovely manners yet was not afraid to step from the accepted mold, witness her thrusting her parasol out to assist him and Algie to shore. His youngest sister would have screamed and fainted. And now this — her calm assessment of a mysterious package containing a small fortune in jewels.

He looked at the jewels resting on the cream velvet and briefly wondered what the sapphires would look like against her pale skin. Then he turned his attention to the matter at hand.

'What is it you wish me to do for you? I fancy I know any number of men whose initials are J.R. What about the name Pamela?' He watched her struggle with her memory.

'I have thought and thought, and confess that I do not know quite how to solve that, even if I found her — and I suspect there are many. As well, I cannot go to Bow Street by myself to see if a necklace such as this has been reported stolen. I suppose it is possible that the necklace was commissioned from a jewelers. Yet I am loath to probe into that, not wishing to inquire at numerous jewelers regarding a sapphire necklace. Can you imagine if word of such a thing reached the patronesses?'

'You fear being cut from Almack's?' That was a ridiculous question; admission to that holy of holies of society was something for which every young woman making her come-out prayed. It said much for Lady Pamela that she had attained such lofty status and intended not to jeopardize it.

'I do not mind so much,' she replied, surprising the duke exceedingly. 'But Mama would be utterly wretched were something of that sort to happen. She sets great store by propriety, and means for me to make a proper marriage. One can scarcely accomplish that without admission to Almack's.'

'You are not promised, I take it? No tacit understanding or anything of that sort?' Had she a serious beau, she ought to have consulted him, unless she found him either a nodcock or trusted Robert more. He found the latter thought far more pleasing.

She blushed again. 'No. I am not betrothed, nor is there an understanding of any kind.' She dropped her gaze to the reins in her hand, then added, 'I fear I have not taken, precisely. Mama scolds, but that changes nothing,' she concluded in a rush and looked as though she regretted her hasty

56

words immediately. He had observed more than once that people tended to confide things in him that they might not in another. He'd never been able to account for it, and now it had happened once again.

'Just wondered. I'd not like to accept your commission, then find some chap is about to run me through in a total misunderstanding of the matter.' He raised his brows with a rueful grimace, exchanging looks with her clear blue eyes. She seemed a most self-possessed young woman.

She smiled at his words, accepting the absurdity of them. Her blush subsided, and Robert wondered what he might say to bring that delightful bloom back to her cheeks again.

'Let's see,' he said by way of winding things up. Her groom could be expected to linger in the distance just so much longer. 'Why do you not retain possession of the necklace, at least for the present? Where have you been keeping it thus far?'

'On my bookshelf, for that box resembles a thin book. I do not know where else to put it, unless it could go in the bottom of a hatbox. 'Tis a fearful responsibility. I'd feel better were they in Papa's new safe.'

'I expect so. However, we cannot talk any longer here. Others may come soon. I've been trying to think where we might meet again. We need to plan our strategy, and that is best done together.'

She blushed again, and Robert congratulated himself on obtaining what he wished. She really was a pretty little thing. He liked the way those soft brown curls feathered around her hat. He also approved of her excellent seat on her mare. She'd been well taught. That habit flattered her figure nicely, too, particularly that generous bosom she was blessed with. Nice, indeed.

'You met Lady Anne Radcliffe yesterday, I believe. I think we could borrow their library when necessary. We would have to allow them in on the secret?' He searched her face for a clue to her inner feelings regarding the Radcliffes.

'I feel certain that if you trust them, it would be most acceptable. I quite liked Lady Anne when we chatted, and I should enjoy meeting her again.' Lady Pamela smiled, a genuine smile of delight, if he was any judge.

'Perhaps you could take your maid for a walk this afternoon at the time when all the world and his wife descend upon the park? I could endeavor to meet you, let you know if our plan is acceptable. That would eliminate the need for another note.'

Her blush deepened, and she said with a

mere hint of an excuse in her voice, 'I had no other way of reaching you, Your Grace. It is most difficult for a proper young lady in a case like this.'

'Do not worry,' he assured her, 'you have not put your propriety in peril. I shall see you this afternoon, my lady.' He tipped his hat and rode off toward the park gate.

Pamela's satisfied gaze followed his retreating figure. Jumping slightly when Timson rode up to join her, she glanced at the groom, then said, 'Mind you, not a word of this to anyone. I'll not be the object of gossip. His Grace and I met yesterday, and I wished to consult him about something. There is nothing more to it.' More's the pity, she added silently.

The groom looked knowing, but simply nodded his head and then discreetly followed his mistress at a proper distance for the remainder of her uneventful ride.

* * *

Knowing that the Radcliffes would not be receiving anyone at this hour, Robert set off toward Bow Street. Lady Pamela had made an excellent point regarding the Bow Street Runners. She could scarcely venture into their domain on her own to inquire about jewelry that might be missing.

Inside the building all was chaos. The magistrates' court was in session, and people of every description came and went. He took care to mind his purse, for thieves were as common as grass in these parts. He finally waylaid a clerk. 'I wish to know if a particular piece of jewelry has been reported stolen.'

'Well, Your Grace, we do have a list,' the gentleman said with all possible deference once Robert had identified himself, 'but there be upwards of three thousand receivers of stolen goods in the city alone. There are countless more in other towns where items can be sold. I can show you our list if you like, but there is little chance of recovering a piece of jewelry once it's gone. If you wish, I can give you a list of likely fences where you might find the piece.'

Led to a small, quiet chamber, Robert scanned the several-page list of stolen items the clerk offered him to read. There was an incredible collection of jewels missing he had not heard about in the papers or elsewhere. Curious. However, nowhere could he find a description of the sapphire-and-diamond necklace now tucked between a couple of books in Lady Pamela's bedroom.

'Thank you, what I seek is not on the list. Perhaps I shall have better luck elsewhere.'

The clerk gave him a puzzled look, indicating that he doubted if anyone could retrieve a piece of stolen jewelry unless he hired a man to search out the particular item. That usually involved hiring an ex-thief — who might still be one when he felt like it — who was willing to locate the stolen item for a fee. It was suspected that in many cases, the thief turned in an item that he, himself, had first stolen in order to receive a reward more generous than he could fetch from a fence.

Robert went from Bow Street to the establishment of Rundle and Bridge. Here he described the necklace to a head of the firm, asking discreetly whether the firm might have had the making of such a necklace. The gentleman allowed as how the description His Grace gave them matched that of one they had made, but understood the necklace had exchanged hands since first commissioned. He had not the least notion as to who might be the present owner.

Another blank wall did not diminish the duke's interest. Rather, it pushed him to find out precisely who that owner was and if, perchance, his initials were J.R.

A glance at his watch revealed the time had flown by and he might now head for the Radcliffe home at No. 6 Upper Brook Street.

He was ushered into the house with the ease of one who is a family friend. Sauntering into the morning room where his friends sat absorbed in the morning papers, he greeted them as usual. He drifted about the room, crossing to gaze out of the window facing the rear of the prime property and the elegant garden.

'Out and about early, this morning, are you not?' Lady Anne said, no doubt taking note of his restlessness.

'As a matter of fact, it has been a busy one. I've been to Bow Street as well as Rundel and Bridge so far. Of course, that followed my morning ride in the park.' He walked over to lean against the mantel, absorbing the slight heat from a small fire designed to remove the morning chill from the room.

Both of the Radcliffes lowered their papers, Lady Anne folding hers to put aside.

'This sounds intriguing. Pray tell what has set you on such an unusual day?' Sir Cecil inquired.

The footman entered at this point to bring a tray set with tea, Madeira, and crisp cheese biscuits. The latter was known to be a favorite of the duke.

Once again alone with his friends, the duke enjoyed a bite of a biscuit, then sat down to face them.

'Do you recall meeting Lady Pamela Taylor yesterday?'

'Of course. Charming girl,' Lady Anne promptly replied.

'I met her again this morning while on my ride. It was prearranged.'

Robert watched his friends assimilate this tidbit before continuing. 'She had sent me a message requesting that I meet her regarding a mysterious package that had been delivered to her.'

'A mysterious package? Oh, do tell us more if you can. I adore mysteries,' Lady Anne bubbled with enthusiasm, quite ignoring the cautioning look from her spouse.

'I saw the package this morning when we met in the park, including the wrapping that had nothing written on it — not even her name. Inside the leather case was a magnificent sapphire-and-diamond necklace that would astound your senses could you see it.'

'No clue as to who sent the thing?' Sir Cecil said.

'Not in the least — unless you count the initials J.R. to be of value.'

'Good heavens, man, there must be dozens of men with such initials around London — this time of the year in particular. What does she propose to do — I take it the contents of the parcel were not intended for *our* Lady Pamela?' Sir Cecil concluded, a twinkle flashing in his kindly gaze.

'Indeed. Naturally, she feels constrained to hunt for the true Lady Pamela the necklace is intended for — whoever she might be. And there's the rub. An unmarried young lady of quality simply cannot be prowling around Bow Street, or asking peculiar questions at a jeweler's shop.'

'Speaking of that, did you learn anything at Rundle and Bridge?' Lady Anne demanded quietly.

'The man I spoke to was far too discreet to reveal who had first commissioned the necklace, but did say he knew it had changed hands — possibly indicating it was meant as a gift. He admitted he did not know the present owner.'

'Oh, bother,' her ladyship said. 'Back to Lady Pamela. I gather she sought your expert assistance?'

'Indeed. However, I do not know what good I can do. Nothing matching the description of that necklace has been reported missing so far. It could be that the owner is as yet unaware that the jewels are gone. You know how many of the *ton* leave their valuables in their home safe while they go off to London for the Season.'

'That does pose a bit of a problem,' Lady Anne said musingly. 'So?'

'We cannot keep meeting in the park. And I believe we need to confer on our findings. Would you not agree?'

Lady Anne, who was quick off the mark as usual, said, 'I believe you had best meet somewhere neutral, a place more unexceptional. How about our library?' The suggestion was made casually, but the duke took note of the gleam in Anne's eyes. The scamp wanted nothing more than to be in on whatever developed.

'That would be excellent. You have an up-to-date copy of *Debrett's*, I imagine? Otherwise, I can bring mine over.'

'Of course we have a copy, but you might require both books, if she is to hunt for a name as well as you,' Sir Cecil said with practicality.

'And the elusive J.R.? Do you think he might be of the peerage as well?' Lady Anne demanded.

'He might be anyone. We will have to scour every list we can find — membership lists, everything you can think of that might be of help.'

'You mean we can partake in the mystery as well?' a delighted Lady Anne exclaimed.

'Could I truly prevent such?' Robert said,

giving his friend that same lazy grin that Pamela had decided would melt one's insides to a puddle.

'What about the necklace? I long to see it,' Anne said with a glance at her husband.

'You could keep it here, you know, old chap,' Sir Cecil volunteered. 'Concealing it on a bookshelf is rather dangerous to my way of thinking.'

'I doubt if Lady Pamela is ready to hand the necklace over to a stranger. Give her time. After all, she doesn't know you as well as I do.'

'I would wager she would have given it to you had you requested,' Lady Anne hazarded. 'You do have a way about you, you know.'

'So that settles it,' His Grace said, ignoring Lady Anne's comment about his way with feminine creatures. 'Once we decide upon a time, I will send along a message to see if it is convenient.'

'Most mornings are open — except next Tuesday. We are having a waltzing party. I do so want to learn that dance and this is a delightful way, is it not? Would you not wish to come, perhaps bring Lady Pamela as well? *You* could convince her mother to permit this. You can study those peerage volumes first, then join our happy little group.'

'You are a party to this, Cecil?'

'I am not about to let another gentleman put his arms about my wife!' Sir Cecil exclaimed.

Robert considered the party, then thought how deliciously Lady Pamela would blush when he placed his arms about her as prescribed while waltzing, and decided in an instant. 'We will be there. Of course, I know that Lady Pamela would like to begin solving this puzzle immediately. Could we come over tomorrow morning? Say, about nine?'

'I shall be delighted to chaperon,' Lady Anne said with a decided sparkle in her fine gray eyes.

'Fine, I shall see you then.' His business concluded, Robert took his leave of his friends, leaving Anne quite bemused.

'I cannot believe he will join us waltzing, and with Lady Pamela as well. Do you suppose?' she wondered aloud.

'If you intend a bit of matchmaking, recall how previous attempts have gone and give up now. Robert will find his mate at the right moment, and she will be of his own choosing.'

'I cannot help but wish for him the same happiness we know, my dearest.'

With that, Sir Cecil smilingly agreed.

★　★　★

Lady Gresham quite agreed that Pamela ought to take a stroll in the park at the fashionable hour.

'I do believe you ought to invite a friend to go with you rather than Rose,' she added to her acquiescence.

'Perhaps next time. It would not be proper to dash off such a request on a moment's notice.' The last thing Pamela desired was to have a witness to her meeting with the duke.

'True, one must observe propriety. Rose must go with you then. The next time you might ask one of the charming young ladies you have met at Almack's to join you.'

Pamela agreed and wondered if her mother might not make more of a push to see to it that Pamela had more friends. It seemed to her that every time she found a girl she liked, her mother had pronounced the young lady lacking for one reason or another. It had made life difficult and rather lonely.

The day was a trifle cool, but there was little breeze so it was quite pleasant while walking. The park was thronged with beautifully dressed women and elegantly garbed gentlemen. The finest in horseflesh drew the most dashing of carriages, while along Rotten Row the bucks and dandies on prime mounts vied for the attention of attractive ladies on horseback.

It was undoubtedly London at one of its finer hours.

Pamela strolled along, resolutely ignoring the odd looks from those in carriages. It was not customary for a young lady to walk alone, with only her maid for company. This was why Pamela had not gone before. She had never been a gregarious sort, making her friends very slowly. If she might have had the company of her dear friend Susan from home, it would have been wonderful.

Suddenly, she saw the duke slowly making his way through the assemblage of people. He drew near, and she wondered if he would smile at her again. She did enjoy that smile.

'Good day, Lady Pamela.' He dismounted, holding the reins while he studied her. He flashed that smile that she was quite certain would melt her insides.

She felt very conscious of her appearance, and wondered if she had been correct to wear her simple rose walking dress and her cottage bonnet bedecked with roses of a deeper shade. Deciding there was little point in worrying about it now, she greeted him politely, 'Good day, Your Grace. How pleasant to see you again. I trust you enjoyed the Venetian breakfast as much as I did?'

'That I did.' He scowled at Rose, who shrank back against a clump of bushes. He continued softly, 'Tomorrow at nine of the clock is agreeable for the project you mentioned. The Radcliffes will be delighted to assist. Go to No. 6 Upper Brook Street.'

'Oh, that will be good. I am anxious to solve the mystery.' She bestowed a smile on him, then took her leave.

Robert watched the most proper young lady in all of London walk away after making an assignation to meet him in the morning — and grinned.

There were a number of gentlemen that took notice of the pretty young thing who had captured the duke's interest, and they resolved to pay her attention as well. He was known to be extremely discriminating in his tastes. She must have something concealed beneath that well-bred exterior. They resolved to find out what it might be.

4

Following dinner Pamela approached her mother in a cautious manner regarding her time to be spent at the Radcliffe home. This was not something she could conceal from her parent, much as she might wish to try. 'Do you recall meeting Lady Anne Radcliffe, Mama? She was at the Cotterell party the other day.'

'She's the Earl of Winterton's daughter; married beneath her as I recall. Radcliffe is nothing more than a baronet.' Lady Gresham looked up from the book of sermons she had begun to read to frown at her daughter.

'I met her and her husband while there. She seems quite delightful.' Pamela wondered if it would help were she to mention the duke, and decided it could only favor her cause. 'They introduced me to the Duke of Wexford.'

'Did they, now? You failed to tell me that.' Lady Gresham gave Pamela a considering look. 'I have not had the pleasure of meeting the young duke. Knew his father, naturally. What is the son like?'

'Quite pleasant,' Pamela managed to say,

wondering how she could ever express her reactions to the handsome gentleman. 'Actually, I wish to know Lady Anne better. She has invited me to her home tomorrow morning. I trust it meets with your approval? I do like her, Mama.'

Pamela could see the war waging in her mother's mind. On one hand was the influence of a young woman who, while she was an earl's daughter, had married beneath her. On the other hand Lady Anne was one of the fashionable younger set who was everywhere seen with not only the Duke of Wexford, but any number of highly presentable lords and ladies of the *ton*. Pamela waited for her mother's response with bated breath.

At last her mother gave a regal nod of her head. 'I believe it might be just the thing for you — to mingle with that set. Mind you, be cautious. I'd not have you adopting some of the affected manners a few of them espouse.'

'Yes, Mama,' Pamela replied demurely, fixing her gaze on the piece of needlework she held in her lap. She suspected it would be better that her mother did not know all that was involved. There was that matter of severe palpitations her mother continually threatened to have.

'But remember, my dear, it is always better to associate with those who are superior to you — in talents as well as position. You can only improve your knowledge and manners by doing so. To do otherwise is to diminish yourself.' Lady Gresham gave her only child a stern look that most likely was intended to intimidate her.

Pamela nodded and thought of how gloriously happy Lady Anne appeared to be with her dearest husband, In her mother's eyes, Sir Cecil had followed her dictum and done well for himself, but Pamela very much doubted if he had given such a notion a thought when he tumbled into love with the beautiful and gay Lady Anne. From everything Pamela had learned, the Radcliffe home was the place to be for that fashionable set Mama placed in such high regard. The coming days should prove most interesting. And perhaps Pamela just might find the gentleman who would sweep her away from the stultifying atmosphere of Gresham House. The very idea of leaving this dull place was enough to bring a hopeful pink to her cheeks.

The next morning Pamela had no difficulty in waking at an early hour. When Rose entered with her chocolate and rolls, she again found her mistress curled up in her cozy chair and ottoman near the windows — daydreaming.

''Tis a fine morning, my lady,' Rose said after settling Pamela with her tray. When the maid swept the draperies aside, the soft light of early day entered the room to cheer the heart and eye.

'I shall be going out directly this morning,' Pamela said briskly. 'I had best wear something practical, for I shall be studying books at the house of Lady Anne Radcliffe.'

Pamela well knew how her maid hoped for excellent connections for her mistress, connections that might lead to being free of her mother. Pamela felt rising optimism that it might be so. Not that she expected for one moment that she might capture the eye of the duke. But where he led, others followed. And she might benefit from that interest.

A soft green walking dress with a dark green spencer piped in cream met with both Rose's and Pamela's approval. It was but a matter of minutes to decide on the rest of her garb for the important morning.

By nine of the clock, Pamela was at No. 6 Upper Brook Street on the steps of the Radcliffe house being ushered quietly in by the most proper butler. He escorted her through the silent house to the library, gesturing toward the other occupant. 'His Grace awaits, my lady.'

'Good, you are on time again,' the duke

said, glancing up from where he was seated at a large, round library table piled with books of various shapes and sizes. 'I told Perkins that you most likely would be here on the dot. No problems arose in regard to coming over here? I suspected you'd not come without your mother's approval.'

He rose to meet her, then politely drew out a chair across the table from his seat for Pamela to use. When she was seated, he returned to his place, dropping casually into his chair to study Pamela with a most disconcerting, almost probing, gaze.

'Mama approved of my becoming better acquainted with Lady Anne. I fear I did not mention that you would be here this morning, nor have I mentioned the necklace as yet. I shall have to face it sooner or later, I suppose. I'd rather have it later.'

The two shared a look of total understanding regarding parents and other problems that faced young people in general.

'Still determined to locate the sender and intended recipient of the necklace?' He studied her from the depths of his gray eyes, the intentness of his gaze bringing a faint blush to her cheeks. 'Any other young woman would be greatly tempted to keep those incredible sapphires and diamonds for herself. After all, it is not your fault the chap who delivered the package took it to the wrong Lady Pamela.' He picked up a pencil and began to toy with it. 'And that is one thing about which I'm most curious. Why did the package come to *you*, in particular? Could there be a Lady Pamela living not far from you? Or perhaps a Lady Pamela with a house number the same as yours, but on a different street?'

'I hope to discover precisely that this morning, Your Grace.' She glanced at her neat little watch pinned to her spencer and then gave him a shy grin. 'Time is flitting by.'

He became quite businesslike. 'Here, you may have the Radcliffe copy of *Debrett's* while I use my own. There is a stack of paper for making notes and extra pencils should you require them. I know they smudge, but ink can be so dreadfully messy — especially around books.'

Gratefully, Pamela accepted the book, a portion of the stack of paper, and a neatly sharpened pencil. She needed a distraction from the duke. Fancy sitting here directly across from such a man and plowing through *Debrett's*! It would take all her powers of concentration.

An hour later, she sat back in her chair to rub the back of her neck. There were limits to one's ability to pay attention to pages of names. She'd developed the ability to skim through the list with fair speed, the name Pamela seeming to leap out at her when it came. However, the names tended to blur; she hoped she'd not missed any.

'I have an impressive list of gentlemen who have the required initials. How are you coming along?' the duke asked, glancing over at the precise notes filling the top page of Pamela's paper.

'I had no idea that my name was so popular. I imagine that Richardson's novel had something to do with it, or so says my grandmother. At any rate, I have compiled a fair list of names, none of which are familiar to me. I fear this is not going to be as simple as I'd hoped.'

'Goodness, but you two look terribly serious,' caroled Lady Anne from the open doorway, breaking into the silence that had begun between the duke and Pamela. She turned aside to say something to someone in the hallway, then drifted into the room bringing the scent of heliotrope with her.

'Each of us is overly blessed with names. It is going to be more difficult than we expected or hoped,' the duke replied.

'Well, it is time that you took a respite from your search. I insist you join me for a light repast.' Lady Anne turned to the door, motioning the young footman to enter. He wheeled in a cart bearing a hearty meal. Ham, meat pies, deviled kidneys, fricassee of eggs, and rolls were revealed when lids were removed from the dishes. Pots of tea and coffee sat atop stands that had candles beneath to keep the contents warm. The sight was unbelievably welcome to a suddenly hungry Pamela. The way the duke tucked into the food, it would seem that he felt the same.

'Good,' Lady Anne said sometime later when an agreeable amount of food had disappeared, with Pamela and the duke wearing somewhat bemused and contented expressions on their faces.

'That was truly excellent and most welcome. How considerate you are, Lady Anne,' Pamela said warmly.

Lady Anne smiled, then turned to the duke. 'Did you tell her about Tuesday?'

Pamela darted a look from one to the other. Tuesday? When the duke shook his head, Lady Anne turned to face Pamela, her eyes sparkling with delight.

'I trust you will join us come Tuesday morning? After you have spent a bit of time searching these books, you absolutely *must* join our waltzing party! There will be quite a number of us, you see. We desire to practice that new dance I predict will sweep the *ton*.

The ladies of Almack's will not be able to resist it once we all know how to dance it, and well.'

Pamela took a hopeful breath. Of course she had heard of the popular new dance that was being introduced all over the city. Princess Charlotte was reported enamored of it, although Pamela's mother felt it disgraceful. And Pamela had heard about the waltzing parties held at Melbourne House, which did nothing to help, for Mama deplored that ménage. 'I should like to join you,' Pamela said hesitantly.

'I hear a 'but' in that,' the duke said.

'I can only hope that my mother will approve.'

'She will,' Lady Anne predicted, a smug look settling over her face. 'I shall call to issue the invitation in a more formal manner. I believe my mother is an old school friend of your mother's. Mama shall join me.'

The duke chuckled. 'I would say that is an unfair advantage, but since I want Lady Pamela to join us, I shan't argue.'

'I will be pleased to meet your mother, and I feel sure that Mama will enjoy chatting with her former school chum.' Pamela exchanged a shy smile with Lady Anne, then rose, preparing to leave, thus ending this morning's session.

'Must you go so soon?' Lady Anne inquired

with what appeared to be genuine regret.

'This afternoon is my mother's at home. I had best present myself, dressed to assist her.' Pamela paused a moment, then added, 'I cannot tell you how much I appreciate your help in this — both of you. You are truly most kind.'

'Our pleasure,' the duke replied before Lady Anne could say a word. He turned to his old friend to say, 'Do you suppose it would be of help if I went along with you on the call?' He had no illusions about his power or the effect his title had on people. At times, it came in dashed handy.

'I believe it might at that,' Lady Anne mused with a perfectly straight face, although a twinkle lurked in her eyes. 'We shall see you later, sometime around three-thirty?'

'I shan't say anything to Mama; it shall be a surprise,' Pamela decided.

Lady Anne summoned a maid and footman to escort Pamela to her home, Pamela having evaded her nosy maid when she slipped from the house. The quiet moments were welcome to digest all that had occurred. A waltzing party! And she might attend? Would her mother permit it?

'Pamela, is that you, dear?' her mother said when Pamela passed the study on her way to the stairs.

'Yes, Mama.' Pamela dutifully went to stand by the doorway, adding, 'I had a lovely time. I hope you may come to know Lady Anne better, for she is a most thoughtful person. Her mother went to school with you, I believe?'

'Indeed, I expect she did. I had almost forgotten that,' Lady Gresham said thoughtfully. 'You were gone rather longer than I thought proper.' There was a questioning note in her voice Pamela dare not avoid.

'Lady Anne persuaded me to stay for lunch. It was simply lovely, all in excellent taste. I felt certain you would approve.'

Lady Gresham said nothing more, and Pamela escaped to her room to change into appropriate attire for her mother's afternoon to receive callers. Pamela would sit quietly, tending to the older ladies with extra care, pour tea if required, and in general see to it that everyone who came to call had a pleasant time — if possible. Never had her nerves been so on edge as today, however. Her mother would be secretly pleased when the duke arrived. Never mind he came with Lady Anne and the Countess of Winterton.

The afternoon went remarkably well from Pamela's point of view. There were an agreeable number of women present when the trio arrived promptly at three-thirty. To

81

make matters even better, two of those attending were gossips of the first degree. The duke's presence would do her mother nice distinction.

The Countess of Winterton and Anne were charming, with the countess happily relating a story of school mischief that turned out to Lady Gresham's credit. The duke must have made her mother's heart swell when he commented that he could see where Lady Pamela inherited her charm and grace, implying that they came from her mother. Pamela wryly accepted that no flattery about her looks was offered. That would have been pouring the butter boat a bit heavy.

'I wish Lady Pamela to join a small group of my friends on Tuesday morning,' Lady Anne said quietly to Lady Gresham before it was time to leave. 'It is a little waltzing party, to allow us to practice in private. His Grace approves and will also attend,' she added artlessly.

Pamela almost smiled when she noted the expression on her mother's face. The war waged within again — decadent waltzing versus the duke and his set.

The duke won easily when he bowed over Lady Gresham's hand, adding in his distinctive voice, 'I believe Lady Pamela will shine quite well, as I feel certain you would should you choose to try the new dance.'

'Of course she may attend,' her ladyship replied with a regal nod that set the Countess of Winterton coughing into her handkerchief.

Lady Anne exchanged a nod with Pamela that might have been demure, but Pamela almost chuckled, for Lady Anne's eyes danced with mischief. 'Tuesday, next?'

Pamela walked with the departing trio as far as the door, pressing Lady Anne's hand in gratitude that she should be so helpful. After all, Pamela reminded herself, this was in aid of finding the true owner of the sapphire-and-diamond necklace — nothing more.

In the meantime, Pamela intended to pore over her father's copy of the peerage in order to expedite the hunt. It took time to check each name and the family listed beneath each titled gentleman. What she might do when she had compiled her list, she had not quite decided as yet. Perhaps the duke would have a solution.

Her heart warmed at the memory of the kind words he had expressed on her behalf. She knew he had gone out of his way to assure her presence come Tuesday, and she thought it excessively obliging of him. Of course, he only wished her there to assist in solving the mystery.

There was a hint of 'so there' in her

thoughts, for as commonplace as were her looks, she had no illusions that the duke might be inclined to look her direction for his duchess — however lovely that notion might be.

The weekend passed with all the usual events taking place. Pamela joined her mother at a concert, attended a rout, followed by a modest ball, then on Sunday accompanied her mother to the chapel the countess favored to hear a sermon that dealt with telling the truth.

In her mind, Pamela defended herself by insisting she *had* told the truth just not all of it. After all, she did not wish to make her mother ill.

Tuesday morning Pamela was up early, as had become her habit. 'I should wish to seem proper and yet have just a hint of the dashing,' she confided to Rose. 'Do I have anything that isn't depressingly proper?'

'We shall see, my lady.' It was clear that Rose harbored raised hopes for her mistress, especially after the duke attended the at home on Thursday.

It was decided that a simple, high-waisted frock with a crossed braid of fabric beneath the bust and little light puffs of sleeves at the shoulders would do. In a delicate printed muslin the dress was elegantly unpretentious, as only one cut by a master hand could be. Pamela worried the skirt might be a trifle short, but had been assured by Rose — who had bothered to find out what might be proper — that that length was all the thing for the waltz.

Feeling a bit like a fairy princess, Pamela set off for the Radcliffe house in the family carriage. Her mother had naturally not come down to see her off; she was preparing to go on her own rounds.

Breathless, although she had not rushed, Pamela calmed herself once she entered the Radcliffe house. The duke approached from the rear of the house, which surprised Pamela.

'I stable my horse to the rear, thus I come in along Shepherd's Court to the mews. Should there be a nosy busybody chancing past, he or she would never connect us together.' His tone was wry.

'How considerate you are,' Pamela murmured, resolved never to allow His Grace to be placed in a position of the faintest degree of compromise. It was obvious that he did not desire it in the least.

She had brought her greatly expanded list with her, and now placed it on the table along with the books and papers that had been set out for their use.

'I see you have continued to work on your compilation,' the duke said with approval.

'If I consulted the peerage only while I was here, it would take ages to complete,' Pamela said, turning her attention to the paper on the table. It was far too tempting to fix her gaze on the duke, for in that direction lay trouble, possibly heartbreak.

Sensibly, she concentrated on the copy of the peerage before her, trying to complete her list as swiftly as possible. How nice of *Debrett's* to offer such a neat compilation of the peerage, although she doubted if she needed to note those of Scotland and Ireland. Somehow, she suspected that the *Pamela* sought was English.

When Lady Anne entered the library, Pamela was only too ready to stop, however. If she studied those lines of print very long, the words tended to blur.

'A hasty bit to eat,' she cried, 'then you must come along to the drawing room where the others will soon be assembled. I have found the most elegant little musical ensemble to play for us. Come now, do partake of this repast I have brought you.' She gestured to the tray carried in by the footman. It contained a lovely salad, rolls, meat pies, and a pot of hot tea.

'More later,' she said while peering at the

sheets of paper containing the neat list of names Pamela had copied out. 'My, there are more Pamelas than I anticipated. I expect a list of Anne's would be staggering!'

The duke chuckled at this. Then he looked to the man in the doorway and said, 'Your charming wife has declared we would be staggered at the number of Annes to be found.'

'Ah, but there is only one like her, Anne Elizabeth Radcliffe,' Sir Cecil declared fondly.

Pamela hastily completed the light meal, glancing at the duke to note that while he did not appear to hurry, he also consumed his food with speed.

The moment she observed the plates were empty and the cups drained, Lady Anne whisked everyone along the hall until they reached the exquisite drawing room, decorated in the height of fashion in delicate gold and blue on a background of pale cream.

Off to one corner of the room sat a trio of gentlemen, one at a pianoforte, the others with clarinet and violin in hand. The dancing master stood center front, watching all.

The gentlemen dancers all wore slender-tailed coats, discreet waistcoats, tightly fitting knee breeches or pantaloons, and black dancing slippers. Their fanciful cravats were the only touch of embellishment to otherwise sober array.

The young women were in contrast like a flock of extravagant butterflies captured in all delicacy of color, their silks and muslins swirling about them in refined elegance. Pamela was pleased to note that her simple gown was most appropriate for the occasion.

Lady Anne introduced Pamela to all of the group, adding bits and scraps about most of them. There were pleasant jests, but Pamela detected, or thought she did, a faint nervousness in the other young women. It made her feel enormously better.

'I know you have not attempted the steps as yet,' the duke said at her side. 'Now, put aside the worries of that necklace and concentrate on what I tell you to do.'

As custom decreed, she wore a pair of spotless white gloves — removed while she wrote and now restored to tense hands. Pamela nervously moistened her lips and stayed close to the duke as they began to form a circle.

'Head erect, chin up, smile,' the duke ordered softly as he led her to a place along the side of the room. He positioned her so they stood face-to-face, slightly to the right of each other. The duke took her right hand lightly in his left, then slid his right arm behind her back, saying, 'Place your other hand lightly on my shoulder. The beat is three-quarter to a measure, as you will soon sense.'

Pamela was quite certain she might expire on the spot. Never had she been in such an intimate position with a gentleman. No other dance required the couple to face one another in such proximity.

Before she might protest, the music began, a beguiling rhythm that compelled her feet to move in time, matching the duke's steps. Around and around they went, breathlessly, almost dizzily. She had no time to think of steps, of what she ought to be doing, or where her feet must be positioned as in the past. She could only dance.

The dancers turned continually while they revolved around the room. There were no steps forward or backward, no change, it was all a continuous whirl of pleasure.

'Do not be so serious,' the duke admonished lightly. 'I shan't allow you to collapse when we cease this spinning about the room.' When he chuckled, she wondered what was revealed in her face.

Pamela wondered whether it was the actual dance that made her feel light-headed or the closeness of the most debonair of gentlemen, the duke.

The music stopped, and the duke did as promised. He retained hold of her a moment, then asked, 'Do you feel quite up to standing on your own?'

'Oh, yes,' Pamela said, while actually wondering if she might collapse in a heap.

Their dancing master, who had been standing in the center of the revolving group, clapped his hands, then said, 'I shall point out a few things to every couple. Please do remain in place until I have spoken with every pair.'

Since the duke held precedence, the man came to them first. 'Your Grace is extremely graceful, as is your partner. If I might suggest this with the hands' — and he instructed what he desired in a change of position.

To Pamela it was incredibly shocking. Now she could understand why the waltz had been so frowned upon, why her mother was so hesitant. It was one thing to observe; it was quite another to stand so close to a man such as the duke, with his arm snugly about her and her body almost skimming his, her own hand resting on that manly shoulder, her other hand held so gently in his. Never mind they wore gloves, she could feel the strength of his clasp in her hand. She was of a height to reach his cheek, so it was not a difficult matter to gaze into his eyes. Indeed, it seemed impossible to look elsewhere.

He smelled manly but clean, she decided,

not at all like some she had chanced to be made aware of while in the press of a throng. It was a mixture of something that pleased her nose very much, whatever the content, and the light tangy scent seemed a part of him.

By this time, the dancing master had completed the small circle of friends. Once again the music began and the dance resumed, revolving around the room.

'One, two, three — you see, it is not so difficult after all,' the duke said lightly, pulling her closer when they were about to collide with a slower couple.

'Not so difficult?' she said, sounding quite as breathless as she felt.

'You are a natural waltzer. I would think you had tricked me and taken waltzing lessons did I not know what an honest little creature you undoubtedly are. I shall make it a point to seek you out as a partner for the waltz when next we chance to grace the same ballroom.' His gray eyes gleamed with his seeming pleasure at the prospect.

Pamela was utterly speechless at this handsome commendation. What had begun as a plea for help from the master at solving crimes had turned into something else, something she could not define if her life depended on it. One thing she knew for sure, her life would never be the same again.

Even if she did not capture the interest and heart of the duke, he had opened the door to the inner realm of society, that fashionable group of young people where Pamela sensed her mother desired her daughter find a husband. One of these gentlemen was undoubtedly destined to be her mate. Who it might be really didn't matter, she supposed. It was enough that she belonged here.

It was a pity that she had a decided partiality for one she could not have. But there you were. Things like that happened. It was enough to have the happiness of his utterly newfound friendship; the dancing and physical closeness were lovely.

'We must change partners now,' the duke explained. 'It will assist you in becoming accustomed to several different styles of dance.'

Another partner, a different style. Pamela strongly suspected that there was not another man in the room who could match the duke for grace and elegance. And although the dancing master had certainly done his job well, she was proven right.

5

She had danced the waltz with nearly every gentleman present. None of the others affected her like the duke. The amiable Sir Cecil had chatted pleasantly. The ginger-haired Algernon Thynne, Esq., was a charming waltzer and made light conversation of the sort that did not demand a great deal of attention.

The remainder had varied between talking and concentrating on their steps. They had been quite charming. None had permitted Pamela to become so dizzy that she required a restorative.

However, her mind kept returning to the nagging question of who the Lady Pamela might be that ought to have received the necklace. And what gentleman would defy convention to present her with such a gift?

Pamela had been offered lovely things and had always refused them as gently as possible. Her mother would have had palpitations had she not. But Pamela had never wished to be under obligation to a gentleman she did not care for in the least. It seemed dishonest.

Perhaps the other Lady Pamela would also

have refused this offering? In her heart, Pamela felt it to be otherwise, for there was that matter of 'dearest' to consider. She had noticed that the duke had a sizable listing of gentlemen with the initials of J.R. Would any of them prove guilty?

'They have all gone,' Lady Anne declared when she returned from seeing the other guests off following the cold collation, which was enjoyed after the waltzing. Dancing tended to make one hungry. 'Did you enjoy your waltzing,' she said to Pamela with a curious gleam in her pretty eyes.

'Indeed, I did.' Pamela smiled politely at her hostess, for she had provided the opportunity for a most delightful time. Then she heard the duke coming down the hall from wherever he had gone with his host. She turned to face him.

'Are we to resume our search?' she inquired when he joined Anne and her in the hall. 'I had thought our efforts over for the day.' She doubted she could concentrate on it.

'Since you do not look the least fatigued after a strenuous afternoon of waltzing I propose we cover a few more pages before we cease for the nonce.'

'It goes so dreadfully slow,' Pamela protested to Lady Anne at the door to the library. 'There are so many other matters demanding attention, and I, for one, find it difficult to creep away to my room to go over those fine lines of print. After a while, it goes all hazy.'

'I imagine it does tend to drag a bit. We shall have to consider an alternative, perhaps.' Lady Anne turned to her husband and said, 'What do you think, Cecil? Shall we consider another means of finding out who the other Lady Pamela might be, as well as the man, J.R.?'

'Give us another day before we decide that,' the duke said from over Pamela's shoulder.

She froze, terribly aware of his nearness. It was almost like the waltzing, only this time he pressed closely to her back. She took a tiny step forward, for the last thing she wished was to make a scene before these lovely people. He immediately stepped away to enter the library.

'Well enough,' Sir Cecil said by way of agreement, walking away down the hall with Lady Anne at his side.

Pamela approached the library table where the Duke of Wexford was now seated with just a bit of reserve. Dancing the waltz had broken a restraint between them. Did it do that to everyone? She doubted it, for she could not detect the least change in attitude from other gentlemen she had partnered. Nor did she feel anything toward them. Not the slightest. Well, she comforted herself, she doubted if His Grace had the least notion how he affected her, so she was safe from discovery.

'I do not think this is going to work,' the duke said quietly from his side of the table.

'Why do you say that?' In a way, Pamela was glad to hear she was not the only one developing reservations about their scheme.

'Who is to say that this J.R. is one of us? Think about the men who would not be listed in the peerage. He might be a distant relation that would never be counted among the immediate family. He might also be a man of a lower class. Had you considered that?' The duke sat back in his chair, fiddling with his pencil again while he awaited her reaction to his words.

'I had not thought of that. I did wonder what we would do with our lists of names once we finished going through the books. Consider — what course do we take if we decide that a particular Lady Pamela is the one we seek? How do we know for certain? Can we straight out ask her if she has a gentleman she considers 'dearest' who would send her such a magnificent piece of jewelry?

96

She might say no merely to deny that she could be in such a position — for it would place her beyond the pale in society. In which case, we are no better off than we were in the beginning.'

Pamela walked to the table and daintily seated herself opposite him. She studied the duke's face while she allowed him to digest her words. It was clear that he was not pleased with his thoughts.

'It most definitely would not be easy for a woman to confess to this,' he mused with the air of one who has spent a great deal of time around women. 'To admit such a thing places her in a bad position and implies a great deal of wickedness.'

'Mama says that wickedness is always easier than virtue. I suspect she is right. We must proceed with the lists. We have gone too far to cease now. But, I believe we had best figure out what comes next. Do you not agree?'

She gave him a worried look, then turned to her copy of the peerage to commence the continued perusal of the pages of names that seemed to go on forever.

Robert coolly appraised Lady Pamela as she resumed scanning the pages for names. She was right. This was not the best solution, and he was at a loss to know how best to proceed. Several things occurred to him, but he suspected that his client, if you might call her that, would take a dim view of what he had in mind.

He continued to toy with his pencil while he considered what he had experienced this afternoon. He had always enjoyed dancing, the waltz being no exception, for it offered a delightful proximity to a lady. He had to confess he was puzzled by his reaction to Lady Pamela. She was demure, proper, all that she ought to be — yet there had been this amazing rapport between them, as though they had danced before, indeed known each other for a very long time. He could not recall being so completely in tune with another woman before.

She appealed to him in the most unusual way. There was an innocent sensuality about her. He was certain she was quite unaware of it. He had known the oddest urge to forbid the other men from dancing with her, as though it profaned something sacred — which was utter nonsense, was it not?

So, where did it place him in this investigation? He quietly snorted in disgust.

'Did you say something, Your Grace?' Lady Pamela said, clearly startled at his sound of impatience.

'No, nothing at all. How do you come?' He

peered over at her top page, depressingly free of names.

'Not well, I fear. Some letters of the alphabet offer better luck than others. I can only keep going.' She sighed, placing her elbows on the table and resting her chin on her folded hands. 'It is so dreadfully boring. That's a terrible admission to make, I fear. But 'tis true, none the less.' She bestowed a smile on him that lit up her pretty eyes in a charming way — made her look like a mischievous angel.

'Do I detect a rumble of discontent among the natives?' Lady Anne cried from the doorway.

Lady Pamela turned, abandoning her pose that made her look so angelic and said, 'If you can find a native willing to slog through these dratted names, by all means pull him over here.'

'Goodness! Is it truly that dreadful?' Lady Anne crossed to the table to peer over Pamela's shoulder at the book and the empty paper. 'Here, allow me to help. I'll scan this page while you write, when and if I find a Lady Pamela.'

'That ought to cheer you,' added Robert.

'I found a Pamela on that page, but she is not a lady,' Lady Pamela said wearily, then looked confused when Anne and he burst into peals of laughter.

When he could stop his chuckles, Robert took pity on Pamela and said, 'And how do you know she isn't a lady? Is there a star by her name implying such in a footnote?'

To his delight, Lady Pamela blushed that absolutely charming wild rose again. 'Oh, dear, I did say that, didn't I!'

'Robert, you are an utter beast,' Lady Anne declared. 'Stop teasing the dear girl at once.'

'You laughed as well,' Robert said in defense of his amusement.

'So I did.' Anne giggled again. 'Truth be known, I believe there are quite a number of women in this book who aren't ladies.' Which remark sent them all into a fit of laughter.

'I believe we might as well quit for the day,' Lady Pamela said with a fond look at her new friend.

'Actually, I have completed my section,' Robert said, pushing back his chair from the table while closing his copy of the peerage with a thud. 'The list is not long, but does not look promising.'

'It is progress of a sort, you must admit,' Lady Pamela said with a disgusted look at the book she used, the marker somewhere at midpoint.

Robert rose from his chair and went around to assist Lady Pamela and Anne. 'We shall think on this,' he said when the two ladies faced him.

'I hope you might come to an interesting conclusion. We need something to force the issue, I believe,' Lady Pamela offered as she turned to the door. As they began to stroll to the front door, Robert slipped a hand beneath Lady Pamela's elbow and sensed her tension.

'Perhaps I might take you home?' he inquired with a diffidence he didn't feel.

'If it is not too much trouble, I would appreciate it,' Lady Pamela said with that delightful hint of rose once again rising to color her cheeks.

Arrangements were made to meet again with the hope of completing the work — this time Robert assisting Pamela. Anne offered her help, which was promptly accepted.

'I shall begin from the back of the book; I am certain to have a bit of spare time later on or early in the morning,' she said blithely.

The Duke of Wexford left the Radcliffe house with the gentle and proper Lady Pamela on his arm, wondering if he had taken leave of his senses. She was not his usual sort of flirt. She was not his usual sort of interest at all. So why did she intrigue him? It would take study, and of course that would take time and exposure to the pretty Lady Pamela.

He would help launch her into society, for although her mother might be a countess and her father an earl of distinction, the fact remained that Lady Pamela had not been seen in the right places with the right people. Even at Almack's she danced with the most dreary of chaps. That simply would not do.

'I suppose you have a full evening?' he said by way of finding out what her plans were for this night. 'Your mother most likely selects the entertainments she believes you would enjoy?'

'Tonight we attend a concert of antique music again. I am growing to appreciate it, I believe,' Lady Pamela said with a doubtful look into his eyes.

'Interesting,' Robert replied, hardly noting his response. He found her eyes held intriguing depths.

While their carriage jogged along over the cobbled streets, Robert said, 'I have checked again with Bow Street, and there has been no report of a necklace answering to the description of the one in your custody. I understand that spy activity has been on the rise of late. The necklace could be in payment for that sort of thing.'

'The term of 'Lady' might even be a joke of sorts, and this Pamela isn't a lady at all.' The young woman at his side chuckled softly, most likely recalling her earlier words about the Pamela that was no lady. 'My governess used to call me Lady Jane Gray when she thought I was acting pretentiously above myself.'

'And did you?' Robert inquired. At her look of puzzlement, he added, 'Act above yourself? Somehow I cannot envision such a thing. You are undoubtedly the most proper young woman I've yet to meet.'

'If I am it is because Miss Osborn saw to it that I knew my manners. Mama would have fired her otherwise.'

She clasped her hands tightly in her lap and looked forbiddingly grim when she made that statement. Had he not seen those hands, and the tight line about her mouth — which relaxed moments later, he'd have thought little of her reply.

And what of it? He had been birched a good many times while at home under the tyranny of his tutor, then later at Eton. Most chaps had known the same treatment. He could sympathize with strict discipline. He had long ago realized that it produced people of fiber and backbone.

'At least you are free of your governess and I of my tutor,' he said lightly.

'What a lovely achievement, although it was most likely because we grew too old to require them,' she said with a wry smile.

'No problem with the jewels as yet?' he said when they drew up before her home.

'I do worry about keeping such a valuable piece tucked up on my bookshelf. Makes my sleep a trifle uneasy. And I especially dislike leaving it there during the day. What happens if my maid decides to dust the shelves while I am gone and finds them? She would take them straightaway to my mother!'

'Are most of your day gowns high in the neck?' Robert had observed that all her gowns to date, with the exception of the charming thing she wore now, had been high-necked. When she gave him a puzzled nod, he continued, 'You could wear the necklace beneath the gown. Put it on once your maid has finished dressing you. Surely, you have a few minutes to yourself in the morning?'

'I do,' she agreed. 'And yes, I fear that most of my gowns are properly high in the neck. Mama demands a demure frock; she believes most unmarried women dress scandalously. Our mantua-maker does as Mama wishes.'

'And what do you wish?' he asked, knowing he ought to escort her to the front door where the butler stood awaiting the young lady of the house.

'It really doesn't matter, does it? At least

for now.' She turned to leave the carriage, then paused, facing him again. 'But someday I shall go to a premier mantuamaker and order whatever is the kick of fashion, hang propriety.' She realized her blunder a moment after she uttered the words, giving a vexed laugh. 'What is it about you, Your Grace? You have the most dreadful effect on my speech!'

He joined her laughter, thinking she was a delightfully mixed bag of womanhood. After he had assisted her from his carriage, he returned to it, but not before instructing his driver to take him off to Rundle and Bridge again.

Pamela slipped past Grimes, dashing madly up the stairs to her room. Rose was elsewhere.

Running to the bookshelf, Pamela pulled forth the leather case and gave a sigh of relief when she found the glittering jewels safe. He had suggested she wear it. Gingerly, she picked the sapphire-and-diamond extravagance from the bed of velvet, then draped it about her neck.

Crossing to the looking glass, she studied the effect of the blue-and-white gems against her bosom. Disturbing, it was, to see those magnificent jewels against her own soft skin. It made her want to possess them, and she could understand why some women would do a great deal to own something like this.

She fastened the clasp, then slipped from her waltzing gown. In the back of her wardrobe she found a favorite dress of soft blue kerseymere piped in ivory with pearl buttons down the front, so she did not need Rose to assist her. It had a frill around the neck and the wrists, and made her feel like a character from a play about old Queen Elizabeth. All she needed was a red wig.

It felt decidedly odd to have the weight of the necklace against her bare skin. There was something almost wicked about the notion of concealing the gems in such a manner. Yet she expected the duke had the right of it. It would never do for the jewels to be discovered, particularly by Rose, who would hurry them to Mama.

And Pamela did not want to consider the questions that would come with them. It didn't bear thinking about!

Slipping from her room, she quietly went down to the drawing room, where she thought she might find her mother.

'Ah, Pamela, my dear,' her mother cried when she saw her dutiful daughter enter the room. 'Tell me about the waltzing party,' Lady Gresham demanded.

'It was quite lovely,' Pamela replied in her gentle voice. The duke instructed me most politely, and I waltzed with almost all the gentlemen in attendance. Everyone there would be found in Papa's peerage. The duke's particular friend, Algernon Thynne, Esq. was there, and he is the heir of Baron Lyndon.'

'I believe I recall meeting the baron. 'Tis rumored he is vastly wealthy. When one does not have a gamester in the family, it is possible to accumulate a goodly fortune,' her mother observed.

'I believe that to be most true,' Pamela agreed, wishing she might escape this questioning, yet knowing it to be inevitable. She went on to name the others who had attended, reeling off a list that sounded like a page or two from the peerage she had been poring over the past days.

'And about the waltz? Did it not seem somewhat wicked in nature?' her mother probed.

'Actually, it was splendid,' Pamela said in a rush. 'I did not become dizzy as I had feared. The gentlemen were most considerate. Lady Anne insists it will not be long before the ladies at Almack's yield to the popularity of the waltz. I wonder who will demand it and succeed?'

'Most likely the Countess Lieven,' the countess mused. 'Or perhaps the Princess Esterhazy. Lady Sefton is not the sort, nor do

I believe Emily Cowper would bother. She is too wrapped up in the doings at Melbourne House. Lady Jersey is a possibility, of course,' the countess concluded.

The footman entered with a tray bearing all the necessary items for a substantial tea. Pamela prepared a cup of tea for her mother, then added the lemon and sugar as desired, handing it to the older lady with all the grace of a lady in waiting.

'Ah, there you are,' the earl said, peering around the door. Spying the tray and tea set out, he proceeded to join them.

Pamela poured for her father as well, mentally preparing herself for whatever was on his mind.

'Your mother tells me that you attended a waltzing party earlier today,' he began after taking a sip from his cup. 'How did you fare? Is it a difficult dance to perform?'

'I believe I did well, and no, it is not difficult. One must only be on guard against dizziness — that constant turning, you know. But despite that, I quite enjoyed it. The gentlemen were all splendidly behaved and the young ladies most proper.'

Pamela sipped her tea, grateful for something with which to occupy her hands.

'Tell us more, dear,' her mother gently commanded.

'There was a dancing master who watched us and made corrections where necessary. The duke was an excellent teacher, for we needed very little adjustment. Lady Anne had a light meal set out for any who wished to partake of refreshments after we concluded the dancing.'

'You say the Duke of Wexford taught you the waltz?' the earl said, his eyebrows shooting up in surprise.

'Indeed, Papa. He is most proper in manner. But then, I rarely find a gentleman who is not.' Pamela wondered what it might be like to have a man behave other than with excruciating propriety toward her. It was beyond her imagination.

'He is a fine young man; I approve the connection,' the earl said with the air of a pronouncement.

'Papa,' Pamela said with a feeling of consternation rising within her, 'the duke was merely my waltzing partner, nothing more. I trust you will not make more of this than is proper.'

'It is fortunate that you caught the eye of so socially prominent a young matron as Lady Anne,' the countess observed.

It was a good thing Pamela had set her teacup on the tray, else she might have splattered all the liquid all over her kerseymere dress. She felt the weight of the jewels again and hoped the outline of them was not discernible. Her mother had always been able to tell when Pamela tried to conceal something, and it was unlikely that she would fail to question her daughter if she thought something amiss now.

As blandly as possible Pamela said, 'You are right as usual, Mama.' And then she excused herself, adding, 'I have several books that ought to be returned to Hatchard's this afternoon.'

She escaped from the drawing room with profound relief, leaving her parents to no doubt dissect the character of the duke, Lady Anne and Sir Cecil, not to mention Algernon Thynne, Esq., and the rest of the younger fashionable set who had attended the waltzing party.

It took but a few minutes to gather up the books that truly did need to be returned. She neatly tied her bonnet, pulled on a pair of York tan gloves, slipped the ribands of her reticule over her wrist, then walked down the stairs and out the front door, Rose trailing properly behind her.

At Hatchard's, Pamela set Rose to looking through a picture book. Then she sauntered along an aisle of novels, for she was weary of improving books.

'I thought I saw you enter the shop. With a brim like that on your bonnet, it is difficult to know for certain, but I was certain I recognized your maid.' The familiar voice belonging to the duke set Pamela's heart to spinning like a dervish she'd read about.

'Your Grace,' she murmured, sinking into a lovely curtsy. 'I did not expect to see you here, especially after having just been in your company at the Radcliffes.'

'I'm particularly glad to find you here alone. I saw your maid happily looking at pictures around the corner, but she cannot overhear us, I believe.'

'I doubt that, nor is she inclined to come searching for me,' Pamela said with a pretty smile.

'Good. I did a bit of sleuthing after I left you. Tried again to persuade the chap at Rundle and Bridge to give me the name of the person who had originally commissioned the necklace, but it was no go. However, he did offer a suggestion that I feel has merit. Actually, it was not a suggestion, he merely said something to the effect that were the person who missed the necklace to view it, he or she would be apt to seek it out.'

'Surely, you are not suggesting what I think you are?' Pamela whispered, fearful that someone might overhear what she said. One hand crept up to touch the necklace where it nestled beneath her gown. The warmed metal felt smooth against her skin.

'You have it on now?' he said quietly, glancing about them in a casual way.

'As you suggested I do,' she whispered. 'You cannot mean for me to wear it in plain view!' She almost forgot to whisper in her concern.

'How many gowns do you own that have suitable décolletage to show off the necklace?' he softly demanded.

'You are utterly mad!' she hissed back.

'How many?'

'Two, maybe three. Mama does not approve low necklines for proper young ladies.'

'Could your maid alter several ball gowns for you?'

'Mama would have severe palpitations!' Pamela softly declared. It was most difficult to conduct an argument with someone while whispering. She felt more like shouting.

He thought for several minutes while Pamela pretended to browse along the shelves of books. From the corner of her eye she watched that lean, beautifully gloved hand rub the line of his jaw. Then he dropped his hand and peered around her bonnet to look at her.

'I am determined this is the best course for us to take. I shall persuade Lady Anne to convince your mother that it is essential for you to be *au courant* with the very latest in style, which of course will be ball gowns with very low and fashionable bodices. I believe they will look quite stunning on you,' he mused softly.

'Sirrah!' Pamela said more loudly than intended, then blushed when a formidable matron frowned at her. She whispered, 'That is a highly improper comment, Your Grace!' She had discovered that an improper remark not only made her blush, it made her feel wicked somehow.

'Come now, surely you are aware that you have a very lovely figure and ought to do fine justice to fashionable gowns. That is an encomium I do not offer lightly, nor to just anyone. Are we not beyond polite acquaintances?' he said with a hint of plaintiveness in his voice. 'Can we not be friends as well as accomplices?'

Pamela almost felt like laughing, for the entire matter was so utterly preposterous that it was more like a dream than reality. Friends with the duke? Was it possible? 'I feel it is better to be an accomplice,' she concluded.

'We shall be both,' he decided. 'And the next thing for us to do — after altering a few of your ball gowns — is for me to escort you to a number of balls. You will wear the necklace and then we shall see!'

'Oh, mercy!' whispered Pamela. How could she explain the jewels to Mama?

6

'Precisely what are we to tell my mother?'
Pamela said while taking a book to the clerk.
She was not sure what the subject of the book
was, for her wits were certainly confused at
this point, but she needed to leave here and
must have a book — she always returned with
one or more. 'You must know Mama will not
fail to notice the rather spectacular jewels I
have suddenly acquired. Since my parents did
not bestow them upon me — who dare we
say did?' Pamela knew that in all propriety
the duke couldn't do such a thing — he had
no intention of marriage, nor was he the least
interested in her except in helping solve the
mystery.

'Hm, that is a problem. Let me think.' He
strolled along toward the front door of the
bookshop, quite obviously intent on the matter.

After the clerk duly noted Pamela's
selection, she motioned Rose to follow, then
with a feeling of unreality walked to the door
where the duke awaited her. Could this
actually be happening to her? Once again, the
sensation was both deliciously dangerous and
exciting.

As they left Hatchard's, the duke motioned to his driver and Rose to trail behind them, then proceeded to guide Pamela along in the direction of Green Park.

'Do you have a rich uncle or some such helpful creature who might endow you with unexpected wealth?' the duke asked, taking her elbow firmly in his clasp when they were to cross a street.

Pamela was so rattled by his touch, she scarcely knew how to reply. 'I don't recall,' she began.

'Is your mother one of those who knows every relative on either side of family trees?'

'She considers family important, but I confess she is a trifle vague when it comes to great-uncles and first cousins once removed,' Pamela said with a smile.

'Good,' he declared. 'You will receive this necklace — in its original box and by special courier — from your eccentric great-uncle on your father's side of the family. He' — and the duke stared off into space for a few moments before he raised a finger in point — 'wishes you to wear this necklace in place of his first love, for whom he originally bought it, who died and was never able to wear it. That gives you an excellent excuse! You will be honor bound to wear the necklace. I believe your mother is a stickler

116

for what is proper.'

'Goodness,' Pamela exclaimed after she had followed his tortuous line of reasoning through in her mind again. 'I do know there is a great-uncle still alive somewhere in Kent, and I recall Mama referring to him as somewhat strange. The necklace proposition will seem rather odd, however.'

'Consider, once you receive the necklace you will be able to store it in your father's safe. That will set your mind more at ease in that regard,' the duke said persuasively.

'I do not know,' Pamela said, feeling there must be something amiss with this mad scheme if she could only think of it.

'Tell me, what mother would not wish to see her daughter arrayed in those exquisite jewels with a legitimate reason for wearing them? I shall personally drop a word or two in Lady Jersey's ear, the others as well, if necessary. Most young women can wear but simple pearls. You not only will wear something different, you will have a most romantic reason for doing so. Everyone likes a touch of the romantic. You will be a *succès fou*.'

The duke sounded so plausible, so convincing, that Pamela simply gave up trying to find holes in his logic. She was not quite certain she wished to be a raving success, but the duke's idea was better than anything she had.

'Very well,' she capitulated. 'My eccentric great-uncle it is. Mama is sure to want to read the message, so I cannot write it. And where will we find a courier?' she queried, frowning at the obstacles presented.

'Leave it all to me. Once you are at home, place the necklace back into the leather box. I shall come to call with Lady Anne this afternoon near the end of the calling hours. You will have to find some reason to give the box to me. Can you disguise it?' Pamela felt an inner glow at the look of regard he gave her. Why, it seemed as though the duke actually thought she had an opinion worth listening to!

'That ought to be simple. It is very like the shape of a book of poetry I own. Perhaps I could lend the 'book' to Lady Anne?' Pamela said, while thinking she was sailing off into rather deep waters, especially for one who considered herself to be as truthful as possible.

'Clever girl,' the duke said with quiet approval.

'I am glad you did not expect me to claim that it was a gift from you,' Pamela said without realizing she had given voice to her inner thoughts.

'My dear girl,' the duke said in dismay, 'I trust you do not hold me in such contempt!'

'I *am* sorry,' Pamela said contritely when she realized she had spoken so foolishly. 'I know you would not be so improper. My wits have gone begging, I fear.'

'Indeed,' he agreed with chilling reserve. 'I shall see you later. Until then, I have much to do.' He turned to enter his carriage with a rush, taking off down the street with alarming speed.

Pamela paused on the edge of Green Park, looking after the departing carriage and feeling quite vexed with the duke. Hurriedly, retracing her steps to the bookshop, she found her father's carriage waiting for her.

'He is the most impossible man,' she fumed to Rose, who merely smiled and said nothing in reply.

Back in her bedroom, she dismissed Rose. Then after slipping off the necklace, she replaced it on the bed of cream velvet with reverent care. It took a bit of searching before she managed to locate some paper in which to wrap the case, but once it was done, it looked sufficiently like the book of poetry to fool her mother.

It was late in the afternoon, almost the time when society took to the lanes of Hyde Park for fashionable drives, when the duke arrived with Lady Anne. Pamela sat at her mother's side trying to conceal her impatience and apprehension.

To say that Lady Gresham was surprised to see them again in such a short time was putting it mildly. Pamela disliked the speculative looks coming her way from Mama during the brief call. If her mother acquired foolish notions, they could not be laid at Pamela's feet. It wasn't her idea that the necklace be transferred in this manner. Of course, if Lady Anne could persuade Mama to change her view of necklines, all to the better.

'Dear Lady Gresham,' Lady Anne said in her winsome way, 'I trust you and Lady Pamela will be attending Lady Sefton's ball this coming week?'

'We have sent our acceptances,' Lady Gresham admitted. Since the Sefton ball was *the* ball that everyone must attend to be considered true society, it was of utmost importance to be seen there. No one would refuse the invitation.

'I am pleased we shall see you there,' Lady Anne said with a touch of complacency. She leaned forward in an attitude of confidentiality and lowered her voice. 'Have you observed how the most proper young ladies have adopted a style that was once considered a trifle daring? Necklines, my lady,' Anne declared with a nod. 'They are dipping lower than in past weeks. Surely, you have noticed such in your latest copy of the *Repository*,' she said, referring to the most recent issue of Rudolf Ackermann's *Repository of Arts* that was placed on a nearby table. It was regarded by society as the essence of fashionable taste and refinement in apparel.

'I had not paid any attention,' Lady Gresham confessed, most likely because she was reluctant to say she did not agree with the fashion to one who was most fashionable.

'I imagine your daughter will be doing the same thing I intend to do — that is, have my maid alter the necklines on my ball gowns so I will be *au courant*. One cannot permit oneself to drift into dull conformity to a past fashion, can one?' Lady Anne inquired with a limpid gaze into Lady Gresham's confused eyes.

'No, of course not,' Lady Gresham said with hesitation. 'I feel sure that Rose will be able to make Pamela's latest creation quite the thing.'

'How lovely. Some maids are not so talented. Lady Pamela is fortunate you found her a maid with such skills.'

By praising Lady Gresham for a small part in the entire business, Anne succeeded in assuring the success of the mission — to lower the ball gown neckline so as to best display the jewels.

Before the guests departed, Pamela insisted that Lady Anne should enjoy a charming book of poetry. While hurrying to her room, Pamela decided that for an incurably honest girl, she was becoming something else entirely!

A short time later, the duke ushered Lady Anne into his carriage with a most satisfied expression on his face.

'You are in danger of growing smug, Your Grace,' Lady Anne said from the opposite seat of the carriage.

'I do have rather good ideas, you must admit,' he replied, forgetting the idea was partly Pamela's. 'Give me the case and I shall tend to the letter and delivery of the same. Her dotty old great-uncle is about to become most cherished.'

'How cynical, to think he could only be loved if he bestows a handsome gift on her.'

'Perhaps not Lady Pamela, but certainly the mother,' the duke replied, silencing his friend. 'I shall consult the peerage to find the precise direction of the old chap, as well as his name. It ought to make the parcel appear most genuine.'

The following day saw the delivery of an

interesting package to Pamela, brought by courier at a time when the entire family was at the breakfast table together.

'A courier just arrived with this, your ladyship,' Grimes said, but handing the parcel to Pamela. ''Tis for Lady Pamela.'

'Whatever can it be?' Lady Gresham said with more than a little curiosity. Life in London had become exciting as of late.

Pamela glanced at the direction on the package, setting it aside for possible inspection later, swiftly opened the package, then the box, exclaiming with delight at the jewels within.

'Who dares to send such an expensive gift to you,' her father roared.

Unfolding the crisp note, Pamela read the contents to her increasingly amazed parents.

'Great-uncle Charles? I had no idea he had a lost love. Chap never married, you know. This must be why,' Papa said musingly.

'Well, I do not recall any such relative on your side, but he would have been a brother to your grandfather, so that is not surprising,' Lady Gresham said while studying the magnificent jewels. 'I do not know about Pamela wearing these . . . ' She gave her husband a doubtful look.

'Of course she shall wear them,' the earl cried. 'It would be an insult for her *not* to wear them. Do not think that because he isn't here, he wouldn't know. Word can reach the most peculiar locations.'

Pamela's heart sank at this pronouncement. 'I will write him a letter and give it to you to frank for me, Papa,' she said at last. Knowing that her parent was fully capable of reading her letter, Pamela took ages to compose the most polite and properly vague letter of thanks that had most likely ever been written. What he could not know was that after franking, the letter would simply disappear.

Then she had Rose alter her ball gowns, particularly the one intended for the all-important Sefton ball.

So it was to be at this ball that Pamela not only would wear the magnificent sapphire-and-diamond jewels, but now her blue satin ball gown had a far lower neckline than when originally made.

'Rose, tell me I do not look like a brazen woman,' Pamela said softly to her maid while she inspected her reflection in the looking glass. The diamonds coupled with the sumptuous richness of the satin gave her delicate skin a soft blushing glow while the sapphires matched the vivid blue of her eyes.

'No, milady,' her gentle maid replied with a smile. 'You look a treat for the eyes in that pretty dress. And the necklace is sure to draw attention.' Naturally, Rose dared not mention her lady's décolletage was made audacious by the recent alteration.

That was precisely what Pamela feared. She was all about in the attic to proceed with this mad scheme. It went against her grain to partake in deceit — yet she must, for she desired to restore the jewels to the rightful owner and it seemed to require drastic measures.

It was evident from the moment she removed her cloak at the Sefton house and came forward to greet her hostess that the duke had done as promised. 'So these are the lovely jewels from your great-uncle! What a charming gentleman, to harbor such love, then do this for you, my dear,' Lady Sefton concluded before passing Pamela along to the earl, who studied the necklace with a connoisseur's eye.

Pamela still felt somewhat undressed, not the least accustomed to a neckline that barely — to her sensitive nature — seemed proper. However, she reasoned that most of the people would be far more interested in her jewelry than the low cut of her gown, so she tried to appear serene.

'Ah, Lady Pamela, Lord and Lady Gresham,' Lady Anne cried. Sir Cecil, the duke, and Algernon Thynne were clustered around the pretty Lady Anne in light conversation when Pamela and her mother entered the room followed by the earl.

Lord Gresham nodded pleasantly to the duke, then headed for the room reserved for cards.

'Lady Gresham, how nice to see you this evening,' the duke said with proper reserve. 'Lady Pamela, I trust you will grant me a dance this evening.' To Algernon he added, 'We will have to fight our way to her side, I expect, for everyone will want to see the exciting new heiress to the fabulous sapphire-and-diamond necklace.'

The music began and before Pamela could think of a sufficiently scathing retort, the duke took her gloved hand, smiled at Lady Gresham, and swept Pamela off to the dance floor.

'I do not recall being asked to dance, Your Grace,' Pamela said in a smothered voice, wanting to say a great deal more but unable because a minuet did not permit much conversation.

He twirled her about, then retreated in the steps of the courtly dance and grinned most annoyingly at her.

When possible, Pamela said quietly to him, 'Have you thought what I am to do when I must give these to the rightful owner? What then to my heiress?'

'Do not borrow trouble from tomorrow,' he said with a frown when able to speak without another overhearing his words. 'We have enough on our plate for now.'

Pamela dipped a regal curtsy at the conclusion of the dance and turned to leave the floor. The duke took a possessive hold of her arm, so her progress was slowed. Before she had reached her mother, Algernon Thynne joined them.

'I have requested permission for your hand for the next dance. I trust you enjoy a Scottish reel?'

Pamela tossed a narrow look at the duke, then graciously placed her hand on Algernon's arm and left with him to frolic on the dance floor.

Robert pensively watched his good friend walk off with Lady Pamela. The sight of the jewels on her skin was even more enticing than he had expected. What incredibly lovely skin, so satiny and soft-looking. She was the perfect foil for the jewels, all blue satin, her brown curls dressed with blue ribands threaded in them and discreet diamond-and-sapphire earbobs to match the necklace — no doubt the notion of her mother. They were excellent, as was her bosom, he added to himself with another look in her direction. She certainly did justice to the gown. He'd had a hard time keeping his gaze from fastening on the enticing view exposed by that low neckline.

Again he knew the feeling that he wished to keep her away from other dashing men who were attending the ball. He gave himself a mental shake and went off to make note of the men who intended to claim the hand of the Earl of Gresham's charming daughter for a dance.

The stir around Pamela began in earnest when Algernon Thynne returned her to Lady Gresham. The press of gentlemen begging the favor of her hand in a dance was unlike anything she had ever known. She would have been a most unnatural creature to be completely unaffected by the attention.

At the introduction prior to each dance she paid close attention to the name of each man who partnered her. Not a J.R. in the lot, it seemed.

An hour later the duke sought her out again. As the strains of a waltz drifted over the heads of the dancers, many left the floor, unwilling to jeopardize their standing and unsure of what would be proper. Though this might be a ball given by a patroness, it did not mean everyone wished to waltz.

Pamela gave the duke a questioning look and asked in a low voice, 'Are you sure this is proper?'

'I asked Lady Sefton if I might have the honor of leading you out in a waltz. She had to be persuaded to allow it. I believe a Scottish reel was scheduled to be next.'

'And you wished to talk without causing comment,' Pamela guessed.

'Clever girl,' the duke replied while gracefully sweeping her around in continual circles. At first they were one of only a few couples who dared to attempt the waltz. Lady Anne and Sir Cecil were another pair, soon followed by Algernon Thynne and others Pamela recognized from the waltzing party.

'Do you have anything to report?' he queried while Pamela tried to cope with his nearness and the feelings that deluged her at his expert touch.

'I have listened carefully and noted each name as a partner was introduced to me, and I am sorry to say that there has been no success to this point,' she replied.

'It is still early in the evening. You will not leave here until sometime around four in the morning. I shall consult with you over supper.'

Pamela dropped her gaze, fastening it on his diamond stick-pin. Monstrous creature, to expect she would fall in with whatever he wished — which, of course, she would.

If she was breathless when they finished revolving around the room, it had more to do with the effect the duke had on her senses than merely circling. Never had she been so acutely aware of a man — his touch, his voice. She could have closed her eyes and immediately known his identity were he to approach her, even before he said a word. It bothered her, for she knew that once they had solved the mystery surrounding the jewels, she would most likely not see him again, except from a distance. Ordinary girls did not attract a man of his stature, not even the daughter of an earl with a healthy dowry. He could have a bird of paradise, and she was a sparrow — albeit a bejeweled one. Her reflection in the looking glass revealed a potential she'd not expected. Perhaps . . .

Her mother sat a trifle straighter as a dashing gentleman in a decidedly foreign-looking uniform of form-fitting white pantaloons, a magnificent blue dolman dazzling with gold braid, and a short fur-trimmed pelisse slung over his shoulders in the manner of a hussar, made a bow before her. The gentleman was blond, with a thin, aristocratic face decorated with an elegant mustache, ice-blue eyes, a generous mouth, and an air of one who is accustomed to having his way. In that he reminded Pamela a little of the duke, although this gentleman was shorter in stature.

'Madam,' he said while fastening his gaze upon Pamela, or more specifically on her necklace, 'Prince Jaroslav Radinski at your service. I beg the hand of this exquisite creature for a dance.' He bowed low before Pamela, and she stifled the urge to giggle because he was so preposterously outrageous in his manner. Mama was impressed.

Within moments Pamela found herself as partner of the dashing prince. They were spinning along the line of a country-dance when it hit her. The prince had the necessary initials: J.R.! Could that account for his fascination with her necklace? It was possible. She must do something to keep the prince at her side so she might query him.

When the dance came to an end, Pamela fanned herself, not without cause, for the room was warm and the dance had been an energetic one. 'Oh, please, Prince Radinski, might we stroll along the side of the room to the central hall? I find the air in here a trifle warm.'

'But of course,' the prince said with delightful enthusiasm. 'You are the most charming of many charming ladies here this evening, my Lady Pamela. It is impossible to take my eyes from such a vision of English loveliness. At home, you would be fêted, heaped with more jewels, betrothed to a prince of the land.' His eyes caressed her, particularly her bosom and the necklace. Were it not for the need to flaunt the necklace, Pamela would have been utterly mortified by his attentions.

'My goodness,' said an undaunted Pamela, thinking he found the jewels more to his liking than her person. 'A prince? Are there many princes in Russia?' Perhaps this might deflect his attention from her bosom and the jewels for a few moments while she probed for information.

'One must be a prince,' he exclaimed, 'to be less is unthinkable. And there is no money in being ordinary,' he said with disarming frankness. 'The army is the way of things for young men of noble rank.'

'So you look for an English heiress?' Or, she added mentally, some sapphires and diamonds.

'It is a possibility, dear lady. But only if she were as beautiful as you.' His voice had the quality of fine honey, flowing over her senses with soft, smooth words. Oh, he was a wily one, she decided. He had to be, to call her beautiful and charming, a considerably un-English thing to do after a first dance.

He continued to cozen her with flowery phrases and high-flown allusions until she thought her head would spin.

After a time spent strolling along the large hall, in company with a good many others who sought respite from the heat of the ballroom, Pamela said, 'I must return to my mother, Your Highness. It would be highly improper for me to remain here much longer. Besides, I must explain my absence to the gentleman who had asked my hand for the following dance. I fear I have disappointed him.'

'He will be desolate, poor fellow. I fear I may have to fight the duel.'

Pamela laughed, thinking that was a good bit of nonsense. Taking her gloved hand, the prince properly returned her to her mother.

The Duke of Wexford appeared to chat pleasantly with Mama, but his gray eyes looked as though a thundercloud had taken permanent residence on his brow.

'Your Grace,' Pamela said, dropping a perfectly proper curtsy before him after exchanging a look with her mother.

He bestowed an icy glare on the prince that must have reminded him of a Moscow winter. 'Prince Radinski, I do not believe we have met.'

'Your Highness, may I present the Duke of

Wexford,' Pamela said with diplomatic tact, removing her hand from the prince's arm with cautious propriety.

'You do not wish to duel, do you?' the prince said with a disarming smile.

Clearly startled, the frown left the duke's noble brow to be replaced by a questioning look at Pamela, as though she ought to explain such odd words.

'May I enjoy a glass of ratafia with you, Your Grace?' Pamela said with daring, knowing it was not at all the thing for her to do, but desperate to isolate the duke from the prince before one of them said or did something stupid.

'I would be delighted, Lady Pamela,' the duke politely responded, his manner again wintry. He offered his arm, and Pamela sailed off with him after giving her mother another look, this one attempting to convey her helplessness, and leaving Mama to deal with the prince.

They strolled through the throng of people clustered near the door to the refreshment room, then paused before the footman waiting to serve them. The duke motioned to a servant to fill a glass with ratafia, another with wine.

'Now, tell me, please, what is going on!' he demanded quietly once they had left the table. 'I thought you a proper young miss and off you go with that run-of-the-mill prince. He looks like something out of a Covent Garden farce.'

'Why, I thought him most handsome, Your Grace, particularly his mustache. And his manners are quite acceptable. However, there is one thing.' She paused to take a sip of the drink he had handed her, becoming most serious.

'And that is?' the duke said, looking fierce.

'His initials.'

There was a moment or two of silence, followed by a sigh. The fierce look disappeared to be followed by an expression that might almost be considered sheepish in anyone less consequential than the duke.

'I had forgotten that for a moment.' How could he have doubted her integrity.

'But it is why we are here?' Pamela exclaimed, annoyed with her escort. This was *his* idea.

'You are right, of course,' he muttered. 'I can't think what was in my mind. Well?'

'I cannot tell on such short acquaintance whether he may be the one or not. He certainly stared at the necklace.'

'It would be difficult not to stare at it,' the duke said, following suit, observing the creamy swell of her lovely bosom rising from the daring dip of the neckline.

With his gaze warming her skin and making her feel somehow as beautiful as the prince claimed she was, Pamela sought with great difficulty to adhere to the subject at hand.

'Be that as it may, what should I do now?'

'Do?' the duke said blankly. 'Oh, *do*'. Well, you had better encourage the fellow. Perhaps a ride in the park some morning? Will you? If he offers?'

'I suspect he is not overburdened with money and would welcome an heiress. I could suggest a ride in the park if he wishes to see me again — with my groom along, of course.'

'Decorous as always, naturally,' the duke said wryly, seeming to tear his gaze from the necklace with difficulty.

'Naturally,' Pamela said with a chuckle. She flipped her fan open and wafted it before her with a languid hand. 'I am finding this all fascinating. I had not the least notion what a sensation the jewels would create.'

'Just concentrate on those initials. Forget the sensation,' the duke growled. She drew more admiration than he wished for, and it disconcerted him to see her bloom under so much attention — given by other men.

He escorted Pamela back to her mother

and to her next partner with what almost felt like reluctance. But that was nonsense. Perhaps he was trying to think of the prince's background, Pamela decided as she was whisked off on the arm of the young and most presentable Viscount Darnley.

Hours later the prince again claimed her hand, this time for a waltz. She wasn't sure she ought to accept, but since she had danced the waltz with the duke, she could scarcely deny the prince the pleasure.

'You are a most excellent partner,' the prince declared with enthusiasm. 'The Russian court would adore you,' he said while expertly circling her about in the proper degree.

'You are wonderfully kind, Your Highness,' Pamela said, finding it not at all difficult to beam a smile at him.

'I must see you again,' he insisted. 'I asked your Mama if I might, and she agreed. A ride in the park?'

'I usually ride in the morning when the air is crisp and fresh and there are not so many about,' Pamela said demurely.

'Delightful girl,' the prince said with clear approval in his smooth, velvety voice.

Pamela shivered a little, wondering what she might be involved in should this continue. 'Tomorrow at eleven of the clock?'

'If that is not too early, my lady. I should not wish to drag you from your bed at an unseemly hour.'

That might be his spoken sentiment, but his eyes sent an entirely different message.

Pamela tried to look nonchalant about the assignation and said, 'Eleven is fine, Prince Radinski. I look forward to a pleasant ride.'

'Until then, princess.' He bowed over her hand, then left the ballroom.

Pamela mulled over his title of 'princess'. She surely had never been given that appellation before. Perhaps . . .

7

'He was most particular in his attentions,' Lady Anne whispered to Pamela following the prince's departure. 'What exactly did he say?'

'Indeed,' the duke chimed in from behind Pamela, albeit quietly. 'I should like to know that as well. His marked interest in you did not escape me, nor — I fancy — most of those attending.' He gestured to those not far away, who studied Pamela and her friends with curiosity.

'He was most gracious, and while he noticed the jewels, his only remark was on the difference between what I wear and that of most of the young unmarried women,' Pamela said with a hint of asperity in her voice. 'I do not like displaying the necklace while other girls wear more seemly jewelry.'

'It is time for supper. I suggest we discuss this further over our plates.' The duke took a gentle grasp of Pamela's elbow, firmly guiding her along to where a marvelous collation had been set out. It defied description, for the food was as splendid to behold as it proved to eat.

Pamela sat with her new friends, catching

her mother's approving gaze while nibbling on a roll.

'Now, word for word as best you can recall,' the duke commanded quietly.

'We spoke little while dancing. A country-dance is not conducive to conversation, you must agree. I requested his company after the dance, for it was a trifle warm in here. He seemed most happy to comply.' Offering a crooked smile, she then continued, 'He said that in Russia I would be heaped with jewels and feted, betrothed to a prince.' The twinkling look she exchanged with Lady Anne revealed what nonsense Pamela thought that to be. 'However — as I mentioned to you before — he spent more time eyeing my necklace than anything else. I concluded that was where his interest truly was fixed,' she concluded wryly.

'What else did he say?' the duke prompted, looking as though something he'd eaten was off in flavor.

'He said 'tis important to be a prince, for to be less is unthinkable. Apparently, anything less offers little money. I suspect he is on the hunt for an English heiress.'

'When do you see him again?' the duke inquired. His manner was casual but his regard was very intent.

'I did as you suggested, and we are to ride

out in the park later this morning — about eleven.'

'Well, as he appears to be the most likely of this evening's suspects, you may as well go home now and acquire some sleep before it is time to proceed with your encouragement of the young prince.' The duke gave a cursory look at the room, as though to see if he had missed anyone of interest in his assessment.

'He is not so very young, Your Grace,' Lady Anne teased. 'I wager he is of an age with you.'

'He is an impudent puppy,' the duke said in a manner that closed the subject, and said more for Pamela's ears than Anne's.

'Well, I am beginning to feel as though I might find my pillow most welcome,' Pamela said, stifling a yawn that threatened.

'Then you must, by all means, head for your home,' the duke agreed, rising to assist Pamela with such promptness that it made her feel as though he couldn't wait to be rid of her.

She was far too astute to point out that even her mother did not appear to be tired and that once revived by the delicious supper, Pamela could have danced for hours. But she'd been trained to be guided by gentlemen — and that the duke certainly was — so she acquiesced.

When they found her mother deep in conversation with a friend, Pamela hated to interrupt, but the presence of the duke captured her mother's attention without a word said.

'Lady Pamela has found the evening fatiguing,' the duke explained after a courtly bow. 'Perhaps you are of a mind to leave as well, Lady Gresham? I shall, of course, see that you both arrive home safely. I noticed that Lord Gresham joined several other gentlemen who went off to White's.'

It was an offer few mothers could resist, and Lady Gresham was no exception. To be seen leaving on the arm of the highly eligible Duke of Wexford would do Pamela great credit. Lady Gresham was too shrewd to expect His Grace to marry Pamela. If he but brought her to the notice of other eligible gentlemen, it would be quite enough to satisfy her ladyship.

Lady Gresham gathered her shawl and reticule, then smoothed her skirt after rising, all of which caught the eye of a number of peeresses nearby. She swept along to offer her appreciation for a marvellous evening to Lady Sefton, then led the way down the stairs to the entry. Since the duke had already sent a message for their carriage — which Pamela thought a trifle presumptuous — it awaited them without.

'What a delightful ball,' Lady Gresham said with a hint of pride in her voice as she settled in the comfortable vehicle.

'Lady Pamela truly sparkled this evening, my lady,' the duke said with that debonair polish he possessed in such abundance.

'That she did,' the countess replied, sounding pleased. She then went on to make polite small talk about the people who had attended and what lovely gowns were to be seen. It was the sort of thing she did well and never had Pamela heard her in better form.

The duke left them in the entry of the Gresham home, after expressing the hope that Pamela would enjoy her morning ride.

'You accepted the prince's company on your morning ride?' the countess queried.

'He said you had given permission, so I agreed,' Pamela said respectfully.

'Excellent, child. I do believe you are going to have a creditable Season after all.' It was obvious the countess was pleased.

'I would like to place the jewels in Papa's safe,' Pamela said before beginning the walk up the stairs to her room. She unclasped the necklace and held the glittering sapphires and diamonds in her hand, where they caught the light from the entry candles. The jewels captured a thousand tiny candles, flaming with brilliance.

'It will have to wait until your father comes home. He failed to tell me the combination or even where the safe is located,' Pamela's mother replied in vexed tones.

Once again, Pamela clasped the jewels about her neck.

Grimes extinguished the candles in the chandelier while mother and daughter climbed the staircase with night candles in hand. At the top, each went her own way.

Pamela had never felt less like going to bed. It had been most exciting, to be the object of such attention — dancing with the duke, the prince. She was not quite certain how wearing the jewels could make such an enormous difference, but it had. Perhaps believing it was the jewels rather than herself that attracted attention made her less self-conscious?

'The necklace! Oh, bother,' she exclaimed, then removing the gems, she restored them to the hiding place in the bookshelf for another night, thankful Rose was elsewhere for the moment.

Before undressing, she studied the effect of her blue gown with its newly lowered neck and decided the jewels had made the difference; there was little change in her.

A huge yawn overcame her, and she crawled into her bed with more contentment than she'd expected. Assured the jewels were well hidden, she fell into a sound sleep.

★ ★ ★

The duke had availed himself of the Gresham carriage to cover the distance to White's. Here he found Lord Gresham. The gentleman was not gaming, but rather sitting with several friends discussing the political situation.

'I took the liberty of having your carriage wait for you, Lord Gresham,' the duke said in that way he had when he wanted someone to do something without suggesting it outright. 'I saw Lady Gresham and Lady Pamela home from the ball, then thought you might wish the carriage as well.'

'Most considerate of you, Your Grace,' Gresham replied, rising from his chair. 'It will be good to have an early night of it for a change.'

'My feelings precisely,' the duke said, turning to walk down the stairs with his lordship.

When it became apparent that the duke was leaving the club as well, Lord Gresham insisted upon giving the duke a ride to his home in Mayfair. The conversation covered many areas, not the least of which was his lordship's attitude toward a foreign prince and the possibility of international complications were the prince to become enamored of an English lady.

★ ★ ★

The morning brought a nasty, cold rain that pounded on the cobblestones with relentless fury.

Pamela sought the warmth of the morning room fire, wrapping a warm shawl about her for additional comfort.

'I have sent a message to the prince that I shall not ride out this morning,' she informed her mother.

'He will no doubt join you on the next presentable day,' her mother said complacently.

'No doubt,' Pamela agreed, but hardly for the same reason. If he sought her out, it would be for the sapphires and diamonds, not for her own sake.

Curious about a number of things, not the least of which were details of His Grace's background, she found his name in the peerage and studied the entry most carefully. Under the listing for the Duke of Wexford was the information that he also carried the titles of Marquis of Huntington, Earl

Stanhope, and Baron of Rathbone, which would be courtesy titles to bestow on a son if he ever married and produced one. She observed that the duke's present heir was a first cousin once removed. His principal seat was Blythwood Park, in Oxfordshire. He also had a number of lesser homes — a manor house in Dorset, a hunting box up north, a home near the sea, as well as his London address. It sat on a most fashionable street in the heart of Mayfair. The Musgrave family had produced prudent investors, no spend-thrifts or gamesters, and wise managers of their lands. All had married and produced heirs — until now.

Not bothering to look for more Pamelas in the book, she turned her thoughts to the prince. Judging from his attire, he did not appear to be penniless. Of course, clothing might be less costly in Russia, but she doubted it. Although she had no knowledge of the matter, she doubted if a London tailor would be inclined to create beautiful garments for a foreign prince unless his credit was good. There was no denying that his raiment last evening was nothing short of spectacular.

So why would a man who was not poor steal the necklace? For excitement? Danger? Why? No solution offered itself.

As the day wore on, the rain abated, and when the time for afternoon calls arrived, it was no more than a faint drizzle. Not expecting any callers, Pamela was surprised when word was sent for her to join her mother in the drawing room.

She recognized the women who graced the drawing room, having met them the evening before, but admitted great surprise to see them in her home.

'Lady Vane, Lady Smythe, how lovely to see you again,' Pamela said with a proper smile pinned to her face. Then Grimes brought in two charming bouquets of flowers from gentlemen with whom Pamela had danced the evening before and conversation turned to the ball.

'How well I recall the days of my own come-out,' Lady Smythe said fondly. 'It seems like yesterday.'

'It cannot have been so very long ago, for you are quite young,' Pamela said courteously.

'What a charming girl,' Lady Smythe said with a delightful laugh.

Pamela listened to the others exchange pleasantries while assessing the two women. They seemed opposites. Lady Smythe looked jaded; an experienced woman of the *beau monde*. From the way she spoke, it seemed as though she was familiar with the duke — quite familiar, in fact. Of course, she had been among his guests at the theater. She must be of his set — or something. On the other hand, Lady Vane was a quiet, genteel woman with lovely manners who seemed eager to further her acquaintance with Pamela. The widow was more of an age and a person with whom one could feel at ease.

'I could not help but notice your friendship with the Duke of Wexford,' Lady Smythe said with a flutter of her lashes. 'He is such a kindly, generous man. Blythwood Park — his principal seat, you know — is quite beautiful. Should you have the opportunity, you must view it.'

Pamela could only describe Lady Smythe's look as pitying, possibly patronizing, and decided she did not like this lady overmuch. And whatever His Grace might be, *kindly* and *generous* obviously had another meaning to this flame-haired madam.

While Lady Smythe engaged Lady Gresham in a discussion of the fabric used in one of the ball gowns seen last evening, Lady Vane quietly asked Pamela how she had enjoyed the Sefton ball.

'Quite the nicest of the Season, I believe,' Pamela replied, hoping she didn't sound pretentious.

'That was such an amazing necklace you wore. So many people commented on it. Is it truly from your great-uncle with a request you wear it in memory of his true love?' She gave Pamela a hesitant, almost timid smile.

'Most assuredly true,' Pamela admitted.

'You must find storing the necklace a burden, for those jewels are so very precious.' Lady Vane smiled in sympathy for such an onerous task. One did not have the keeping of such fabulous jewels every day. 'The newspapers contain stories of thefts so often.'

'Quite so,' Pamela agreed, but did not reveal what her methods were. That would be imprudent. Naturally, Lady Vane was unconnected to the jewels — such a gentle, sweet woman would never be involved in something so horrid — but an innocent might allow a word to slip out without realizing it.

The two women were preparing to depart when Grimes ushered in another guest — the Duke of Wexford.

Lady Vane turned to Lady Gresham, saying quietly that she must leave for she had several duty calls to make. She slipped from the room with no more than a murmur to Pamela and a simple curtsy to His Grace.

Across the room Lady Smythe sank back on her chair with a flirtatious smile at the duke. 'What a lovely surprise to see you again so soon, Your Grace,' she said with what Pamela considered to be a purring note in her voice.

Pamela decided that she liked Lady Smythe even less.

'Good day,' he said politely. Then the duke turned his attention to Pamela. 'I suppose you did not ride out this morning, what with that rain. I imagine the prince will make arrangements for another day,' he suggested. He did not appear to particularly enjoy the thought.

'La, the prince is quite the latest rage,' Lady Smythe said with a flutter of eyelashes. 'How clever of Lady Pamela to have attracted his attention.' Her ladyship turned a charming smile on His Grace. 'I was truly impressed to see how taken Prince Radinski was with Lady Pamela. Oh, to make the conquest of such a dashing gentleman. He quite took the breath away of any number of ladies. But it was plain to see only Lady Pamela captured his interest.'

Apparently detecting something in Lady Smythe's manner that she could not quite like, Lady Gresham inserted her thoughts on the subject. 'I feel certain that with such perfectly splendid friends — such as the duke and the Radcliffes — and the support of her family that my dear Pamela will have the opportunity to meet a number of highly eligible gentlemen before the Season is over.'

The implication was clear that Lady Gresham fully expected Pamela to be able to choose from a presentable selection. It was almost as though a gauntlet had been tossed on the floor, Pamela thought with humor.

'I do believe Prince Radinski admired my necklace more than my company,' Pamela said modestly. 'How lovely that my great-uncle elected to send me the jewels to aid in my come-out.'

'A girl can never have too much help, I fancy,' Lady Smythe said with a smile that implied much.

'You married at the end of your first Season, didn't you,' the duke said in a quiet voice. 'Lord Smythe was a gracious gentleman. Pity he died so soon after your marriage.'

'Indeed,' Lady Smythe said with a total lack of expression in her face or voice.

A rather shocking thought crept into Pamela's mind that Lady Smythe did not appear all that desolate at losing her husband. She decided to check the peerage to learn more about the woman if possible.

The time considered proper for a call had passed for Lady Smythe, and she reluctantly rose from her chair. 'I must bid you adieu, madam. Lady Pamela as well, but only for the nonce.' She turned to the duke, clearly expecting him to accompany her, but she was disappointed in this and left the room in an annoyed flurry of skirts.

Pamela thought the notion of Lady Smythe in a huff because she did not have her way utterly delightful.

The duke chatted politely for a moment longer, then rose to depart as well. 'Walk with me to the bottom of the stairs, if you please, Lady Pamela?'

She glanced at her mother for approval, then graciously walked with their guest while wondering what he intended to say that he didn't want her mother to hear.

'You know there is cause for caution,' he said just before Pamela reached the last step.

She paused, looking at him with concern. 'I am more than a little aware of that, Your Grace.'

'The prince will seek you out I feel sure. He likes a title, and you have the extra advantage of the jewelry and dowry.'

'I imagine you experience a great deal of that sort of interest, Your Grace,' Pamela said with a daring she didn't know she possessed. 'There must be any number of women who try to find ways to attract your attention.'

'Toadying sycophants are all too common,

I fear,' he admitted. Then he smiled, that charming sort of smile that lit his eyes so they gleamed like gray satin. 'Do not worry, we will find out the truth one of these days. I shall hie myself off to Bow Street to see if I might learn anything new there.'

'Fine,' she managed to say after recovering from the impact of that glorious smile. She stood at the bottom of the stairs after he had left the house, thinking about that smile and wishing she were even more daring.

The following day proved quite lovely. As anticipated, Pamela received a note from the prince requesting the pleasure of riding with her that morning. She returned an affirmative reply with his servant and went to dress.

In a riding habit of purest sky blue trimmed with black braid *à la militaire*, Pamela thought she looked more than presentable. Her hat was a dashing version of the shako, only more petite. The admiration she saw in the prince's eyes made her efforts well worth while.

'A royal princess!' he exclaimed softly when he bowed, then took her gloved hand to place a light kiss in the air somewhere above it. He added a few words that presumably were in Russian, and she wished she knew what they meant. For all she could guess, he might be saying that the hunt for the sapphires would

154

not be so painful after all.

They clattered along the streets until reaching the greenery that was Hyde Park. Once there, they were able to comfortably converse while ambling along at a pleasant walk. If the prince were impatient for a dashing ride, he didn't show it. His costume for the morning consisted of a deep blue coat over white pantaloons and waistcoat, and Hessians that reflected the sun in their black leather. His manners were quite as polished as his boots, his words as well.

Pamela's cheeks had turned that wild rose pink with the flurry of flattery pouring from his lips. It seemed that he had a wealth of encomiums if not money.

'Do you attend the theater this evening?' he inquired while looking about the area at the other riders who were joining in early morning exercise.

'No, I believe my mother fancies attending a rout at Lady Beckert's. Is there something of particular interest?' Off in the distance Pamela noticed a familiar figure astride a pale gray stallion. He controlled the magnificent animal quite as easily as he appeared to control everyone around him.

'I had hoped to see you there, my princess,' he said with a burning look at Pamela that was so outrageous she felt it highly insincere.

155

What a mercy she was not a green girl straight from a Bath school and that she suspected what truly prompted the prince's behavior and words. She would have been far and away in love were she not protected by her knowledge. No English gentleman would behave like this.

'Good morning, Lady Pamela, Prince Radinski,' the duke said with exquisite politeness as he rode up to them. 'A pleasant change from yesterday, I believe.'

They chatted about the weather for some moments while the duke studied Pamela. Then he rode off after bidding them an agreeable ride.

Robert wondered what that scoundrel of a Russian prince had said to Lady Pamela to bring that blush to her cheeks. The delicate tint of the wild rose enhanced her prettiness, even more so with the added contrast of that rich blue. Blue became her, he decided. She ought always to wear blue and would if he had the saying to it.

Then his thoughts returned to the reprehensible foreigner, and he wondered what effort, if any, the prince might make to claim the jewels. He couldn't demand them after the story that had been put about regarding the great-uncle and his unrequited love affair. So what might he do? Steal them, of course. Pamela must be warned to be on guard against a burglar. Sensible girl that she was, she would no doubt have them safely in her father's vault by this point. Or would she?

Determined to protect his little friend, the duke decided he had best call on her as soon as possible. The earliest a gentleman might make a proper call was after eleven in the morning. Presumably, nothing would happen until then.

★   ★   ★

Pamela had half expected the duke to contact her to find out what occurred on her ride with the prince, so she was prepared when a message was brought to her that he awaited her in the drawing room.

'Your Grace,' she said breathlessly, although she had not really hurried. He simply had that effect on her, taking away what little breath she had saved up with his polished magnificence and presence.

Rose sat herself down just inside the door, knowing better than to attempt to listen or watch.

'You looked very charming this morning in your blue habit on your pretty little mare. She suits you.'

Startled at his fine words, she blushed and

stammered something in reply that must have pleased him for he smiled very nicely at her.

'The prince?' the duke said with a raise of his brows. 'I did a bit of sleuthing, and I could not find anything of particular help. All we know for sure is his interest in the jewels and you.'

'The prince was all that was proper — which I venture to say is more than can be said about Lady Smythe,' Pamela said with a suggestion of a snap to her voice. 'She hinted that she is *very* well acquainted with Your Grace, going on about the beauties of Blythwood Park.'

He frowned as though utterly perplexed. 'She has never been there to my knowledge. However, she may have been escorted through the house by my housekeeper in my absence. Quite a lot of this country house visiting goes on, you know.'

'True,' Pamela agreed, feeling absurdly pleased at this explanation. 'As to His Royal Highness, Prince Radinski, he is most assuredly a flirt, but a nice one. He alluded to the necklace again, but most circumspectly.'

'You are not tumbling for that chap's sham charm, are you?' the duke said with apparent alarm.

Pamela was tempted to tease him a trifle, for he deserved it — he was assuming far more than he ought. But relenting, she demurely shook her head.

'You need not worry on that score. His words of praise are too fulsome; flattery becomes silliness when overdone. I have tried to guess what his intentions might be and confess I am at a loss.'

'I think he might attempt to steal the necklace.'

Pamela gasped at the very notion of a man entering her room while she slept in her bed. 'What should I do?'

'Is the necklace in your father's safe?'

'He came home after I had gone to bed, and Mama forgot to take it along to give him. When I arose, he had already left for the day. I fear the necklace is still sitting on my bookshelf,' she confessed, feeling quite stupid.

'Well, best see to it that it is carefully stowed before nightfall. Little chance it would be taken during the day, but come night, well . . .'

'He did question me about our plans for the evening. He hoped to see us at the theater. I told him that Mama planned to attend Lady Beckert's rout. But after I returned to the house, I learned I had the wrong date — the rout is tomorrow evening. We are to be at home this evening.'

'Take extra care, then,' he cautioned.

Pamela escorted him down the stairs to the front door, pausing on the bottom step while silently clasping her hands in worry.

When he took note of her concern, he smiled at her — a kindly, brotherly smile that Pamela was most accustomed to receiving from gentlemen — and said, 'I wish I might be here to assist you, but you know *that* would not be the least proper.'

'And I am very proper,' she said with a resigned sigh, watching as he took his leave.

She set about taking a few precautions for the coming night. She slipped down the stairs and into the scullery, grabbing the first heavy thing in sight. Silently, she returned to her room, just missing an encounter with a footman, Grimes, and Rose. Then she carefully concealed the jewelry in the box that resembled a book and hoped it looked innocuous.

The heavy object proved to be an iron skillet. She placed it close to hand where she might seize it in an instant should someone attempt to enter her room. With the toe of one slippered foot, she nudged it out of sight, lest Rose spot it and ask embarrassing questions.

That night she curled up in bed and found herself unable to sleep. How silly she felt with the skillet on the floor. The prince wouldn't actually try to steal the necklace, would he? She sincerely doubted it — or perhaps wished it not so. But she was prepared for any eventuality.

In a way it was almost an anticlimax when — with no moon to light the area and the streetlight but slight — Pamela heard a scraping noise at her window. She silently slipped from her bed, snatched the skillet, and hid behind the draperies.

A figure all in black slithered into the room with so little noise that had it not been for that first scrape and the fact that Pamela expected someone, she would never have heard a thing. Her heart pounded madly. Her palms felt damp, and she wiped them one at a time on her gown. She swallowed with difficulty, her throat extremely dry.

The man began a search of the room while Pamela assessed the size and possible strength of the intruder. She was not so foolish as to try to do battle with someone twice her size. From the faint outside light, he appeared close to her in height, so much the better. She could hear him paw her things with little regard for the delicate objects, and she grew angry at this base intruder. How dare he!

Gathering up her courage, she stepped

from behind the draperies, tiptoed across the room, and raised the skillet. Her aim was off. She hit the person a glancing blow, causing him to stagger slightly.

Before Pamela could gather her nerve again, the figure in black spun around, pushed Pamela aside, then dashed to the window and was out as silently as he'd entered, albeit somewhat worse for the bump on the head.

Pamela leaned weakly against her bed, thinking that while she had foiled the burglary, she knew no more as to the identity of the figure in black. Who was it? Could the slender figure actually be the prince? In the pitch-dark of the room, she had barely been able to make out the man. It could have been anyone, she thought, dispirited. Except for the duke. She'd know him even in the deepest of nights.

That left a goodly number of possible suspects.

8

Returning to the warmth and safety of her bed, Pamela trembled at the realization of what had just so swiftly happened. It had taken but moments! Her room had been shockingly easy to enter. At that thought, she whipped back her covers and dashed to the window to look out at her dainty balcony of wrought iron added just last year to decorate the façade of the front of the house. Without it, the intruder would have had a great deal more trouble. She fastened the window lock.

She vowed that come morning she would find a way in which to secure that window against further intrusions. It was utterly intolerable! To think she was so vulnerable! Indignant and angry, her trembling ceased, replaced by a determination to outwit and best this thief.

Following a restless night, Pamela was still abed when Rose entered with her tray. Obviously surprised at this change from the new pattern, Rose said nothing, merely setting the tray before her mistress and offered a cheery good morning to her.

At the sight of the skillet on the floor near

the window, Rose halted and cast a dismayed look at Pamela.

A skillet on her bedroom floor merited an explanation, so she might as well tell the truth. 'Someone tried to enter my room last night just after I had gone to bed. I frightened him away.'

'Mercy!' the maid cried. 'Why did you not call for help?' She picked up the skillet, taking it to the door with the obvious intention of returning it to the kitchen, along with a suitably embellished tale.

'It was not necessary. But I intend to do something about that window, I can tell you. I do not like having intruders when I want to sleep.'

Giving her mistress an awed look, Rose left the room, skillet in hand.

'Silly gudgeon, you were so frightened you could not have called for help had you tried,' Pamela scolded herself.

She received a lecture on foolishness from her father at the breakfast table some time later.

'I had not realized you had taken to keeping a weapon of sorts in your room. Amazing you managed to use it. I must investigate the matter,' he said in his usually vague manner. After her father concluded his admonitions, he inquired, 'Why was that

164

necklace not in the safe box?'

'Mama and I do not have a key. For that matter, we do not know where the safe is — and *you* were not here.' This was the closest she had ever come to openly criticizing her father's conduct or his apparent lack of faith in their intelligence.

'I should have taken the necklace, but I forgot — unaccustomed to Pamela having valuable jewelry in her possession,' Lady Gresham added with no real apology in her voice or manner.

It was immediately decided that Pamela and her mother would be provided keys, knowledge of the safe's location in the paneled study, and freedom to use the safe. Indeed, Lord Gresham exhorted them to place anything of value in the safe.

'All I have to consider is where to hide my key,' Pamela muttered on her way back to her room. When she entered, she found Rose and a footman placing a metal bar within the sash box, bracing it in the upper portion of the window. It would quite effectively prevent the lower part from being raised.

'If you please, milady, we think this might help. His lordship, the Earl of Hampton, has such bars for his windows,' Rose said with a nod to the footman. 'Henry served at that house before the earl sold it.'

'Thank you,' Pamela said, thinking that she could not wait to leave London and all the threats posed by living in the city. She would be glad when the necklace could be handed over to the true owner, whomever that might be.

However, escaping the house for her morning ride brought other complications. No sooner had she entered the park than she was joined by Prince Radinski. She examined his face, looking for a sign that he had been the one who crept so silently into her room late the night before.

'Ah, my fairest princess,' he softly exclaimed in greeting, bowing so low that Pamela feared he might unbalance and fall from his horse. He looked somewhat the worse for wear — as though he had a headache?

'Good morning, Your Highness. It is lovely to see the sun shining at this hour, is it not?' She gestured to the pattern made by the dance of lacy leaves overhead. 'Shall we progress?' Star moved forward with little prompting from Pamela. The mare didn't like idleness at this hour anymore than did her mistress.

The prince joined her, giving a lazy glance at Timson, who rode behind with marked vigilance.

'Your groom does you credit,' the prince remarked. 'He guards you with great care.'

'Mama selected him for me. He comes from our country home and has known me all my life.' Pamela glanced back to bestow a smile on the devoted Timson. 'There is no chance that ill might befall me with him on watch.'

The trio rode through the early summer green with every evidence of amiability. Pamela had just decided that the prince could not be the thief when he brought up the subject of her necklace.

'I trust you have that magnificent jewelry kept in a safe place?' Was there an intent to his query?

'Of course. My Papa is most insistent upon that,' she replied. She wondered what had prompted his question. Was he truly concerned? Or piqued that he had been foiled in his attempt to steal the jewels?

'So many people in this city are lax in storing beautiful, priceless things. In Russia, we have small vaults to house our precious items,' he said by way of explanation.

'I suspect that we do as well, at least some of the people.' She hoped that was sufficiently noncommittal.

'Do people place them in their libraries or a bedroom?'

'As to that,' Pamela said prudently, 'I could not say.'

Again she saw the handsome, distinguished figure of the Duke of Wexford riding across the park in seeming indifference to those who also rode this morning. Pamela suspected otherwise. She was beginning to know his methods.

'Good morning, Your Grace,' she said with a proper deference when he joined them.

'Lady Pamela, Your Highness,' he said with a glance at the sky. 'It looks to come on rain before long. I trust you will be home before then, as I should not wish that delightful hat to be ruined. I wonder,' he said to Pamela, 'do you attend the Kingscote affair this evening? Lady Anne mentioned it is to be particularly nice.'

'I believe so, Your Grace,' Pamela said with a glance from one man to the other. Would the prince have an entrée to the elegant Kingscote party? Most likely. Better to have him there than attempting to enter her bedroom again — if, indeed, he was the culprit.

The duke maneuvered the trio with the most casual of moves. Without knowing quite how it was done, Pamela found they were retracing their path and leaving the park, headed for her home. When they reached her front door, the duke swiftly dismounted and helped Pamela down before the prince realized what was afoot.

'Trust you do not mind, old chap. I have a matter to discuss with Lady Pamela. We shall see you this evening, I hope?' He gave the prince a bland look that somehow suggested His Highness had an appointment elsewhere.

'Indeed.' The prince bowed, then rode off, stiff-backed and looking a trifle insulted.

'Pouting pigeon,' the duke muttered, escorting Pamela past Grimes and into the entry. Timson ably took charge of the gray stallion. Star followed with an undergroom.

'Many gentlemen affect that style,' she gently admonished, although privately agreeing with the duke's assessment.

While they walked up to the drawing room, the duke quietly said, 'You wear the necklace again this evening?'

'Of course. Fortunately, I still have it despite an attempt last night to steal the thing.'

This shocking remark necessitated an explanation, bringing forth a look of disgust for the villain and respect for Pamela. 'I cannot believe entry could be so simple. Please have a care for your safety, my lady.'

'Take comfort. I shall now have a key, and I know behind which panel in the library wall the safe hides. There will be no repeat of the attempt to enter my room.' She explained what the footman had installed and barely restrained the duke, who wanted to see it for himself.

Instead of marching up another flight of stairs to her room, they entered the drawing room, where the duke suavely greeted the countess. 'What a pleasure to find you are still to home, Countess. I understand you are frequently to be found with Lady de Clifford and the Princess Charlotte.'

Gratified by his acknowledgment of her high position in society, the countess rose to greet her guest, then led him to the most comfortable chair in the room, close to hers.

They chatted some, then the duke said, 'I trust you attend the Kingscote affair this evening. I should like to escort you if I may?'

The countess recovered her speech with amazing speed to murmur, 'We should be most pleased, Your Grace.'

Having accomplished what he wished, the duke soon left the house.

Lady Gresham sat with a bemused smile before marshaling herself to plan for the evening. 'Pamela, what do you intend to wear? How will it look with the sapphires?'

'I thought to wear the cream satin with the deep blue bows and trim.'

The countess relaxed. The most recent creation from the mantua-maker was undoubtedly one to rival that of any other young lady

170

— and Pamela would have the necklace. The countess might be forgiven her complacent expression.

That evening while driving along in the duke's carriage, Pamela adjusted the puffed sleeves of her gown, thinking the little inserts of deep blue most becoming against the cream satin. Even her slippers were pretty blue satin. She glanced at the duke, arrayed in white satin breeches with a deep blue coat over a white satin waistcoat. Mama wore mulberry faille trimmed with lace. They were all splendidly garbed for what promised to be a lovely evening.

Once past the receiving line, she became aware of the stares cast in her direction from a good many people, since the duke was obviously arriving as one of the Gresham party. Pamela walked into the drawing room with a new confidence.

The first gentleman to be presented to her was a German diplomat, Baron Johan Ruchoven. With a meaningful glance at the duke, Pamela walked off, hand properly placed on the baron's arm, to join in the next dance.

She hoped the duke had taken note of what had struck her immediately. The baron's initials. This J.R. had made a dead set at her the moment she entered the room. He was, if

171

anything, purposeful. He also was charming, for a German. Pamela had found that too often they tended to be pompous and overbearing. The baron might be a trifle pompous, but he did try to please. He danced well, too.

'My lady, you are the most charming sight in the room, I vow,' the baron said with a gracious smile.

'How kind of you,' Pamela replied while wondering how he would manage to arrive at the topic of her necklace. It did not take him long.

'That is a magnificent necklace. Such a heartwarming story it has,' he said, his accent lending a certain charm to his words. He gazed at the jewels with what she thought to be a covetous look. But then, that gaze also roamed over her upper torso as well, causing her bosom to swell with indignation. Really!

'English ladies dress with such style,' he commented. 'You obviously know how to best display that pretty bauble.'

Pretty bauble, indeed, thought an irate Pamela. He probably was calculating precisely how much the necklace was worth, right down to the pence. The effect of all this was to cause Pamela to lose her customary attitude of reserve and made her appear infinitely more desirable. With flushed cheeks and sparkling eyes, she was dazzling.

The duke stood on the far side of the room, watching the progress of his little 'protégée' with the foreign diplomat. What was the bounder saying to Lady Pamela to make her color up like a wild rose? Only fulsome compliments could do that, he knew. She was delightfully graceful, and it must be admitted, the baron danced well.

That perfectly splendid bosom was such a charming resting place for the sapphires and diamonds. He felt a stirring within as he watched her lithesome figure swing about in the pattern of the dance, knowing an urge to hold her in his arms again, experience her touch. For such a prosaic little creature, it was amazing how she had become such a part of his life. He couldn't explain his feelings in the least, and it certainly puzzled him. He resolved to claim the next waltz. He would hold her, and soon.

When the baron returned Pamela to her mother, he bowed low, then commented, 'Lady Gresham appears more your sister than mother, I vow.' As a compliment Pamela thought it a trifle heavy-handed, but Mama adored it.

The duke stood behind the countess, determined to have his way. Having spoken to the bandleader, he moved to take possession of his quarry. He quietly remarked to Pamela, 'I trust you noticed what I did. The chap's initials.'

'Was he on your list?' Pamela inquired, her tones dulcet. 'The prince wasn't. Odd that neither of us considered foreigners in our calculations.'

'No convenient list of them,' the duke grumbled. 'And no, in answer to your question, he was not on my list. No one on that list has come near you, in fact.'

Oddly annoyed with His Grace, Pamela dared to say, 'If we do not dance, people will place more importance on our association than warranted. You must not spend much time conversing with me, or they will gossip.'

Since the strains of a waltz had begun — as requested by the duke — he simply slipped his arms about her and swept her into the dance. He noted with gratification the displeased look on the baron's face. Pompous diplomat.

Pamela chided herself for goading His Grace into dancing with her. What a deliciously naughty thing to do. Her eyes sparkled with delight as they revolved slowly around the room in a graceful swirl of her skirts. His touch was just as sure as before, his effect on her just the same. If anything, she had fallen more deeply under his spell.

And she was determined that he would not know how she felt, for that would be a disaster.

'Could the baron have been the one who attempted the theft of the jewels?' the duke inquired.

'It was too dark to tell for certain, although he is of the proper height. Maybe I ought to go about checking gentlemen for lumps on their heads?' she said mischievously, a smile dancing in her eyes as she looked up at him.

The image of her bending over gentlemen to examine possibly wounded noggins while their eyes were level with her lovely bosom did not set well with the duke.

'I doubt that would work,' he muttered. 'Just keep your eyes and ears open. You are a clever girl, I feel certain something will occur to us in time.'

How lovely to be called clever — which she might or might not be. It was nice to be treated as though she had something other than cotton wool in her head.

The duke seemed reluctant to return her to Mama's side when the dance concluded. Perhaps he had not finished with his suggestions? A minor battle waged within her at the moment. On one side she relished the attention from His Grace, no matter that it was in aid of hunting out the truth. On the other, she wished most heartily to have the mystery of the jewels solved so that life would return to normality. And didn't that have a dull ring to it?

At this moment the charming and proper Lord Raeburn modestly asked Pamela to dance, quite beating out the prince, who had arrived late and looked highly displeased at the growth in competition.

'Good chap,' muttered the duke as he more or less handed her over to Lord Raeburn, quite ignoring the prince.

How marvelously kind of the duke to vet her partners, she thought, faintly tired with the efforts of men to rule her life. Naturally, her father set forth rules to be supplemented by her mother. And she supposed that once married, her husband would follow suit. Yet that did not mean she did not yearn to make her own decisions or to have a husband with whom she might jointly discuss problems and reach decisions.

Her present partner looked kind and undemanding; a pleasant, unassuming fellow, by all accounts. She'd wager he would be a nice match, gentle and understanding. Why could she not be attracted to someone like him?

When he returned her to her mother's side, Pamela was intrigued to find a dashing gentleman of moderate height wearing the very cream of fashion. She gave her mother an inquiring look, expectant.

'The Vicomte Jean Reynaud requests the pleasure of your company for the next dance, my dear.' There was no mistaking the satisfaction in Mama's voice as she uttered these words. The vicomte was known to dangle after the diamonds of society, those belles of every ball. Had Pamela really ascended to these heights? Was it the necklace, or had the attentions of the duke drawn the eye of these notable gentlemen to herself? Whatever it was, she was delighted to be in fashion for the moment, happy to accept the civility showered upon her by these sophisticated men.

'Vicomte Reynaud, I am pleased to accept your hand for the next dance,' she said with shy courtesy, even though she grasped the significance of the man's initials almost immediately. First there was Baron Johan Ruchoven and now Vicomte Jean Reynaud. She wondered if all the other men with those particular initials would be attracted to her as well? How very, very odd.

'Ah, mademoiselle, you are *très charmante*. There is no other to compare to you this evening.'

His smile made her uneasy. She also knew his words were pure flattery of the most blatant sort. He went on, blithely extolling virtues she was becoming accustomed to hearing. Yet, she had to confess it *was* charming. The duke issued directions and was all business. He would not sully her ears with such nonsense, more's the pity.

The dashing Frenchman gave the proper baron a bored look of disdain when the German diplomat attempted to reclaim the hand of the charming belle of the evening. The prince couldn't come close to Pamela. From afar the duke watched the display of masculine outmaneuvering with a grim smile. If this failed to turn the head of the pretty Lady Pamela, she would be a most unusual girl. The duke resented the Frenchman's attitude almost as much as he disliked the baron's proprietary manner. Being watchdog to an heiress who possessed a stolen sapphire-and-diamond necklace was more than a little wearing on a chap.

She was laughing at some nonsense that Reynaud tossed off, as the duke knew he was rather good at doing. Wit and charm were Reynaud's stock in trade, as it were, and it appeared he was set to charm Lady Pamela. How could she resist such foolery? Far more sophisticated women than Pamela had tumbled to that facile bewitcher.

The duke sought her out the moment he

had the chance. 'I do not suppose you had an opportunity to learn anything about our Frenchman? He seemed to do most of the talking, which means he controlled the conversation, which also means he asked many questions, particularly concerning the necklace. Am I correct?'

She clapped her gloved hands — in mock admiration, he suspected.

'You are precisely correct, Your Grace. He poured flattery over my poor head until I thought I should sink beneath it. Never have I been so praised. It makes me very suspicious of his motives, you see.' Pamela gave the duke a frank, open look. 'And he asked a great number of casual questions about the necklace. He wanted to know who had created such a masterpiece. Was it true that my great-uncle had commanded I wear it in memory of a lost love? And of course, did I guard it properly? How odd that everyone desires to know how it is kept safe,' she declared in a wry voice. 'Not to mention where.'

Robert placed her hand on his arm and led her toward the refreshment room, thinking it a pity they had so little freedom to meet for discussions during balls.

'We must plan carefully to trap the guilty one. Could you meet me tomorrow at the Radcliffe library? There we will be able to discuss this without the worry of listening ears.' He instructed the footman to place a number of delicacies on two plates, then took them to a small table near the doorway.

Pamela glanced thoughtfully at the duke. How her life had altered since the necklace had been mistakenly sent to her. Before, her days had been tediously the same. Now she scarce had a moment to work on her needlepoint. And she was certainly mixing with the *crème de la crème* of society!

'The Radcliffe library? At ten of the clock? Of course. I shall come directly when I return from my morning ride.' She placed a morsel of lobster salad in her mouth and almost choked at the duke's next words.

'Doubtless both the baron and Vicomte Reynaud will pursue you. Do you feel up to handling the situation? Diplomats are trained to be very persuasive. You might find yourself agreeing to something outrageous before you know it.' The duke's gaze seemed to be sympathetic.

Pamela found his understanding to be far more dangerous to her senses than the foolish flattery the others had heaped upon her. The warmth in his eyes possessed far more power to seduce than empty phrases.

'Thank you for your concern. I promise you that should I feel things are a trifle out of hand, I will summon your able assistance.' She gave him a speculative look, then added, 'It is reassuring to know I may depend upon your help. I could not attempt this otherwise.'

Robert looked deeply into the honest blue eyes of pure cerulean that gazed so directly into his. How confident she was now. No coquetry, no flirting, just a straightforward appeal and an appreciation he'd swear was genuine.

'Tomorrow at ten, and please know that I would never fail you, should you seek my assistance,' he found himself saying — something he'd never said before.

'Well, if it isn't the belle of the ball in hiding,' Lady Anne cried with glee as she rushed up to Pamela. 'Are your poor slippers worn through? Or perhaps you have to brush out the flattery from your hair?' She giggled at Pamela's amused expression and seated herself on a chair pulled forward by her ever-attentive husband.

'We will be meeting at your library in the morning to discuss what must be done,' the duke began. 'There are now three suspicious gentlemen who have presented themselves to Lady Pamela. They have the right initials, are the proper height, and ask improper questions about the necklace,' the duke said with a lift of his brows.

'You poor darling,' Lady Anne said, placing a hand over Pamela's. 'How dreadful to suspect every word said to you and know that one of your admirers could have been the burglar in your bedroom.'

'I can trust the duke . . . and you two. Indeed, all others are questionable. It is most amusing, however, to change from being a wren to a swan.' Pamela laughed at herself, exchanging amused looks with her friends.

'Time to return to duty, my lady,' the duke insisted.

Pamela chuckled at his mock seriousness. 'Aye, aye, sir,' she murmured, walking at his side to the ballroom.

Once with her mother, she wondered what might happen next. It was not long before the prince claimed a country-dance and the baron his waltz. And then it was time to leave.

The ride home was quiet, with the duke in a reflective mood. He said little when he left her.

Pamela took her new key and carefully placed the necklace into the safe before going to her room. Once there, she gave the protective bar that slanted across her window a resigned look, then pulled the draperies to hide it. Still, she'd sleep better tonight.

The following morning at ten in the Radcliffe library, she faced the duke with a

182

merry smile and lighter heart.

'You were quite correct last evening,' she reported with a beguiling grin. 'The baron and the vicomte vied for my attention this morning until I almost lost patience with them. What a pity they cannot learn from you that a lady appreciates a few well-chosen words far more than an ocean of false flattery.' She gave him a soft smile.

'You think their praise false flattery?' the duke asked, oddly touched by her tribute.

'You were not there to hear them' was her only comment, one she'd not have dared say in the past.

The duke appreciated her discretion. She did not do as so many women would — confide the private conversation of others like so much trite gossip. Had their words been meaningful and important to the solution of the mystery, she would have reported it without failure.

'Have you thought about what more we shall do to lure out the villain of the piece?' she inquired, restlessly strolling about the room, glancing out the window, before turning to look at him.

'You will have to go on as you have been, I believe. Encourage them all. Sooner or later someone is bound to make a move. When he does, I will be waiting for him.'

Not understanding how this would be accomplished, Pamela gave him a nod, drawing closer to say, 'I do not understand why this other Lady Pamela has not wondered where her necklace is — unless it was to be a surprise.'

'Very few chaps would send such a costly surprise gift by delivery. I would prefer to give sapphires and diamonds to my lady in person.'

'But,' she countered breathlessly, 'it might be dangerous.'

'Dangerous? I suppose it might at that.'

Pamela stood still, studying the duke in his casual perfection. He always seemed so well turned out, garbed appropriately no matter what the occasion. But more than that, she admired his attitude toward her. He was the perfect gentleman.

Robert watched the expressive face so close to him. What thoughts were flitting through that pretty little head? She entranced him, beguiled by her winsome grins and her forthright speech mixed with proper manners. He had wondered for some days what it might be like to gather her in his arms and know the touch of her pretty lips. His thoughts proved irresistible in the quiet privacy of the library.

In one swift movement he swept her into

his arms and pressed his mouth to hers. Her softness was like heady perfume to his senses. He deepened his kiss and thrilled to her response.

When she pulled away — or he let her free, depending on whose view one took — she gave him an adorable look, then backed away from him.

'I suspect we had best forget that happened,' she said in a quivery voice. 'I want no additional complications.' She heard her voice — calm, rational, but her heart and pulse were racing wild. The delicious warmth of his kiss lingered on her sensitive mouth.

9

'Do forgive me for being so tardy,' Lady Anne cried, breathlessly entering the room. 'I am being very remiss in my chaperonage! Time seems to pass so quickly in the morning, and though I had but a short list to do, every clerk in town seemed to be as slow as treacle.' Apparently sensing none of the tension in the room, she dropped her swansdown muff on the desk, then gracefully sank on to one of the comfortable lounge chairs placed about the little room, fanning herself with her handkerchief. 'Well?' She darted little looks from His Grace to Pamela, then back again.

Pamela clutched the back of a library chair, willing herself to become calm, serene. Her cheeks still felt on fire, and her limbs still trembled. How dreadful if she were to collapse in an ignominious heap. The duke might find it amusing to kiss her, but he would deplore any sign of the vapors, she felt certain.

Pamela said hesitantly, 'I reported on the results of my morning ride, which was a lot of nonsense from the prince and the baron — who vied for honors, silly gudgeons.' She looked anywhere but at the duke.

'We have been discussing the matter of how best to proceed while waiting for you,' the duke said in a wild stretch of the truth. 'Lady Pamela just suggested that it could have been dangerous for the fellow to present the necklace in person. Under what circumstances might that be?' One of those powerful, lean hands reached up to stroke his chin, and when she glanced at him, Pamela found she again must look elsewhere. He could unnerve her so easily.

With utter confidence, the dratted man leaned back against the table and crossed his arms over his manly chest against which Pamela had so recently been drawn.

'Perhaps she is married? Or she's an heiress and her parents will not countenance marriage with this man?' Pamela began, thinking of her own situation and potential problems. She was determined not to permit Lady Anne to see what a ninny she'd been for allowing the situation to develop to the point where the duke felt free to take the liberty to kiss her. Why, if they had been discovered, he might have been forced into marriage with Pamela — the last thing he should wish — because he had compromised her. A gentleman did not go about kissing the daughter of an earl — or any young single woman, for that matter — in a private library without facing serious repercussions were he found out.

'Or she is watched by an evil guardian,' Lady Anne added with enthusiasm for the game.

'Who most likely wants to marry her to snabble her fortune for himself,' Pamela said darting a glance at the duke. He looked as cool as an ice from Gunter's. 'Do you have any suggestions, Your Grace?' she queried with a shrewd look at this man who had turned her world upside down with his touch.

'I submit it could be a spy who has received the necklace in payment — either for work accomplished or in progress. Or possibly it is someone who is blackmailing another after learning a secret — and we all know that is quite a likely possibility. Scandal lurks behind every door in this town — unless one is careful.' That hand reached up to stroke his chin again.

Pamela turned from the sight, thinking there must be something amiss with her senses, for she had never felt like this before in her life.

'Why, Your Grace,' Lady Anne said with an amused laugh, 'do you mean to say there could be scandal lurking even in this house? Gracious! I had no idea.'

Pamela thought he was playing with fire to

skirt so close to the issue of kissing her and the danger that could so easily overtake him. She waited to hear what sort of answer he would give.

'I doubt your house could be a scene for scandal, but one never knows. For example, what if I had been found alone with Lady Pamela in this room? We are innocent of any wrongdoing, yet because she is young and single and I am unmarried, there would be a scandal. How simple it could be for an unscrupulous person to arrange.'

Lady Anne gave him a speculative look and said, 'One could think you have been subjected to precisely such an arrangement, the way you speak.'

'I am grateful that not even one of the servants has seen us unchaperoned while we waited for you,' Pamela said earnestly. At least, she amended, she had not seen anyone. Could a footman have walked silently past that door and neither she nor the duke been aware of it? They had been totally caught up in that kiss, brief though it was. Or at least, Pamela had been enraptured. She couldn't guess what the duke had felt, but he had worn a most bemused expression on his face when she'd stepped away from him.

'And I am such a tardy soul,' Lady Anne said with a naughty grin. 'Now, what have you learned that is new?'

'I have nearly finished the peerage in my search for every Lady Pamela in the book. Of course,' Pamela admitted, 'I may have missed one or two. Sometimes the listings are very confusing.'

'And the type tends to blur after a time,' His Grace added with an amused look at her.

'I shall simply have to encourage the three who now dangle after me,' Pamela said with a shrug of her slim shoulders. The dainty ruff at her neck tickled her chin when she gave the duke an oblique glance to see what his reaction might be, noting that a frown was hastily replaced by the most bland of expressions.

'Lovely!' Lady Anne exclaimed somewhat gleefully, Pamela thought. 'That ought not be a difficult task. Each of them is rather handsome in his own way. The prince is so romantic with his tall, blond, dashing good looks and those fabulous light blue eyes. He looks just as a prince should look — as a sort of St George, if you know what I mean,' she concluded with a vague wave of her hand. 'The vicomte is also of a height with Pamela, his black hair curls becomingly about his face and his dark eyes seem to find one's inner person with no effort at all. One can easily imagine having an *affaire d'amour* with such a man — were one not already happily married, that is.' She gave Pamela and the duke a serious look, then continued.

'The most distinguished of the three is the baron. Although of medium height, he has that interesting tinge of gray in his brown hair and gray eyes to enhance it. Ah, Pamela, how many women in the country would gladly exchange places with you!'

'Well, they cannot,' Pamela said sensibly. 'Not that I do not wish this done and over, mind you.'

'Tonight you attend what?' the duke inquired lazily.

'The Lockhart *soirée*. Wednesday evening will find us at Almack's per usual. Thursday evening is the opera — the baron has already requested to escort Mother and me. Friday night is the Henson rout.'

'And Saturday?' the duke prompted.

Pamela studied her gloved hands a trifle before raising her head so she might look at the duke. 'Mama is having a quiet little dinner party just some intimate friends. Of course I must attend, but I expect Mama will pair me with that general who is always trying to persuade Papa to sponsor some bill for the army.'

'It sounds dreadfully tedious, poor darling,' Lady Anne said with sympathy. Daughters and young matrons often had to perform political functions from time to time — partnering an elderly gentleman merely to please a parent or spouse.

'He is a very dashing general,' Pamela said in his defense. 'I also think gray hair can be very distinguishing, and he is quite trim.'

Putting aside the Radcliffe copy of the peerage, the resolute duke exclaimed, 'I expect we can proceed. I would like to look over your list, Lady Pamela. If I may?'

She handed over the neatly written list of names.

'Not as many as I expected,' Lady Anne said, peering over the duke's arm to scan the list as well.

'Perhaps twenty. As I said before, I do not know . . . ' Pamela began, then halted when she heard footsteps in the hall.

'You think some may be missing,' the duke said for her.

'What ho?' Sir Cecil said, entering the room like a fresh breeze.

'We have the completed list of names to peruse, three very good candidates who have yet to stake a claim on the necklace, and one of whom has attempted to enter Lady Pamela's bedroom,' the duke declared.

'You never said a word,' Lady Anne cried, giving Pamela an accusing look. 'How horrid for you!'

192

'Fortunately, I had stowed the jewels in an innocuous place. I tried to hit the intruder with an iron skillet. Pity my aim was so bad, I might have been able to pick him out by the lump on his head.' Pamela grinned at her friend.

'Time I take you home,' the duke declared, looking grim. 'May we continue to use your library as a meeting place should it prove necessary?' he asked Sir Cecil. 'I'm beginning to have a fondness for the place.'

'By all means,' Sir Cecil replied, glancing for Pamela's approval before turning to walk them to the door.

'What do you wear to the Lockhart *soirée* this evening?' Lady Anne demanded when they reached the entry hall.

'Silver tissue,' Pamela said with a soft smile. She had been rather pleased with the new gown, one made particularly to show off the sapphires and diamonds. 'It has but the tiniest of puffs for sleeves and a pretty border of silver embroidery at the hem.'

'I cannot wait to see it,' Lady Anne said, her eyes lighting up with delight.

The duke accompanied Pamela to her home, saying little. He looked as if something said had displeased him.

'I trust you will be at the Lockhart *soirée* this evening,' Pamela said hesitantly. 'As I've

193

said before, I do depend on you to support me should I need it. I find the prince, in particular, rather daunting in his enthusiasm. The vicomte is also a trifle overwhelming.'

'Of course. It will be my pleasure to keep a watch over you,' he said, seeming to brighten.

'There is something especially gallant about our own English gentlemen that the foreigners simply cannot match.' She prudently ignored the duke's kiss in the library. That was best forgotten for the moment — if possible. 'Our *gentlemen*' — and she thought to remind the duke of his honor and nobility — 'have a sincerity of manner not to mention a restrained elegance. As Lady Anne pointed out, the prince is dashing, the vicomte quite volatile, and the baron is, I admit, a trifle pompous or perhaps merely dignified,' she said in a considering way.

The carriage drew to a halt before her door. Alighting from the carriage, the duke placed his hand over hers and smiling down into her intent face spoke softly. 'Until this evening, fair lady.'

★　★　★

The silver tissue gown with its very low neckline, tiny puffed sleeves, and the exquisite embroidery in heavy silver thread was perfect, so Lady Anne declared when she admired Pamela. 'Who had the making of such elegance?' she demanded while touching the fabric with gentle fingers.

'Madame Clotilde,' Pamela confided, noting the duke somewhere close behind her, although he had not said a word so far. 'Mama said I must go to the best, for to do otherwise would not give proper honor to my great-uncle's jewels.' She turned slightly and with a hint of mischief in her eyes added to the duke, 'Think you that I am sufficient bait this evening?'

'Scamp,' the duke growled. 'The baron is likely to offer you one of those little kingdoms in Europe for your very own once he sees you in that gown.'

'What a charming thing to say, Your Grace,' Pamela said with amusement. She tapped him lightly with her fan, then left to seek out the vicomte, thinking he would most likely appreciate her new elegance. However, the person she had most wished to impress had been the duke, and he liked the gown. Pamela knew a glow of gratification at that.

'She is definitely becoming more sure of herself,' the duke murmured mostly to himself.

Lady Anne agreed. 'A lovely girl. Proper, loyal, and sensible, but with a true appreciation of beauty. She is not shallow, as are so many of the young girls today.'

'And you are so very ancient, my dear,' he said with a laugh at her expression.

Robert slowly made his way about the high-ceilinged room, keeping an eye on Lady Pamela all the while he mingled with friends, absently greeting others he knew slightly. She dazzled, shimmered, glittered, all for that blasted Frenchman. Did she care for the man? Or was it merely all a game?

It was a good thing Anne had entered the library at such a fortuitous time. It would have been far too easy to be carried away with such an agreeable armful as Lady Pamela — who had proven to be highly responsive to his kiss. He'd been surprised at that. Who would have thought that Lady Pamela would have a fire banked beneath that cool pose? He envied the man who would ignite the emotional blaze that merely waited to explode. What a passionate young woman she promised to be. Had he really thought her prim and proper? She might seem that way, but within . . . ah, something else entirely.

When the duke saw the vicomte fawning over her, almost drooling over the extremely low-cut gown — or was it over the sapphires? — he felt like punching the chap in the nose.

Spying Pamela, the prince moved to her side, forcing the vicomte to retreat slightly.

The duke was able to relax, but not much. She depended upon him, she'd said. He'd not let her down.

Anne had declared Prince Radinski to be sort of a St George. The duke wagered that there was nothing saintly in that fellow's thoughts at the moment, not from the manner in which he gazed at Pamela. Zounds!

'La, sir, you are both shameful flatterers,' Pamela said with a flicker of her fan in their direction.

'You are truly a princess this evening, garbed in silver mist, shining like the moon in all its splendor,' the prince insisted.

'Bah,' the Frenchman countered as though disgusted at his rival's lack of imagination. 'Lady Pamela has more vibrance than the cold moon, I vow. She possesses a warm heart and generous spirit that cannot be likened to the moon in the least. She is the three graces in one — the brilliance of Aglaea, the grace of Terpsichore, and the joyfulness of Euphrosyne.'

Pamela wanted to laugh at this nonsense. It was a good thing she didn't believe a word they said or she would be utterly impossible to live with. She might know joy and grace at times, but brilliant as a Greek muse she was not.

'Gentlemen, how naughty you are, to try to turn the head of one of our lovely young ladies,' Lady Vane said softly, with a charming and gentle smile.

'How nice to see you again, Lady Vane,' Pamela said, noting that the lady appeared pale, perhaps a bit tired. 'Are you feeling well?' The lady was garbed in a sober plum gown with a turban to match in which she wore a discreet gold pin. A small matching brooch was modestly centered at her demure neckline. Only a black curl escaped from beneath the turban.

'A mere nothing. I suffer from the headache — so inconvenient when I wish to attend a party. I am sure to be better by the morrow,' she concluded with a small smile.

'You poor lady,' Pamela said, ushering her to a chair nearby while urging the vicomte to obtain a glass of wine for her ailing acquaintance. She perched on a small gilt chair next to the turbaned and pale Lady Vane, who appeared as though she were indeed in pain. Her dark eyes flashed with gratitude when a footman brought the wine, and the vicomte, himself, offered it to her with a bow.

'How courteous you are, kind sir,' she murmured in a high, sweet voice. 'I shall be quite fine in a few moments. Are you enjoying the party?' she asked of Pamela.

Looking at the two gentlemen hovering over her, Pamela laughed lightly and nodded. 'Indeed. My evenings are quite full of late, and I find these gentlemen wherever I chance to go. They flatter one quite incorrigibly, however,' she said in a tone of mock scolding.

'But they are doubtless full of good intentions,' Lord Raeburn declared with a roguish smile, having silently joined the group when Lady Vane was ushered to the chair.

'Ah, Lady Pamela, I find you in excellent spirits this evening,' Baron Ruchoven declared as he sauntered up, a hint of superiority in his manner. 'Pity you must extend your graciousness to these poor men, my dear lady.'

'Goodness me,' Pamela muttered, then rose to greet the baron. He was garbed in the height of German elegance, his blue sash covered with medals decorated his chest with great distinction. In a moment of distraction, Pamela wondered what it would be like to endure being held close to that cold array of metal.

The duke inserted himself into the heart of the group, commanding the lovely Pamela's attention. 'Allow me to offer you some refreshment, Lady Pamela.' She accepted his arm to the murmured regrets from the other men.

'I trust you will be feeling more the thing, milady,' Pamela said with concern to the quiet lady still seated.

'I shall see to it that she has a breath of fresh air and a morsel of food, Lady Pamela. Your consideration is most appreciated by all, I am sure,' Lord Raeburn said, his manner one of admiration and deference.

Gracious, did these people think she was about to become a duchess? Pamela thought that somewhat amusing. She walked at the duke's side, glancing at him from to time. What a curious notion, to be sure. She turned her attention to the array of pretty foods arrayed for their enjoyment in the refreshment room.

He selected two plates of appealing viands, then escorted Pamela to a tiny table on the far side of the room, next to a window. 'This seems to be the only time I can spend alone with you,' he grumbled.

'I see Raeburn is as good as his word. He is seeing to Lady Vane's care quite dutifully.' Pamela suspected there was an underlying intent to the duke's words, but couldn't imagine what it might be. 'Poor woman, she obviously has a dreadful headache.'

The duke turned his attention to Pamela. 'You must realize that having all those chaps clustered about you at one time is not going to help our hunt in the least. The thing is to be alone with each in turn, much as I dislike saying that.'

'That could present a problem, Your Grace,' Pamela said thoughtfully. 'I would not wish to marry any of them, should we be accused of an impropriety.'

The duke gave her an arrested look, then sipped his wine before saying, 'Why not? They are most likely well to grass, have *entrée* to all the best places, travel widely, and seem to adore you. What more could you wish from a possible husband?' His words hung in the air as delicately as ice crystals on a winter morn.

'I suspect that so-called adoration has more to do with the necklace and my dowry than me,' she said bluntly. It was a remark she would never before have made to a man; however, she and the duke had transcended the polite trivia that passed for conversation. 'While I admire traveling to interesting places, I would rather do so with one who has a similar English background, so we might share our appreciation of what beauty is to be seen.'

'I see,' he said with a reflective note in his voice.

'That notwithstanding, I shall make an effort to be apart with each of them if possible. Note that I said apart, not alone. It is possible to speak almost privately with a gentleman even in the midst of a party. Witness how we are able to converse without the likelihood of being overheard,' she pointed out.

He stared at the necklace — or was it her neckline? Pamela was becoming accustomed to having her bosom and neck eyed by one and all. While she might prefer to display the jewels against a background of fabric, a part of her was elated that she possessed an acceptable foil for the jewels.

'Those stones are magnificent,' he said quietly. 'I trust you will not be accosted on your way home this evening.'

'Mama has an extra groom along,' Pamela confided.

'He has a pistol, I hope?'

'I would expect so, but I really could not say,' she confessed.

'Your parents are not to be believed. They ought to protect you better,' he grumbled, quite astounding Pamela. She had not heard him criticize his elders, especially her parents, before.

She popped the last of the pretty tidbits in her mouth, sipped the rest of her wine, then rose from the table. 'Until later, Your Grace,' she said by way of farewell.

Robert watched her glide through the throng of guests, wondering how she would manage to separate her admirers one by one. That she would do it, he had no doubt. When Lady Pamela gave her word, she was to be trusted.

It was refreshing to meet a woman such as she, he reflected. She seemed not the least awed by his title; his rank usually reaped the gushing regard of every unmarried woman around. And to her credit, she had little care for the eminence of her beaux. Her wry acceptance of the most likely reason for their interest disturbed him. Did she attach so little importance to her charms? Surely, no one so lovely could be so unaffected by the admiration and flattery being constantly proffered. Or could she?

He vowed to impress on Pamela the true value of her allure. It might not be a simple task, but he felt it one well worth pursuing. How odd that he had missed this delightful woman in the past. He must be slipping — or not really looking in the right places.

Pamela found the vicomte crossing the room. 'Will you walk with me a bit?' she said with a demure glance in his eyes, pleading most prettily.

'Mademoiselle, I would find it the greatest pleasure,' he said ardently, but glanced off to the main door before turning to join her.

They chatted about the trivial inconsequentials she had deplored moments ago with the duke. However, she bore it with fortitude, intent on her mission.

'You ride again in the morning,' he inquired at last.

'Indeed. You must enjoy riding at home,' she said in the effort to draw him out about himself, a subject he seemed reluctant to discuss.

'It has been some time since I have been able to ride in the parks of Paris,' he said simply.

'Bonaparte rules,' she replied.

'That he does.'

At that moment, someone claimed his attention, and Pamela found herself drawn to the side of the duke, who had been hoping for this intrusion to bring Pamela some new and interesting information.

'I have discovered that the vicomte has Bonapartist contacts. Try to find where his sympathies truly lie.' The duke faded into the crowd.

When the vicomte returned his attention to her, Pamela baldly asked, 'You approve the Corsican's ascendance in France?'

'He has made contributions, that is true.' He looked across the room, paled, then said,

'Excuse me, my goddess, there is someone with whom I must speak.'

Pamela watched him weave his way across the room to a man standing by the hallway door. They turned to leave together.

'Excuse me. I believe I shall follow that chap,' the duke whispered.

'Not without me,' Pamela insisted. 'I'll tell Mama you wish for my help.' She sought her mother, confident that that good lady would not object to anything the duke suggested. How marvelous it must be to be a duke, Pamela thought as she returned to his side. He always had his way!

'Where is your shawl?' he demanded as they lightly ran down the stairs.

'A moment,' she whispered, then caught up her shawl and they were out of the house and into the hackney before she could blink her eyes. 'Do you have a remote idea where we go?' she demanded as she caught her breath.

'We are following a most interesting pair. Your vicomte met a chap who looked French. After some conversation he turned white as a sheet, then left with him immediately. I would say that is dashed suspicious behavior.'

'It could be anything,' Pamela objected.

'Hush,' he commanded as the carriage ahead of them halted. He signaled their hackney to stop as well some distance away.

They waited a few moments, then carefully exited the vehicle, intent on the pair standing in front of a nondescript house.

'I wonder what those papers are that he is giving that fellow,' the duke whispered, shoving Pamela behind a stout tree that grew along the walkway. Fortunately, it was dark where they stood. The pair they watched stood beneath an oil lamp in front of the modest house, revealing all actions to the two who watched with narrow-eyed concern.

'Could he be one of the spies that plague our country now?' Pamela whispered. 'You suspect him of Bonapartist sympathies, and he said that the Corsican has done much for France — hardly the remark of one who detests the man.'

The two Frenchmen shook hands, then the vicomte hurried into his carriage and sped off. The man took the small packet of papers and slowly walked into the house.

'We won't learn anything more now.'

Pamela felt gentle warmth when he put his arm about her in a protective manner. Did he know how his touch affected her? How the sound of his voice entranced her? What a dilemma, to fall in love with the duke! For she did love him, she acknowledged. She'd known it for days but refused to admit such folly.

The duke hailed a hackney that had clattered around the corner. Within moments they were headed back to the Lockhart soirée.

'Are you frightened?' he asked, his arm still about her as though he liked having her close. Perhaps he meant to keep her warm? Her shawl was insubstantial.

'No, but most curious, Your Grace. I shall endeavor to learn if either of the other two have any secrets up their sleeves, such as the vicomte.'

What a plucky girl she is, thought Robert with admiration. The hackney halted, the duke opened the door, then turned to her, swiftly placing a kiss on her lips before she could guess what he intended. 'Be careful,' he said, his voice deep and husky.

Careful? She was far past prudence.

10

The following morning Pamela rode into the park with some apprehension, Timson dutifully behind her. So far nothing had been made of her brief disappearance from the *soirée* last evening. It was no more than the time she might have spent in the withdrawing room, and her remark about her hem needing tending had seemed to satisfy even her mother.

But this morning she would see the vicomte — if he followed his previous attentions. What would she say to discreetly draw out more information? How could she conceal her knowledge of his peculiar behavior of the evening past? Ordinarily, one did not leave a party to exchange a packet of papers with another in a dimly lit street, particularly if he was a potential enemy.

Even Lady Vane had been concerned about his absence, commenting in her soft, hesitant voice. If the widow was anxious, it could easily explain Pamela's concern.

The park was devoid of riders, it seemed. The weather was not good, coming on to mist before long. Only one familiar gentleman on a gray stallion rode her way.

'Your Grace, good morning,' Pamela said when he drew close. 'It seems we are the only riders out and about.'

'Slugabeds, most likely. An excess of wine can do that, you know, or a late night of gambling.' He shared a smile with her of the sort she treasured.

Pamela suspected there were other, more intriguing things that might cause one to oversleep as well. She did not say this, naturally. Once in a while prudence still reasserted itself.

'It is Almack's this evening, if I recall,' the duke continued as they walked their horses along the Row.

'Yes. I am prepared,' she said, thinking she sounded like one about to be sacrificed, and that was not the case. 'I truly enjoy the dancing, for the music is delightful — even if the refreshments lack a certain something. And you know Almack's is where one can find a suitable husband. I shall require one once this riddle is solved and I am free of the necklace,' she added.

'Husband,' he repeated as though the word, indeed the concept, were foreign to him.

'Yes, silly man,' she dared to say. 'It is not surprising that I must marry, is it? Every young woman knows it is her duty. Since Papa did not have a son, I am to pass on the very ancient family estate to my son. It is a great responsibility, and one of the prime reasons I wish to wed, and soon. I suppose I'd best look for a husband who comes from a large and prolific family. I suspect it might prove a sensible approach to the matter, as I do wish for many children.'

Since the duke had remarked that those with large families seemed to produce the same while flipping through his copy of the peerage, he merely grunted something incomprehensible in reply. That he would certainly qualify in the last respect, he did not mention. Having four sisters and three younger brothers ought to fit Pamela's requirements — were he interested in such a thing. But then, it was possible Pamela knew of his family, for she had studied the peerage book with intensity.

'For example a man — such as yourself — who comes from a family with eight children would be a possibility. I understand Lord Raeburn is from a family of ten siblings. I'd find that most encouraging,' she declared with a serious nod.

'No money, however,' the duke pointed out. 'You would do better to look in my direction.' Why the devil he said that he couldn't understand. Surely, she would not take that as an indirect proposal? He slanted her a cautious look.

She laughed, a silvery, fluting sound that irritated him, for it sounded suspiciously as though she thought the idea of anyone marrying him preposterous.

'You are a wonderful jokester, Your Grace,' she said with an infectious grin lighting her pretty face. 'You have remarked that I am a sensible, practical girl, and so I am. One as practical as I knows better than to sigh for the moon.' She turned her attention to the approaching gate and the traffic beyond. The mist that had held off now began to fall, creating a cool, damp curtain around them.

There ought to be a feeling of relief within him, and there wasn't — which was odd when he considered it. Was he coming to realize that what his family had been saying for some time was correct? That he must find a proper wife? He glanced at the pretty young woman at his side, and knew that if propriety were the deciding factor, he could do no better than marry this girl.

'What do you mean — sensible?' he seized upon one word she had used. 'You who are involved with a diamond-and-sapphire necklace of mysterious origin, political intrigue, and international flirtations?'

'Why, and so I am,' she said prosaically. 'I have passable looks, do needlework quite well, ride properly, and can perform all the other tasks required of a countess — but I do not believe I have special qualities to make me stand out beyond my peers. That is, until the necklace came my way,' she added in a considering afterthought. 'I believe it affects the way men perceive me.' She looked at the duke with a frank, speculative expression on her face.

He wanted to tell her that she was truly exceptional, but he doubted if she would believe him. It would scarcely be proper for him to mention her splendid bosom and charming figure as points in her favor. A gentleman simply did not say something like that to a young unmarried woman no matter how he might think it.

They drew to a halt before her home, and the duke assisted her before the groom could dismount.

She stood close to him for a few minutes, the damp air bringing her scent of carnations to tease his nose. The rich fragrance seemed at odds with her propriety, but hinted of a deeper sensuality that he knew lurked beneath that prim exterior.

'Thank you for your company and conversation,' she said with a delightful smile.

'Not having had a brother, I appreciate the frank and open words we exchange, Your Grace. I value your friendship and assistance with the necklace.'

'There is much I could say in regards to the absurdity you spout, but now is not the proper time.' He glanced at the sky, where it seemed the clouds had decided to rain in earnest. 'I shall see you this evening.' He turned to remount his steed, then paused, looking back at her. 'What is your attire this evening?'

'In addition to the necklace?'

He thought of the necklace gracing her figure and nothing more, and gave himself a mental shake at the sensual image that produced. 'Indeed,' he responded dryly.

'It will be a gown of pale blue aerophane crêpe — the sheerest made — over a white taffeta slip. I am acquiring quite a wardrobe of gowns in white and blue. I wonder what other color would enhance the sapphires and diamonds?' She gave him a rueful smile and dashed up to the door, which had been opened for her by the sourfaced Grimes. 'If you think of anything, do let me know,' she called out before the door was shut behind her.

He sent her a wreath of forget-me-nots and white carnations to wear in her hair for that evening. When he viewed the results, he felt unaccountable pride in his choice. She looked utterly lovely. Wild roses bloomed in her cheeks when her gaze met his across the ballroom at Almack's. The gown she'd mentioned floated about her in sheer delight, the pale blue emphasizing the stones and the purity of her skin. Her neckline dipped in a very low vee in the front, meeting at a point somewhere between that magnificent bosom. At his side Lady Jersey glanced at Pamela, then tapped Robert on his arm.

'Do I smell the scent of June roses in the air?' she inquired archly.

'If you refer to me — not that I know of, Lady Jersey. There are many ladies I admire, and I suppose some year I shall have to select one of them for my duchess. At least, my mother reminds me it is necessary.' He gave the countess an absent glance, then pretended he didn't know or care when the baron led Pamela on to the floor for a country-dance.

'We are considering allowing that naughty dance, the waltz, to be permitted here,' Lady Jersey said in a teasing voice. 'I understand you partake in waltzing parties?'

'True,' he admitted. 'I look forward to it here, you may be sure. I suspect you would be exceptionally graceful while performing it,' the duke said courteously. He then excused himself, and was about to head in the direction of Lady Gresham when he was waylaid by his own mother on one of her infrequent appearances at Almack's.

'I am pleased to see you doing your duty, Robert. If you find a young lady that meets your standards, do let me know in time to plan a wedding. I want no hole-in-the-wall affair,' she said with a wry smile, knowing how her son detested pretentious display, yet desired proper ceremony.

He nodded perfunctorily — it was far better than arguing, he'd found — and instead inquired of his mother, 'Can you tell me anything about Baron Ruchoven?' Not that he expected his mother to be particularly helpful, but it was an excellent diversionary tactic.

'I had considered him as a possible match for your sister Susan. However, I discovered an unsavory bit of information about the gentleman. Although he comes from a fine old family, he is extremely short of funds. And, upon additional inquiry, it appears he has spent German government money on his own pleasures.'

Robert decided he had best never underestimate his mother again. He had not expected her to assist in his investigation! By her stress on the word pleasures, the duke assumed she referred to a mistress, or certainly the petticoat line.

'Were he doing what was expected of him, he would be bribing officials in the usual manner, obtaining information useful to the German court. Fool!' The dowager duchess flicked a disdainful look at the baron before excusing herself to join a cluster of friends on the far side of the room.

Could it be that the *baron* had purchased the necklace for his paramour, and it had been misdelivered? Might that account for the hungry expression in his eyes as he stared at Pamela during the pattern of the dance? Robert found he did not care for the fatuous expression on the baron's distinguished face as he ogled Pamela's admittedly splendid bosom.

The moment the dance concluded, Robert intercepted the pair on their way to Lady Gresham's side.

'Good evening, Your Grace,' said Lady Pamela, giving Robert a heartfelt smile.

He took her hand from where it properly rested on the baron's arm and drew her along with him, giving the baron the curtest of nods. He did not ask her if she wished to dance, for he had never in his life been denied what he wished and didn't expect to now.

'The flowers are lovely. Thank you so much,' she said as she flashed another smile at him before resuming the proper mien expected at Almack's.

'I thought they would complement the jewels. And to return to a point that you made this morning, surely you do not credit your flare of popularity solely to the necklace — even if it is splendid.' He began the pattern of the minuet, executing the steps with the casual elegance that came from familiarity and an inborn grace.

'Of course not,' she agreed. 'I fear some of the credit must be laid at your feet, bringing me into fashion as it were. It is known that where the Duke of Wexford goes, others follow. For that I thank you again.' Her eyes sparkled, and she executed the intricate steps with consummate grace. Lady Pamela was very light on her feet.

'Rubbish,' he grumbled, but not without a modicum of pleasure in her evaluation of his influence.

'As you wish,' she said just loudly enough for him to hear.

'I spoke with my mother. When the dance is over, walk with me — I suppose it must be the refreshment room again. I have something to tell you, and we can speak there.'

Pamela's heart fluttered for a moment,

then resumed its normal beat. Whatever the duke had to say doubtlessly had to do with the mystery surrounding the necklace, nothing more. She had better remember that no matter what she wished, she'd not likely have her way in things as it seemed the duke always did.

When the strains of the music faded away, she turned to His Grace and asked, 'Tell me — out of curiosity — do you always have your way?'

He reflected a minute, then nodded. 'I suppose I do. It becomes a habit after a time.'

'I suspected as much.' She gave him a look that Robert interpreted as a rebuke.

'I am a duke,' he reminded her as they walked.

'A very spoiled one, I make no doubt.' Her words were softened by a beguiling smile. 'Now, what has happened?'

He explained what his mother had learned, and Pamela exclaimed with amazement.

'Goodness, your mother ought to be working as a spy for the government. But then, I expect my mother would do the same were she considering a particular gentleman for me.'

Robert thought it curious that she had not done so.

'What do we do now?' she said.

'Ah, the sapphire lady that has London society wagging tongues,' exclaimed Algernon Thynne come seeking a dance. He tilted his head and gave Lady Pamela a comprehensive look that would have earned him a set-down had he not been Robert's best friend. Even then it annoyed the duke. He tossed Algie a warning glare.

'Is it true?' she said in a dismayed tone. 'Oh, dear, that does not seem very proper. What is being said?'

Algernon looked a trifle uncomfortable and glanced at Robert with uneasy eyes. 'There is always more than a little speculation when people gossip, my lady. However, I come to tear you away from this fellow. I beg your hand for the next dance. You perform the Scottish reel very well.'

'But, of course,' Lady Pamela replied.

Robert wondered how long it would take for her to worm out the rest of the story from his friend. While the music of the country-dance flowed about him, Robert looked over the current crop of girls making their come-outs. There were a few stunning beauties to be seen. Most were a trifle ordinary and would require someone superior to bring out their specialness. The rest were dreadful. Heiresses, most likely — platter-faced, freckled, plump, or graceless. He noted

Lord Raeburn paying court to one of them and wondered if the chap was being kind or thinking of his empty pockets.

Interesting how so many of the men who paid attention to heiresses were in need of funds. He suspected that Pamela's necklace also played a part in her attraction, but to what extent he could only speculate.

'I should like to know what else is being gabbled about me, Mr Thynne,' Pamela said with determination when she met Algernon in the pattern of the reel.

'Nothing of import,' he replied with maddening insouciance. 'Sometimes it is better not to know.'

She digested this remark while dancing and weaving through the reel, until she lightly clasped her partner's hand again. They skipped down the line to the bottom of the set and faced each other. Pamela noted his eyes were sparkling with what she suspected was mischief and resolved not to make an issue of the gossip.

Upon returning to her mother, Pamela was glad to rest a few moments while the musicians selected the next music.

'My dear, I heard the strangest thing,' her mother said, looking confused. 'Rumor has it that you are to be the next Duchess of Wexford. It seems His Grace has never shown quite so much interest in a young, unmarried, and highly eligible woman before.' It was plain that the Lady Gresham couldn't fathom the duke's interest in her daughter.

'Do not bother your head about it, Mama. The duke is merely being kind. I think he believes he can bring me into fashion — it is but a whim of his.' Pamela would have liked to explain about the necklace, but she was too involved at this point to make a simple clarification of the matter.

'Well, he comes again, no doubt to claim your hand for the next dance. It will add fuel to the fire,' her mother murmured to the air, for Pamela had risen to accept the duke's hand. She found she really did not care what the gossips said. She knew the circumstances, and she was going to enjoy herself while she could.

Robert gave her a quizzical look. 'And did you find out anything more from Algie?'

'No,' she admitted. 'I decided to leave well enough alone, although my mother heard a few rumors that I suspect would match his. I know the truth, therefore I shall ignore all gossip.' She darted a prim little smile at him, then added, 'You might pay attention to one of the diamonds that shine here this evening. That would drive the gossips into a tizzy.'

He gazed at her perfectly beautiful bosom

and sighed. 'If I do, it will be under protest. I would rather enjoy our repartee than the trite remarks of those beauties.' He discovered that this polite observation was quite true, much to his surprise. He gave her a thoughtful look. 'Egad, why don't they have two original thoughts to rub together?' he complained in a highly improper confidence. 'How is it that you have such delightful conversation?'

'I suppose it is because I am not trying to impress you,' she said when next she took his hand in the dance. 'You see, I have no expectations where you are concerned. I think of you more as a brother,' she concluded in what had to be the most outrageous lie she'd ever uttered.

The duke looked annoyed, frowning in that way he did from time to time. Pamela couldn't begin to guess what went on in his mind.

The baron again claimed Pamela's hand, but requested they seek refreshments instead, for the room was stuffy — as crowded as it was. 'I feel certain that you must desire a glass of lemonade or orgeat, my lady,' he concluded suavely.

She sensed he wished to converse, so agreed to his suggestion. 'Indeed, they never open the windows here, and it can be a trifle warm. Now, if they could chill the lemonade, it would be quite nice.'

She walked at his side in silence, waiting.

'You are rather different from the other young ladies,' he began.

Pamela inwardly agreed, for none of them had received a package with a priceless necklace inside it.

'You do not prattle nonsense, nor do you simper and sigh. It makes for pleasant conversation,' he said with a civil smile at her.

The duke had remarked on a similar vein. Perhaps she ought to rent herself out as a conversationalist? Then she took pity on the baron and smiled gently at him. 'It cannot be that bad, surely?'

The baron chuckled, a low growl, actually. 'You are most amusing. I have a friend in the German court much like you,' he confided.

'Do you miss your home?' Pamela said. 'Or is it quite similar to London?'

'The climate, the people, the atmosphere are all different, although there is a similarity in some of the court — your king being of German descent. And yes, I miss it very much. At times, being an ambassador for one's country is lonely.'

'I suppose you are required to seek out helpful information for your government?' she asked in what she hoped was an innocent manner.

He gave her a sharp look, then relaxed as though he decided a young woman was not to be feared. 'Indeed. It is time-consuming.' He picked up a glass of lemonade and handed it to Pamela. 'Would that this be vintage champagne, my lady.'

She accepted the glass, not commenting on his courtly remark. 'But you must have staff from your homeland with you — people with whom you may share a liking for particular foods and habits. Even a newspaper from home must help,' she observed.

'Ah, newspapers,' he exclaimed softly. 'That is how one finds out a month or so after the fact that a dear friend has married or died.'

From the wistful expression on his face, Pamela wondered if perhaps a particular woman he found to his liking had married in his absence. 'That is a pity. I have never traveled, although I believe I might enjoy it, given the right circumstances.'

'And they would be?' he asked as though surprised at the direction of her conversation.

'I might wish to explore the world were it at the side of my husband,' she said softly, unable to refrain from a darting glance at the duke. Then she resolutely turned her back on him, which was a shame, for she missed his concerned stare in her direction. She placed an empty glass on the table, then said, 'Perhaps we could stroll about the room. I enjoy watching the dancers.'

'I am yours to command,' he said, offering his arm.

They did not wander very far, for the prince came to her side, followed by the vicomte. Both men had outdone themselves in dress this evening. The prince, in white with dazzling embroidery and a display of medals guaranteed to impress all but those who knew what each medal signified, was complete blond effervescence. He almost shimmered, to Pamela's way of thinking.

The vicomte was French understated elegance and of a certain dark moodiness this evening that must have caused a number of female hearts to beat more rapidly.

'Good evening, gentlemen,' Pamela said, smiling on all three men. She caught a glimpse of the duke studying the foursome with hand at his chin, looking almost as moody as the vicomte. The other men appeared to discreetly study the necklace, and she longed to tell them that it had not altered since the last time they ogled it.

'It is not fair of the baron to monopolize you, Lady Pamela,' the prince protested.

'How fortunate I had the foresight to ask your lovely mother if I might have your hand for the next dance,' the vicomte inserted.

'The sapphire lady will be mine after that,' the prince added with a dazzling smile at Pamela. She was certain that a good many other young ladies must utterly hate her for cornering three of the most entertaining gentlemen at Almack's, if not necessarily the most eligible.

Upon leaving Almack's that evening, Pamela felt no closer to knowing which of those three had been the sender of the necklace, much to her disappointment. She could only hope the following evening at the opera would bring better results. She wondered if the duke would again share his box with the spectacular Lady Smythe.

★　★　★

Lady Vane called upon Pamela and her mother the next afternoon with an invitation for dinner the coming week. 'If you must know, I shall invite His Grace, the Duke of Wexford — for he quite makes a party — and if you attend, he will as well,' she confided to Pamela in a soft aside.

'We do not live in each other's pockets,' Pamela protested. She exchanged a look with Lady Vane, thinking that was quite the oddest invitation she'd received in some time.

The widow smiled with gentle charm, then turned the subject to Pamela's modest success. 'I suspect your jewels must play a part in your conquests. They are truly magnificent. Would that every young lady might have such a great-uncle as yours.'

'But then, none of them would be unique, would they?' Pamela replied with amusement at the notion.

'They would have to be endowed with your other assets, as well, to achieve your *succès fou*.'

'What a lovely French accent you have,' Pamela noted, wondering if she was not being overly aware of anything French nowadays.

'I spent a brief time in Paris when I was a girl,' the widow admitted. 'And a good governess does wonders. Do you also speak the language?'

'Of course,' Pamela said simply. Every young lady of the *ton* sought to acquire a basic knowledge of French. It was the language of fashion and food.

'How nice. Perhaps when this dreadful war is ended, you will have an opportunity to use your language skills.'

The duke was ushered in just as Lady Vane was about to depart. They exchanged polite greetings, and the quiet woman exited the room, head meekly bowed.

'She was here before, I believe. A friend of yours?' the duke inquired with a frown.

'Not actually,' Pamela said. 'She is charming, but I confess I do not know why she has sought us out.' And yet she did know. Had the lady not admitted that she sought the Duke of Wexford and thought to reach him through Pamela?

The duke chatted briefly, asking Pamela to accompany him down the stairs when he left.

'Did you learn anything at all last evening?'

'The baron misses his home, and perhaps a certain lady who married after he left. Maybe that explains his foray into the petticoat line while here in London.'

'I'll pretend you did not say that,' he scolded.

'Nevertheless, it may be so. And Lady Vane is sending you an invitation to a dinner next week. We are to attend as well.' Pamela paused at the bottom of the stairs to examine his face when he turned to look down at her.

'I shall be there, then,' he said, flashing a grin at Pamela that quite melted her heart.

Since his acceptance was precisely what Lady Vane hoped for, Pamela merely nodded. Truth be told, she'd welcome him, too, but only because she valued his opinions she told herself. Then she wondered if Lady Smythe would be at the dinner as well.

The duke left the house, jauntily swinging his cane while examining the odd feeling he realized when he'd chatted with Pamela. It was not brotherly in the least. Rather, he'd wanted to hold her, and know the feel of that delightful form in his arms again.

Then — rather than dwell on something that might prove impossible for one who always had his own way — he wondered about the woman who had left as he entered. He knew next to nothing about Lady Vane and thought it might be prudent to look into her background since he had the time.

Some hours later the duke had his information, but was puzzled as to what to do with it. Lady Vane — as so many widows today — had been left in a precarious situation by her late husband. She lived on the fringe of society, accepted mostly because of her agreeable company. The only point that seemed odd was her befriending Pamela. Doubtless he was making a mountain from a molehill, but he took few chances. The lady would bear watching.

11

The opera glittered more than usual, or so it seemed to Pamela that following evening. It was not simply the gentle glow she felt around her from wearing the magnificent necklace again with the soft luminescence of the silver tissue gown to enhance it. It was the first evening she had been the cynosure of all eyes — at least for several moments. She shifted uneasily under the probing gaze of so many of society, even though she well knew that the attention would transfer to another shortly. Still, she found it auspicious in her future search for a husband that she had gained the attention of so many, at least for the nonce.

It took her awhile to examine all the boxes to see a familiar face she had met in her recent forays into the upper strata of the *ton*. Fans fluttered before faces of women she recognized. Gentlemen turned aside to comment on something to their companions. She was silly, for it was unlikely they spoke of her — yet she wished she knew the topic of their gossip.

Suddenly, a disturbance occurred in the

box across from the Greshams, and her attention immediately focused there. She watched as the duke entered his box, ushering the splendidly enticing and lushly endowed Lady Smythe to a chair. Garbed in deepest red that surprisingly flattered her hair, the lady wafted a large black feathered fan that matched the black plumes in her hair. She smiled and chattered away sixteen to the dozen to those in the party.

Pamela froze, nose tilted slightly in the air. She would not permit a soul in this theater to guess her reaction to the scene — should anyone be curious.

Scolding herself, she remembered that she had told him she thought of him as a brother, a friend. A gentleman did not lavish attention on someone who regarded him like that. And in addition, all he agreed to do was to try to solve the mystery of the jewels. Nothing more. If she had been so foolish as to tumble into love with the man, it was not his fault. Nor could he be expected to notice the quiet, well-bred young woman who at times assisted him in his quest.

'I see His Grace has arrived,' Lady Gresham pointed out — most unnecessarily. 'Lady Smythe joins his group this evening. He is polite, but I believe I detect a lack of ardor in his attentions. Sometimes a gentleman escorts a lady for other than the obvious reason, my dear,' she said softly to Pamela.

She was astounded that her mother would be so perceptive as to realize that her daughter was distressed by what she saw. Usually, Mama fixed her interest elsewhere.

'The duke is merely a friend, Mama,' Pamela said quietly, turning her gaze toward the stage, where the curtain began to rise while the orchestra struck up an overture.

A rap on the door was followed by the return of the baron. Pamela was ashamed that she had briefly forgotten he joined them this evening. He placed a box of comfits in Pamela's hands, then offered a glass of ratafia to Lady Gresham.

'Fräulein, I trust these are as sweet as you,' he said in a smooth manner, glancing at the pretty box.

Pamela smiled gratefully at the distinguished gentleman who so politely sat at her side. It was not his fault that she found him tedious. What man could compare to the duke and emerge victorious?

However, he bestowed such devoted consideration on her that Pamela found she was almost enjoying the evening when she had expected it to be dreary. During the first intermission she chatted amiably with the gentleman, persuading him to tell them about his life in Germany and the countryside there. He lost some of his pomposity as he described his home and family. It was quite clear to Pamela that he longed for his home.

When it came to the second intermission, Lady Gresham requested the baron to escort her to a neighboring box so that she might have a word with Lady de Clifford.

Pamela sat quietly, aware that the duke had left his box, leaving Lady Smythe talking with a great deal of animation to Algernon Thynne. Her gestures with that enormous fan brought a reluctant smile to Pamela's face.

'And what is so amusing? Your devoted escort is away for the moment. Yet you entertain yourself?'

Although she'd not heard the door open, Pamela did not have to turn around to know the duke stood in the shadows at the rear of the box. His rich, deep voice haunted her dreams too often for that.

'My escort is the ultimate of civility,' she said with an effort to be gracious. She turned, her back stiff with annoyance, and pinned him with a cool stare. 'And you, sir? What do you here?'

'I do not make a cake of myself ogling the low-cut gown my companion wears.' He fixed his gaze on her necklace — or something — and positively glared at her. 'And what have you learned from him this evening? I'd swear the gentleman pays more attention to your neckline than the play. What has he revealed of his actions and possible motives?'

Stung, she fought for composure, wondering what in the world would make him attack her in such a vile manner. Her bosom swelled with indignation at his innuendos. 'At least I am not in danger of being overcome by feathers,' she replied with a faint smile at the thought of the duke buried in black plumes.

'At least Lady Smythe is not involved in your necklace affair.'

'Is she involved in another affair?' Pamela snapped before she considered how her words might sound.

'That, I could not say. And I thought you such a proper girl,' he gibed. 'If we were not so public . . . ' He propped himself against the frame of the door, looking at her as though he wished he might scold her or do something equally interesting.

'You mock propriety, Your Grace. Yet, it is doing what is proper that holds the fabric of our society together,' she said, utterly furious with him and his unseemly insinuations. 'I am unaware of any impropriety committed by the baron — in my regard.' She was greatly tempted to add that it was more than she might say for him, but didn't.

'Not because he hasn't thought of it,' the duke retorted in a husky growl.

'Thoughts are not quite the same as deeds, are they?' she said with false sweetness.

'I shall discuss this with you tomorrow.' He cut his words and slipped from the box.

Her mother returned shortly, the baron ushering her into the box with great solicitude. 'I am sorry we took so long, dear. Lady de Clifford wished to speak with the baron as well. I was happy to see the duke attending you while the baron and I were out of the box. Such a thoughtful gentleman.'

'I found much to amuse me in looking about the theater, Mama,' Pamela replied, omitting comment on the duke. She had been so absorbed in wondering what the duke might have to say to her tomorrow that she had scarcely noticed the passage of time. He would issue a scold, she had no doubt of that — but why? What had she done to infuriate him? Or the baron, for that matter? She discounted the words about the baron staring at her necklace. True, he had glanced at it and remarked how well it became her, but he certainly had not *ogled* her.

She smiled and nodded and pretended to listen to the remainder of the opera, but she was relieved when the curtain fell and they might leave.

She learned nothing more of the baron or his interest in the necklace on the way home. Perhaps he simply admired pretty jewels?

★ ★ ★

'He may merely admire jewelry, Your Grace,' she explained the following morning when she encountered the duke in the park while on her customary morning ride.

'That is not all he admires,' he muttered. At least that was what Pamela thought he said.

'He certainly did not *ogle* me,' she declared firmly. Then she sighed and said, 'I will be glad when I am able to go out of an evening and not fear catching an inflammation of the lungs.' Pamela wondered why the duke laughed.

'My dear girl, I trust you do not speak like this to the baron?' He turned his horse, and hers followed. They headed back to Gresham House.

'No. You are the only one to whom I can confide my thoughts. I daresay I am a trifle . . . open?' she confessed. 'Perhaps precipitous — at least to you. So much for that overweening propriety you complained about last evening.' She wondered at the pleased expression on his face. How in the world had her admission that she spoke her mind too freely with him met his approval? She did not understand men in the least.

'Tonight you attend the Henson rout, as I recall,' the duke observed as they clattered along the cobblestones to the Gresham home.

'I should imagine you will not attend. It shall be a fearful crush from what Mama says.' Pamela darted a glance at the duke, wondering what went on in that head to make him smile.

'I *must* be there and at your side. What if someone in that crowd attempts to steal the necklace?' He gave her an impatient look, then went on, 'What do you wear this evening to display the jewels?' He dismounted and assisted Pamela from the saddle, holding her only a trifle longer than necessary.

'A dark blue spotted-net gown over a white underdress,' she explained patiently, knowing she ought to step away from him and yet treasuring their closeness. Oh, she was a silly widgeon, to be sure. 'It has net rosettes around the hem and bows at the top of the sleeves.'

'And I suppose the bodice barely covers you,' he said wryly.

'Mama would not permit anything indecent,' Pamela said, feeling that she ought not have to apologize for her gown. Then she ruined that thought by adding, 'I confess that the neckline is extremely low, but I would *not* have people think I am vulgar.' She searched his eyes to see what his reaction to her description might be. He looked smug. Smug? How odd. She must be mistaken.

'I will be there to lend you propriety,' he reminded. 'No one dares to think ill of my companions.'

Pamela thought of the exotic beauty who had sat at his side last evening and held her tongue.

★ ★ ★

The Henson rout was overflowing with guests as Mama had predicted. Lady Henson must be enormously pleased. Pamela wished she were at home with her needlepoint. Being constantly stared at was losing its appeal.

'I see the jewels hold their customary place of honor,' the duke commented from over her shoulder.

She glanced back at him, twisting slightly, her beautiful bosom displayed in profile. 'Indeed,' she replied, following with a sigh.

He studied her, that same smug smile on his face again, then grew sober. 'Are you weary of this game?'

'Only of displaying the jewels because I

wish to lure someone into the open. Why is it taking so long? Why does he not see them and want them returned? I would, were they mine.' Frustration rang in her voice, however soft she kept it.

'Ah, Lady Pamela,' the prince exclaimed, suddenly appearing at her side and taking her hand in his to waft a kiss somewhere over her glove. He clasped her hand to his chest in what appeared to be sincere admiration. '*Très charmante!* You have cast a spell over me with your beauty.'

'Over every basket-scrambler in London as well,' the duke muttered so softly that Pamela was certain only she heard him.

'How sweet of you, Your Highness,' Pamela said with a kindly smile, wishing she might dig an elbow into His Grace's firm chest.

'You have created the sensation — wearing a necklace of such magnificence every evening with a gown that more than does it justice. Your Mama must be most pleased with your achievement,' the prince concluded, allowing Pamela's hand to be freed from his grasp at last.

Pamela felt the comforting clasp and warmth of the duke's strong hand on her elbow. She leaned against him just a little, justifying her weakness by the press of the throng. She no longer wished to jab him in the chest. What she wished, she dare not think.

'How gracious you are, Your Highness. I must say it is a lovely compliment.'

He continued in the same vein for some time before departing.

Robert scanned the throng, noting the prince now paid court to another heiress. If he'd had any doubts about the prince's needs, they had gone. The prince remained in the running, as it were.

He felt Pamela stir at his side, and his eyes sought the softness of her shoulders. There was much to be said for standing in this position. He had an unobstructed view of her, ah, assets — that is, the necklace. No one might reach the clasp while he was pressed against her slim body.

Her skin was so pure, like fragile cream silk, perfumed lightly with carnations. He glanced down at the line of her bodice, wanting what he knew he could not have. He admitted that he would very much like to turn her around and gather her into his arms for another kiss. It was dashed difficult to be a proper gentleman when his body inclined him the other direction.

At last they inched their way toward the door and waited in the front of the house for Lady Gresham to follow them. The duke took a protective stance by Lady Pamela when a somewhat foxed gentleman ogled her on his way out of the house.

'Wrap your shawl more closely about you, my lady. It is possible some rogue might try for the gems while we wait out here.' The duke tugged her shawl over one shoulder, permitting his hand to linger one moment on her delicate skin.

'How tiresome,' she said quietly, but without anger. 'I must thank you for standing guard this evening, Your Grace. I could not have managed without you.'

Her confession caused a curious reaction within the duke. It touched him deeply, for he had never experienced such simple gratitude for a minor thing he'd done for a woman. Usually, they had ulterior motives. Especially, when it was a matter of pleasure for him! And he had to admit that he enjoyed being at her side, listening to her gentle voice and intelligent comments.

'I am only too pleased to assist,' he said thinking of the delectable view that had been his. 'However, if I am required to listen to that Russian again, I may throttle him or both of you. You need not encourage him quite so much, you know.'

'Oh, just when I am in charity with you, you say something that makes me long to do something wicked to you.' Pamela turned to glare at him.

What lit his eyes and made him chuckle at her words? By rights he ought to be as angry as she. Pamela could think of nothing amusing in what she'd said and told him so.

He was prevented from replying when Lady Gresham joined them. 'I shall explain to you one of these days,' he managed to murmur in her ear when he assisted Pamela into the carriage.

And with that she had to be satisfied.

★ ★ ★

The dinner at Lady Vane's gracious town house proved to be a surprise of sorts. She had snared Prince Radinski, the Duke of Wexford, Vicomte Reynaud, and the ever charming Lord Raeburn as guests, as well as a selection of very lovely women, all of the best society, and including Lady Smythe.

Pamela was seated between the prince and the duke, with the vicomte placed directly across from her. It was, to her way of thinking, the best of all possible worlds at the present. Lady Smythe claimed the attentions of the vicomte at her side with practiced ease.

Since the pleasant Lady Vane lacked a host, she had asked Lord Raeburn to assist her.

Pamela overheard the request, phrased in the most polite and charming manner. Really, it was a pity that the lady was confined to London and not permitted to retire to the country, if rumor was true. Apparently the heir — a first cousin once removed of Lady Vane's late husband — permitted her the use of the London house, but she was not allowed to return to her beloved home in the country at any time. Men, Pamela decided, were decidedly peculiar in their demands.

During the time for dinner conversation with the duke, Pamela hunted for something innocuous to say and failed. She nibbled at her fish, glancing at his plate to see he ate well. Her stomach was churning with nervousness, and it unsettled her, preventing her from enjoying her excellent meal.

'I have not explained my annoyance of last evening, have I?' he said quietly as he placed his fork on the plate.

'I am waiting,' she admitted.

'It was not so much with you as the others, and the necessity that you must display the jewels in such a manner. If I could think of something more likely to snaffle our man, I would, believe me,' he said in an undertone.

'Well, it is a relief to know you are not angry with me, per se,' she replied quietly after a sip of wine.

'You remarked that the thief — or whatever he is — ought to have come forward by now. I agree. I confess it disturbs me as well. I expect he will strike again soon.' He dropped the quiet little bomb in Pamela's ear before turning his attention to their hostess at his other side.

The plates were removed, and Pamela turned to the gentleman on her left. At least, she pretended an interest in the effusive flattery pouring forth from the prince. It was utter nonsense, of course, but it surpassed being told the thief might strike again and soon. She would have to test the metal bar and keep something handy so she might again defend herself against attack.

Following dinner, the ladies drifted into the drawing room. Lady Vane begged Pamela to play her pianoforte, newly tuned for the occasion.

She naturally agreed, for all young ladies were expected to perform when asked. It was one of those social duties one acquired, like riding well, nice needlework, correct manners, and the like. She was not terribly gifted at the piano, believing her voice her better talent, but she'd been asked to play, so play she did.

The men joined the women in short order, causing Pamela to wonder who suggested the departure from normal. She studied the prince, who paid attention to one of the Hardesty girls — a platter-faced creature of no charm and even less taste, but sizable dowry.

'The port was barely tolerable, so we cut that part of the evening short,' the duke quietly explained while he leafed through a pile of music atop the pianoforte. How he managed to move about with such quiet speed mystified Pamela. She wished she had that ability.

'It seems the last Lord Vane did not believe in leaving a well-stocked cellar behind him,' Pamela said.

'That is not all,' the duke said. 'There are indications of missing pictures here and there. I suspect the gentleman left his widow none too plump in the pocket, either.'

'There is nothing terribly unusual in those circumstances, you must admit,' Pamela said with sympathy clear in her manner.

'I cannot decide what part Raeburn plays in her life.' He picked up some music, pretending to examine it.

'He assisted her by playing host for the evening, nothing more,' Pamela said, glancing up to see the duke watching her hands hover over the keys. Her fingers moved downward creating a discordant sound. Aware a number of people stared at her, she smiled, then began a sprightly Mozart air.

'Sorry,' he apologized in her ear. 'I did not mean to cause you problems.'

Pamela almost stopped midpoint in the musical selection. Problems? The man obviously did not know the meaning of the word. She completed the piece, then rose from the bench.

The duke slipped into her place. 'Sing something,' he commanded in carrying tones.

She could scarcely refuse, having agreed to provide a bit of music. When he played the introduction for a light, popular tune, she nodded and sang with what she hoped was good grace. It was one of those ditties that had a catchy tune and somewhat ambiguous words that Pamela suspected might be taken more than one way.

But she would not perform again, in spite of the applause. Enough was enough, and she rarely sought the limelight. Slipping away from the pianoforte and the duke, she crossed the room to gaze at a picture on the wall. From where she stood, she noted that two others were obviously missing. The duke had been right. Pamela felt compassion for the pretty Lady Vane, then she wondered about something that seemed most peculiar.

'And why do you frown?' the duke said,

who had casually strolled her way following his own brief performance on the fine instrument provided for entertainment.

'If Lady Vane is hard-pressed for money so that she must sell some of the paintings, why give this elaborate dinner for a goodly number of people?'

'A need for display? Or perhaps she seeks to find a new husband, and this is her avenue?'

'Lord Raeburn?' Pamela glanced in his direction, returning to the hint made by the duke earlier. The gentleman in question now conversed with Lady Gresham.

'Not likely, but one never knows about motives, or what goes on in another's head.'

'How true,' Pamela said with heartfelt agreement. 'You had best circulate, Your Grace,' she added after a speculative look sent their way by Lady Hardesty. 'It would be unwise to encourage any conjecture regarding us, do you not agree?'

He nodded and drifted away from her side with unflattering speed.

Abominable creature, she thought, feeling decidedly grumpy.

The prince and the vicomte compensated for the duke's defection, both descending upon her with their charming words of praise and elegant encomiums.

The prince, in particular, seemed to take it

247

in his head that he could claim her sole regard. He tucked her hand through the crook of his arm and proceeded to amble about the room, Pointing out various objects of beauty, and avoiding comment on the missing paintings with correct civility.

Pamela considered his conduct most fitting, though he tended to dominate her company. However, she was content to be in the company of one of the more sought-after gentleman in London — after the duke, naturally. The prince's polish and Russian charm wore a trifle thin after a time, but she'd not complain about that in the least. Not when the duke glowered at her like a overzealous guardian.

As they were rejoining the main group, the vicomte claimed her attention from the prince with a laughing admonishment.

'You want nothing to do with that fellow,' the vicomte declared with a suave smile. 'You would hate the Russian winters. Moscow is bad, St Petersburg is little better. In summer, there are millions of little bugs to drive you insane. In winter, the wolves haunt one everywhere.'

'I had not realized you knew Russia so well,' she said. 'I confess, I find the Continental wanderings of the various gentlemen perplexing. Baron Ruchoven seems terribly homesick for Germany and his family, and yet he must remain here in his government's service. Do you not long for your home at times?' She recalled that exchange of papers and wondered what else he had been up to lately.

'Perhaps. Until the war is over there is little point in yearning for something I cannot have. Life is a gamble.' He gave her a hooded look, which seemed far too sober for a polite social gathering.

'Were you able to bring some assets with you when you left France?' Pamela sought to find out what she might from this man of whom she suspected something. After all, he was — along with two others — of a height with the thief.

'My family has had investments in England for many years, most prudent, as it turned out. I cannot live in the first style, but I am comfortable enough. I am flattered at your concern, my lady.'

Lady Smythe claimed the attentions of the duke, leaning against him in a highly intimate manner that Pamela thought indecorous. But then, a widow seemed to be able to do a great number of things that an unwed maiden might not.

'You have many friends in this country, Vicomte?' she asked turning her attention back to the gentleman at her side.

'It is pleasant to be invited here and there, both in the country and the city. My only difficulty is that it is almost impossible for me to reciprocate.'

'I suppose so,' she said vaguely, trying to think how he might accomplish entertaining a group while living at Albany House as he had mentioned. Impossible. Grillion's, perhaps, but that was expensive and most likely above his touch.

Pamela excused herself to retreat to the ladies' withdrawing room. Upon exiting, she discovered the duke pacing the hallway. At least she could think of no better word to describe the way he wandered back and forth just beyond the drawing room.

'There you are. I was beginning to think you had done a flit down the back stairs,' he said impatiently.

'Nonsense. As if I would ever do anything so stupid.'

He took her arm and walked with her along the passageway. 'You are courting disaster, my girl.'

'I am doing nothing of the kind,' she replied with quiet heat. How dare this man think he might make such personal observations about her behavior!

'First you disappear with the prince — who was paying you such outrageous court before you left the room that I can scarce imagine what happened after.'

'Not one thing!' she declared emphatically. 'Not that it is any of Your Grace's business,' she added, irritated at his high-handedness.

'Well, then you left with the vicomte in much the same manner.'

'And *now* I stroll along with you!' she exclaimed haughtily. 'Forgive me if I point out that this is scarcely less odious than the others.'

'But you are with me,' came the self-satisfied reply.

'More's the pity,' she snapped. 'I shall return to my mother's side immediately. As the hour is late, I will also suggest we leave at once. I, for one, have had enough of the company!' She glared at him, leaving no doubt of her feelings, then turned sharply about and disappeared into the drawing room.

12

The Duke stared blankly at the morning paper. With his reputation as the most polished of gentlemen when it came to dealing with the fair sex, how had he made such a mull of things last night? For that matter, what was the trouble with him? Never had he acted in such an utterly fatheaded manner — making wild accusations of the proper Lady Pamela! He charged her with unseemly conduct, when she was obviously attempting to solve the mystery and coming a sight closer to it than he was.

The duke was becoming obsessed with the most extraordinary creature, that's what it was. Her pretty little nose tilted up in a beguiling way when she was annoyed. And her luxuriant hair of softest brown curls sparkled when the sun blessed its strands with its golden rays. Those incredible cerulean blue eyes did not coyly flirt with him, but gazed candidly into his own, revealing unsuspected depths for a girl her age.

Her straightforward, frank manner might be considered daunting by some, but he found it enormously refreshing after being toadied to all his life. And that was another aspect about that young woman he'd considered so ordinary to begin with — she didn't give a fig about his rank. The Wexford silver gilt coronet with eight golden strawberry leaves apparently held little appeal for her. She treated him much as she did Algie Thynne, who was no more than heir to a barony. For the duke, who had been accustomed to the deference due his title from birth, it was a highly novel experience to say the least. She might have the confidence of being born an earl's daughter, but that couldn't compare to the title of duchess. The notion that he might be found wanting in any manner piqued his pride.

Considering her further, she possessed a number of charms that set her apart from other young misses. Uppermost in his mind was the image of that magnificent figure. She was perfection in all those delicate curves and quite deliciously formed — particularly her splendid bosom.

In truth, she had requested his assistance in solving a mystery. No flirting, no guile, only proper manners, which placed her in the realm of those women with whom one did not dally, but married. Then he had taken advantage of her, kissing that delectable rosebud mouth when unable to resist the temptation — another inconsistent part of his behavior. He was beyond that sort of thing — or so he believed.

In turn, he had done blasted little to solve that mystery. Oh, they had searched the peerage, narrowing the field, and had latched on to the three most likely men, but had done precious little since then. Where had all his analytical abilities gone? All he had managed to do was parade this lovely young woman in that necklace, wearing daringly low-cut gowns — never mind that most society women wore gowns with similar necklines; she was special. And by now he had hoped that someone would have shown an excessive interest in the jewels.

But truth be told, Robert had been so diverted by Pamela's exquisite body that a chap might have shown an extravagant interest in the necklace and he'd have missed it.

It was definitely time to pull himself together. There were reputations to consider — not only hers, but his. As a debonair gentleman of the *ton* and successful amateur sleuth, his standing could not come into question.

It was crucial to ascertain *if* a crime had been committed. Bow Street had no report of missing jewelry that matched the necklace.

No fellow had quizzed Pamela regarding the story of her great-uncle and his lost love. So where did it all lead him? In a bit of a pickle, that's where. Frustration was becoming an integral part of his life, and he couldn't say it was particularly pleasant.

What was even more unpleasant was the probability that Pamela would not even speak to him this morning. He was reluctant to take his customary ride for fear she'd snub him. It would be a new experience, and one he was anxious to forgo.

Steps in the hall brought his attention to the doorway. He was pleased to see a grinning Algie saunter into the breakfast room.

'I take it you are having a good morning?' the duke said with a trace of cautiousness. Algie looked a trifle too pleased with the world.

'Thought you might want company on your ride today.' He glanced at the duke's untouched plate of food, the near-empty cup of coffee and nodded. 'As I thought, you need help. Heard all about it.'

'I need your help? What did you hear?'

'You made a cake of yourself last evening at the dinner Lady Vane gave for a select few. Word reached me that you gave Lady Pamela a dressing down that did not please her in the least.'

'If you heard about it, I had best attempt to

255

mend my fences immediately.' He crisply folded his paper, setting it aside.

'It will take more than a dozen roses to do that if I make no mistake,' Algie said complacently, helping himself to a plate of ham, buttered eggs, with toast and marmalade.

'Naturally, I cannot placate this proper young woman with jewelry. Perhaps a book?' The duke studied the expression his friend wore, trying to estimate how much Algie exaggerated.

'You're losing your touch, my friend,' Algie said with a grin between forkfuls of the excellent ham.

'I'll have to think about a suitable atonement to the lady in question. When you finish stuffing yourself, be prepared to ride.' He'd ride today; he was no coward where ladies were concerned.

On this sunny day the park was more popular than it had been for some time. He spotted Pamela immediately. She had a precise seat that no other woman matched.

'Good morning, Lady Pamela,' he said, greeting her effusively. 'It is nice to see an improvement in the weather.'

Pamela gazed fixedly at him, and for a terrible moment Robert believed she intended to cut him dead. With an amiable look, she nodded. 'It is indeed a lovely day. In fact, 'tis far too pleasant to hold to grudges or anger. I quite forgive you for the words spoken last evening. I trust you were merely concerned for my reputation. What woman would not be flattered at such consideration from a fine gentleman.'

Feeling as though someone had punched the air from his lungs he took a deep breath. 'You are most gracious, my lady, far more than I deserve. My wretched tongue . . . ' he began, then recalled that Algie was there, all ears. 'Shall we ride?'

Lady Pamela nudged her mare into a gentle canter along Rotten Row. At such a brisk pace, there was little chance for conversation, and Robert felt he needed to talk with her.

However, no opportunity presented itself to chat privately with her as had been the case in days past. Algie remained as close as a limpet, and others paused to greet the trio. Robert noticed that he received more than the usual number of speculative looks and fumed in silence as to their possible cause. How could a supposedly private conversation be known to everyone in town this morning? He'd wager that Pamela had not confided in a soul.

'What are your plans for this evening?' he casually inquired as he assisted her from her saddle in front of Gresham House, thereby taking advantage of the practice he'd begun and refused to relinquish.

'Lady Anne has planned a quiet evening of music. I understand she intends for you to play for us. I would enjoy that very much. You are extremely talented,' she said softly, with a direct look from those cerulean eyes that cut straight to his heart.

'If you will sing, I will play,' he replied, not caring in the least what Algie or anyone else might think as he stood gazing with rapt awareness at her face.

'Agreed. I am pleased we settled our differences, Your Grace,' she replied adding a sweet smile. 'Good friends are few and far between. I should not wish to lose your kind friendship.' With that, she slipped into the house.

A friend! She considered him no more than a friend? He was worse off than he'd suspected.

Algie chuckled; it struck the duke as a particularly insulting little sound. He glared at his friend, who immediately subsided.

'Roses wouldn't hurt in any event,' Algie mused.

His cautious look gratified the duke, who resolved to send a succession of flowers. Immediately, he'd send carnations, for they always came to mind when he thought of Pamela.

Arriving at home, the duke found Sir Cecil waiting for him.

Knowing it was safe to speak in front of Algie, Sir Cecil said, 'I happened to overhear something you may find of interest. The vicomte mentioned to a good friend that he is off to some little town east of here — just off the Dover road. I thought it curious he'd leave town at this time.'

At last, an irrational bit of behavior, something to grasp at. Robert said, 'When does he go?'

'Today,' Sir Cecil replied.

Robert, a man of action when he wasn't beguiled by this slip of a girl, took command of the situation and retrieved his pistols. 'I'll go alone. Less conspicuous that way. If I'm not back in a day or so, your assistance will be greatly appreciated.' He grinned, and they all left the house in high spirits, Algie knowing better than to take umbrage at being left behind.

While anxious to reach the Dover road, the duke rode to the Gresham House to tell Lady Pamela what had transpired. She was alone for her mother was calling on Lady de Clifford and his lordship was at his club. Pamela, not having had time to change from her riding habit, was in the morning room when Grimes announced the duke. Robert briefly explained his mission, but was totally unprepared for her reaction.

'Wait here, I'll go with you,' she said.

'You cannot! That would be the height of dangerous impropriety.' Robert stared at her, shocked. Having a delicate female along was not part of his plan.

'I'll not be left out of the most interesting part of this, I'll have you know,' she declared with a tilt of that determined nose. 'Timson could join us. He's discreet and helpful in a pinch.'

'No.'

'You are being stubborn for no reason,' she countered.

'I have every reason in the book! Woman, consider your reputation!' She hadn't time to think of possible repercussions. He must make her see reason. However, it was very hard to be angry in a whisper, he found.

'Surely, the vicomte would not suspect a couple followed by a groom are chasing *him*. It is too unlikely,' she reasoned. 'Now, were you alone, he might be more suspicious.'

'Your reputation,' he repeated, grasping at straws.

'Nonsense. No one would believe anything amiss between us, particularly with Timson in tow. You are being silly and wasting time. I shall be with you in a few moments.'

Why had he not disagreed more vehemently and refused her assistance was beyond him. Perhaps he secretly welcomed her presence. Oh, he did, but not to chase a spy.

* * *

It was an easy matter to locate the vicomte, for Albany House was not all that far away from the Gresham house. When the vicomte exited, it proved simple to follow him to the Dover road.

'I think you are mad to insist upon coming with me,' the duke chided Pamela, though Timson maintained a proper and discreet distance behind them.

'Not mad, merely determined. My life has been so humdrum. I refuse to miss the excitement after being used as a lure all this time.'

The duke looked at her trim figure, neatly attired in her proper habit, and sighed. She was a lure, all right.

'Don't worry. We shall discover what is going on,' Pamela said in a placating manner.

'I hope so,' the duke muttered, thinking not for the first time that she had a dashed good head on her shoulders.

Pamela glanced at the duke. She had been right not to rail him about last night. He had expected anger, even a snub. Instead she had done the unexpected and won the day, or at least the hour. As to the vicomte, she wondered where he'd lead them. How odd that he left the city in broad daylight, not taking the least precaution to escape detection.

As they entered a village, cattle thronged the roadway, blocking their passage and raising a cloud of dust in the air. Pamela coughed, quickly covering her face with her handkerchief.

The duke motioned her to the far side of the road, edging into a side lane where they could wait for the cattle to pass. The lowing of the animals and general activity fascinated her, but the dust made it difficult to see. She wondered where the vicomte concealed himself, for he was nowhere in view. When the last of the cattle passed, Pamela moved forward.

'He is nowhere to be seen, Your Grace,' she said, exasperation ringing clear in her voice.

'Given us the slip. Had I been alone, I'd have ridden behind the village and likely caught him.' He bestowed an impatient look on Pamela.

She began to turn her horse when she was attracted by a familiar figure. It was not the vicomte.

'Do you see what I see, Your Grace?' she said just loud enough to be heard.

'Baron Ruchoven!' the duke exclaimed in a tone to match hers. 'What do you suppose he's doing here?'

'He did not attend the dinner last evening. Obviously, he had other interests,' she concluded as she took note of the small valise he carried in his hand.

A woman appeared in the doorway of the cottage, bringing something the baron had apparently forgotten. The gentleman bowed over her hand, then captured it in his while searching her face. The bonnet she wore protected her face from exposure, but it did not prevent the baron from giving his amour a very thorough kiss.

Pamela froze, embarrassed to be witnessing such an intimate scene. At her side, the duke also watched intently. After that tender farewell, the baron entered his carriage and headed back toward London.

Pamela was about to move forward, when another carriage — drab and unfashionable — pulled up before the cottage, one with a crest blurred with mud, but a crest nevertheless. The baron's amour waited by the front entrance for a maid carrying a satchel from the cottage to join her. When the woman turned, Pamela saw her face and gasped in recognition. 'Lady Vane!'

The two women entered the carriage and also set off toward London.

'A tryst!' Pamela exclaimed. 'And he pretended to dance attendance on me while all the time he was having an affair with that woman!'

The duke looked at her, surprise on his face. 'You sound more indignant than angry.'

Pamela dismounted. She sent Timson to arrange for a small repast, then ventured her theory. 'I have no illusions about any of those three. They may each have a different reason for courting me, but it is not what it appears, that is obvious. I am sorry we lost the vicomte,' she said in apology.

Robert curved his hand about her elbow, intending to lead her to a more secluded place. Nothing on this trip, on this case, for that matter, had gone as he wished.

Suddenly, catching the hem of her habit on a low-lying branch, she stumbled and would have fallen had not the duke caught her. She looked up at him and whispered, 'Thank you. You seem to save me from my folly at far too frequent intervals.'

His arms still encircled her lithe body. Robert was too far gone at this point to resist temptation. Indeed, it didn't occur to him until later that he ought to withstand it. He ignored those warnings in the back of his mind and captured her lips with his in the most ardent of kisses. She fit so neatly in his arms, her mouth so sweet, her shape so utterly delightful.

When her arm crept around his neck, pressing her body more closely against him, he thought it possible to lose what decency he had left. Sanity returned with a rude jolt, and he swiftly ended the passionate kiss.

What was he doing? Kissing a proper young lady in the middle of a village, just off the Dover road? She could be ruined, and it would be his fault. Taking her pretty scarf, he drew it across her face so no one might easily recognize her. There were times when it paid to appear commonplace.

'I apologize, my lady. I fear I have compro . . . ' he began, then was forced to stop when she placed a hand across his mouth, shaking her head most emphatically.

'If I hear anything that sounds remotely like 'I fear I have compromised you', I shall have strong hysterics!' Pamela firmly declared. 'I think it a silly business when friends cannot ride off to the country with a groom in attendance without causing a dust-up of the first degree.' A womanly warmth burned throughout her; it required determination to appear so cool after such a flaming encounter. She'd not comment on that kiss. Best to ignore it, even if she would treasure it in her heart forever.

Robert found his fears dissolving in her resolute declaration. 'Perhaps you have the right of it,' he said, unwilling to totally agree, for he had felt the kiss to be mutually enjoyable.

Timson arrived with a full market hamper. 'All is ready, my lady.'

The groom had arranged for cool cider and fresh buns with cheese, a surprisingly welcome treat. Robert remembered he'd neglected his breakfast and ate with a hearty appetite.

The meal completed, there was nothing left but to return to London. With a glance at her groom, she said, 'What a lovely excursion into the countryside, Your Grace. Just what I needed to chase away a megrim.'

Since he knew nothing about any megrim, Robert assumed that her words were said for the benefit of the groom. He agreed, and they set off for town at a good clip.

That evening they again met at the Radcliffes. Robert was pleased to note that their pleasant amiability remained. Pamela greeted the duke with cordiality. No hint of his impropriety this afternoon was detected in her demeanor. She was a downright proper girl that was true, but what a brick, Robert thought with pride and admiration. Not that her eyes didn't send a message of sorts when they met with his briefly while deciding which song to play. For his part, he'd rather have been back in that dusty village lane with her in his arms.

The evening went charmingly. As they were a select group, no one raised an eyebrow when Robert insisted upon playing accompaniment for Pamela when she sang.

Lady Anne offered a second helping of a delicious lemon tart for refreshment when they had finished their music. 'Tomorrow you will attend the Chetwynd-Talbot ball?' she inquired.

'Indeed,' Pamela replied sedately.

'We hope to learn something more substantial,' Robert said, indicating he'd be with her.

'Well, I never thought I would say that I am tired of balls and dancing and rushing from one party to another, but I am. The country appeals more and more,' Pamela said while studying the teacup in her hands.

Robert looked at Pamela, her innocent gaze rising to meet his with only the faintest hint of a blush staining her pale cheeks. He'd rather be in the country as well — that village. He continued to wonder whether she'd been affected by their kiss. So much for wounding her sensibilities.

In this he was wrong. Pamela felt an awareness of the duke that surpassed anything she had imagined. As to that kiss! She vividly recalled every moment and wished he might be serious in his attentions. Bracing herself, she recalled just how sensible a creature she was and that a duke could have the pick of this year's crop of eligible females — especially the *haute monde* Lady Smythe.

★ ★ ★

Seeing how well her formerly prosaic daughter was coming along in society, Lady Gresham decided to surpass all her previous efforts. The gown chosen for the Chetwynd-Talbot ball glistened with tiny silver-and-blue sequins sewn in patterns of flowers and leaves on a sheer, silvery sarcenet. The skirt floated softly about Pamela; the bodice draped across her in beautiful folds. Above that lowest of necklines, the diamonds and sapphires sparkled enticingly in the candlelight. The diamond earbobs and tiara belonging to the countesses of Gresham looked spectacular with the necklace — so well Pamela almost wished she might forget about finding the true owner of the necklace.

She had been paid court before, but tonight she attracted even more attention. Of course, everyone who was anyone was here. All the eligible young men flocked to her side in droves.

Turning her head she noted that tall, well-muscled body still guarding her from any assailants. All evening the duke had been forced to listen to the flattery likening her to a goddess and a vision of heaven itself. Poor man.

'Thank you for standing guard, Your Grace. Who knows what might happen tonight. I have never had such flummery poured in my ears in my life. A vision of heaven, indeed,' she said with amusement. 'Do keep an eye on me while I dance, if you can. Although I imagine you will be dancing, too. Perhaps I ought to enlist Algernon Thynne's help as well? To spell you, as it were. I feel certain we can depend upon Sir Cecil to aid us. That ought to cover me quite nicely,' she concluded. She accepted the hand of her first partner for a minuet and walked away.

Robert followed her progress with a narrowed gaze. Covered nicely? Certainly that, perhaps splendidly, or magnificently? He shook himself from his mood and sought out his friends, asking them to do as Pamela requested. They agreed with a promptness that warmed the duke's heart — until his suspicions were raised about Algernon. Did he seem a trifle too eager to watch Pamela?

It was after the sixth dance concluded that it happened. He met Pamela, intending to escort her to the refreshment room, when they were confronted in the hallway by Lord Chudleigh and his plump, overbearing wife, Eudora. She glared at Pamela as though she had sprouted Medusa-like snakes.

'I knew it,' the woman snarled in a thankfully low voice. 'When I heard of that necklace, I suspected it would match the one described on this slip, and it does.' She pulled a piece of paper from her reticule to wave beneath Pamela's nose. 'You are beneath contempt! And you pretend to be so proper.'

Thank heavens Lady Chudleigh's tones were modulated befitting their public position. While she might accuse Pamela, she hardly wished to jeopardize her standing — not to mention Chudleigh's — in society.

Pamela stood her ground, refusing to give an inch to the obnoxious woman who towered over her meek husband. 'And what am I supposed to have done, my lady,' she said, her soft voice frozen with anger. This was a very serious accusation to be made in public at a society ball.

'Do not take me for a fool, my girl. *You*

were the recipient of the necklace my husband bought not long ago. *You* are the mistress Lord Chudleigh has lavished his fortune on these past months!'

Pamela was not certain whether she should take such a ridiculous charge in jest or seriously. Heavens! The image of the meek and mild Lord Chudleigh lavishing a fortune on a mistress was a trifle difficult to grasp.

'You are most frightfully mistaken, madam,' the duke vowed in his most intimidating manner. He turned to look at the timid lord. 'You purchased this necklace?' the duke demanded of the little man who looked as though he'd rather be hiding.

Lord Chudleigh squared his sagging shoulders and said, 'Never,' in a voice that was barely audible.

'I am innocent of any such accusation,' Pamela declared, reaching up to place a protective hand over the beautiful necklace.

The duke looked narrowly at the pair that confronted them, then said, 'Lord Chudleigh, did you or did you not present this necklace as a gift to Lady Pamela?'

Without glancing at his wife, his lordship shook his head and uttered one syllable. 'No.'

Turning to the by-now, apoplectic Lady Chudleigh, the duke said, 'I know Lady Pamela to be of the highest *ton* with impeccable behavior, not to mention lineage. Her character is of the finest, and were more women to share her values, this would be a better world.' Then he studied his lordship, suspecting he had more than a little to do with the necklace, but doubted the man would reveal anything, particularly with his dragon wife present.

The meek little man flashed them a look, then said, 'I believe you have said quite enough, Eudora.' With that, he clasped his wife by the arm and pulled her after him, surprising both Pamela and the duke — and most likely Lady Chudleigh — by his decisive action.

The situation had been handled discreetly, drawing scant attention from the few who traversed the hallway.

'That was most unpleasant,' Pamela said even as she trembled with rage that she should be accosted in so horrid a manner.

'Your excellent breeding shines through, my dear. You handled that nasty woman's charges with considerable aplomb,' the duke said with great admiration. 'But I'd give a monkey to know who he bought that necklace for. You may be sure I will see him later about it.'

'You believe he lied? That he gave it to his mistress and won't admit it now? But of course, how could he?' she concluded, glancing after the Chudleighs. 'I wish this dreadful evening were over.'

'If it is any consolation, the mystery can only become clearer,' he said, taking a couple of filled plates to a nearby table. When they faced each other over the delicacies offered by Lady Chetwynd-Talbot, he added, 'It is fortunate that all involved kept their voices lowered and that others saw nothing greatly amiss in our little conversation. For all the world knows, Lady Chudleigh was merely admiring your necklace. Everyone knows Chudleigh lives under the cat's paw, and wouldn't expect much from him. I believe we scraped through without disaster.'

'I have never been so humiliated in my life — to think that anyone could believe a thing like that about me!' She raised her gaze to reveal eyes sparkling with unshed tears.

'Steady on, my dear.' Robert found he wanted to gather this precious girl in his arms — to comfort her, nothing else. 'You know that only the poisoned mind of that woman could possibly think ill of you. Were she in her right mind, even she must admit your sterling qualities.'

With a cry, Pamela rose from her chair and walked from the room, leaving the duke staring after her in total confusion.

13

The most uncharacteristic behavior of Lady Pamela spurred the duke's decision to mend his fences soon if possible. This might best be accomplished by returning with the family to Gresham House following the ball. He resigned himself to a long wait. That young woman he'd once considered so unassuming had acquired a respectable court.

He'd returned to the ballroom to find Pamela romping through a country-dance with Algie. Lady Pamela was besieged with partners and as resplendent as she was, would most likely remain so until the very last.

He bowed to Lady Gresham. 'Your daughter is making quite a splash this evening.'

'I do believe she is. I suspect that she will wish to remain until the last dance,' her ladyship concluded, seeming overcome by the mere thought. Catching sight of his questioning frown, she added — most impulsively for her ladyship — 'I have the most dreadful headache, and I'll not spoil her evening because of it. But, Your Grace, I do wonder if I can survive that long.' Realizing what she had revealed, she gave him a stricken look. 'That is,' she murmured, taking a deep sniff from her lavender-scented handkerchief, 'I may persuade her to go home early.'

'That seems a pity,' he replied, whilst watching Pamela swing about in the measure of a cotillion. 'She appears to be enjoying herself immensely.'

'That she does,' the countess agreed in faint tones, looking as though a wave of pain had washed over her.

'My mother always reclines with a lavender cloth on her forehead and takes an infusion of feverfew for her headache. Says it is like a miracle,' he offered in the hope it might help the lady he could see suffered silently.

'Really?' Lady Gresham brightened for a moment, then sat watching her daughter, obviously torn between wishing to try the remedy praised by the dowager duchess and remaining at the ball as propriety decreed.

'I am aware it is not what you might wish, but were you to go home now, I feel certain that Lady Anne Radcliffe would be pleased to stand in your place for the remainder of the evening. And I would make certain that Lady Pamela is returned to your home safe and sound,' he said in the most languid of manners.

It said much for the state of Lady

Gresham's distress that she did not question this suggestion in the least.

'Would you speak to Lady Anne for me?' the countess said as the sound of laughter made her wince.

'Of course. You need to be in a quiet, dark room with your feet up and the herbal to soothe you,' he counseled.

Lady Gresham looked at his departing figure as though he had just acquired a halo — a bright, shining one.

Shortly thereafter, Lady Anne hurried to Lady Gresham's side with flattering concern. 'Dear Lady Gresham,' she said in her pretty voice, 'you must go home immediately. I will be delighted to stand guard on your darling daughter. She is so dear to me — like a sister. Please, ma'am, do go.'

Lady Gresham needed no additional urging. She collected her things and was whisked from the room by the duke. In minutes she had settled in the carriage he'd thought to summon for her and was on her way home to peace and quiet.

Pamela knew nothing of these events until the end of the cotillion when Mr Phillpot brought her to the seat vacated by her mother and she found Lady Anne in her place. Lady Anne explained the situation in a trice.

'Grandmama says it is all a hum, but I

believe Mama suffers dreadfully,' Pamela said. 'Dear Mama, it is like her to not want me to miss this ball. I really ought to go home,' she concluded.

'Nonsense,' the duke found himself saying, to his surprise. 'There is nothing you can do for her that her abigail cannot do better, most likely. I suggested she try a remedy that my mother uses with effect.'

Expecting she might be called to account for her hasty flit from his side earlier, Pamela was wary of the duke. How could she explain that he made her sound utterly boring with his talk about her sterling qualities?

The strains of a waltz floated over the room. The duke gave her that debonair smile that had so appealed to Pamela when first she saw him and said, 'I believe this is our dance, my lady.'

She was not quite so sure about that, but as no other gentleman claimed her, she willingly went off with the handsomest man in the room to share the waltz they had practiced at Lady Anne's. Although Pamela had danced it a few times with other partners, she was certain no other man could come close to His Grace's fluid elegance. And wherever he touched her, she felt tingly. The dark blue velvet of his coat harmonized with the blue in her gown and had she not been sensible, she'd have thought he did it on purpose. She hoped her feigned coolness masked her true feelings for the duke; she would not have him think she languished over him.

'I am pleased your mother confided her state of health to me,' the duke said while circling Pamela about the room. 'She was concerned for you, that your evening not be ruined. Lady Anne convinced her that she would watch over you. I shall as well.'

'How tedious for you,' Pamela said, unable to forget the sharp words spoken earlier at the table. She was not a paragon of all virtues, she was simply a girl who had been properly reared and didn't know how to behave otherwise. To act in a seemly fashion was ingrained in her. That is, except when she was around the duke. Then all those admonitions drummed into her head all too often appeared to slip away, only to haunt her later.

'Piqued, are you?' he said in the most odiously patronizing manner.

'Not at all,' she sweetly replied. 'I simply dote on having my life arranged for me.'

'One of these days your parents will inform you of the husband they've selected for you. What will you say then?'

'I do not know,' Pamela said, quite horrified at the notion of walking down the aisle with a virtual stranger. She had not met a gentleman with whom she would willingly spend the remainder of her life. The duke didn't count because he was beyond her reach and she knew it.

'No? But you must expect it before long. Is there no gentleman who has caught your fancy?' He whirled her about while watching her expressive face with an intentness not missed by anyone looking on except Pamela, who was busy staring at his neck cloth.

Her pause, along with that wild rose blush and lowered lashes, would make anyone think she had found precisely the man she desired. The duke waited for the name, wondering who the chap might be and if he'd be worthy of her.

'No, not that I could mention,' she finally replied, looking anywhere but at the duke.

Quite certain she was not telling the truth of the matter, he reluctantly escorted her back to Lady Anne, who now looked like a drooping pansy.

'Dear Lady Anne, what is the matter?' Pamela cried, unaccustomed to seeing her friend looking other than perky. Sir Cecil stood at her side, looking decidedly anxious.

'Did I not know better, I should think the headache can be catching. I hate to disappoint you, my dear, but I fear I must also go home.' She looked so woeful that

Pamela would not have had the heart to look sad at the thought of leaving the ball.

'To tell the truth, my lady, I am feeling a trifle weary, myself,' Pamela politely lied. 'We had best leave at once before Lady Chetwynd-Talbot thinks her ball a calamity.' She smiled winsomely at her friend, then assisted her to the hall where a maid was dispatched for their cloaks.

When they came down the front steps, two carriages awaited them. First in line was the Radcliffe vehicle. Sir Cecil assisted his wife into that one, then turned to face Pamela and the duke, a quizzical look on his face.

'I decided that it is best for you to take your ailing wife home without having to go out of your way. I shall see to it that Lady Pamela safely returns to Gresham House,' the duke informed him.

Sir Cecil nodded, climbing into his carriage at once. 'I'll see you tomorrow at White's.'

The duke waved him off, then assisted Pamela into his open carriage. Within minutes they followed the other vehicle to the corner, then turned the opposite direction.

'This is highly improper, you know,' Pamela said with a teasing smile. 'I am amazed you would countenance such a thing. Although I know this is an *open* carriage, you do not have a tiger along. Why, if someone saw us, we could be in a bit of a pickle.'

Before the duke could reply to this saucy remark, a rider dashed up to the carriage, brandishing a pistol at them. 'Stand and deliver,' the fellow growled in a husky voice, yet keeping his distance from the carriage.

It said much for London's lack of protection that this could happen in the middle of a residential area. There was no one about, particularly none of the Charleys, although the night watchmen were more often asleep in their boxes than patrolling the streets.

'Remain covered, and slip that necklace down inside your gown,' the duke murmured. 'I trust your stays will keep it in place.' While Pamela obeyed, the duke surreptitiously pulled from his pocket one of a pair of traveling pistols he always carried — primed and loaded. One never knew what a London evening might bring. He fired a shot, narrowly missing the chap whose horse danced nervously about on the ill-lit street.

Her shock at having her stays mentioned was forgotten when the duke fired the second pistol, after tossing her the first to hold. He'd aimed lower this time and seemed to hit the man's arm. The thief shot back at the duke, but the bullet missed its mark. The would-be robber wheeled his mount and headed out of town, unable to reload. The duke seemed to hesitate, most likely worrying about convention with the gently bred miss at his side.

'Follow him!' Pamela cried, quite ignoring the impropriety of the situation. 'You cannot let him get away.'

They jounced over the cobblestones at bone-jarring speed. In spite of the weight of the carriage that might have slowed them, they kept the horse and its rider within sight, thanks to the light offered by a half-moon above and some very skillful driving.

Pamela clutched the side of the carriage, hoping they might reach wherever it was the would-be thief intended to go without falling apart in a heap. When they attained a smoother stretch of road, she managed to reload one pistol after finding the bullets, Timson having taught her the skill some years ago.

'Give me the other one,' she called out. He didn't question her, but handed the other pistol and accepted the reloaded one in its place.

The rider in front of them veered off the road and into the shadows around a large country inn. In a twinkling he was lost to their view.

The duke swore softly, bringing the carriage and horse to a halt, then jumping down to search the area. He checked the side and rear of the inn, finding no sign of a recent arrival.

Unwilling to remain alone in the carriage and vulnerable to who knew what, Pamela clambered down and followed him as he entered the inn.

Once inside, the duke gave the common room a searching look, noting the boisterous patrons and teasing serving maid. The landlord scurried back and forth with trays of foaming tankards of ale. The people appeared to have been there for some time. He grabbed Pamela by the hand with the obvious intent of going up the stairs. They were near the top when he paused. The latch on one of the doors clicked, and the door swung inward.

'Cover your face,' he whispered, and pulled her into the shadows of the staircase where they waited.

A slim fellow — about the size and height of the would-be robber — left one of the bedrooms. He paused, glancing in both directions. Instead of coming their way, he hurried down the back stairs, and was gone in an instant.

'Why did you not stop him?' Pamela demanded, freeing herself from the duke's light hold.

'He wasn't our man — wore a different

coat, and I'd swear he was stouter.' The duke pulled her along the hall to the room that the man had left so abruptly, pushing the door open with the toe of his dancing slipper. There was no sound within. 'I am curious, I'll admit.'

They slowly entered the room, Pamela clutching the duke's arm, leaving the door open. A candle sputtered on a bedside table. Evidence of a struggle could be seen here and there. Then Pamela halted, gasping in dismay. On the floor a pair of boots angled toward them from the far side of the bed. They did not look to be empty.

'I do believe,' she began in a quavering voice, before the duke placed a warning finger to his mouth.

He went around the end of the bed and bent over the figure on the floor, rolling it to one side. 'Well, I'll be,' he murmured, checking the body for signs of life.

Unable to withstand this intriguing comment, Pamela followed him. 'Dear heaven!' she whispered, mindful of the need for silence. There on the floor, and very dead, was the baron with a knife in his chest!

A noise in the hall brought the duke to his feet. He glanced about the room and saw what Pamela also noted. There was no place to hide, the floor on the far side of the bed being well occupied at the moment.

In a flash the duke swept her into his arms and — keeping her hood carefully over her hair — proceeded to kiss her, crushing to her in a passionate assault that caused Pamela to forget everything else in the world.

If she'd known tingles when waltzing, they were nothing compared to the feelings that swept through her now. It was impossible not to yield, submitting to his expertise with something akin to abandonment had she considered it, which she couldn't, being far too occupied.

The footsteps paused a long moment, then slowly continued along the hall. Then all that could be heard were the normal sounds found in a busy inn.

Pamela was abruptly released, staggering slightly as she sought to regain her self-control. The duke carefully checked the hall, then beckoned to her.

'Shh,' the duke cautioned. 'Keep your hood down as much as you can and come with me. We must leave here at once.' He grabbed her hand and hauled her along the hall, down the stairs, and then outside until they reached the carriage. No groom had attended the poor horse, and he stood with stoic patience for his owner to return.

The carriage clattered away from the inn

back toward London, continuing along the road until they reached the outskirts of the city. Here he stopped, getting down to check the horse, then rejoined her.

'Whew! That was close.' He turned to look down at her, frowning. 'It would never do were we to be identified. Think of the scandal. We had nothing to do with that poor fellow's death, but who would believe it? The kiss provided excellent cover.'

'It all seems exceedingly odd,' she began, ignoring the kiss for now. 'Do you know,' she said slowly, 'this is most bizarre, but it is almost as though that thief wished us to follow him, wished us to find that body and be entangled in an investigation.'

'Impossible. The man who most likely killed the baron left as we stood in the shadows. I couldn't recognize the fellow. As to why he'd kill the baron, I can only guess.'

'You think it involves Lady Vane?'

He gave her an admiring look. 'Yes, I feel sure that she is mixed up in this somehow.' He thought for a few moments, then adjusted the reins, obviously intending to go on. 'Now, we had best return you home. As it is, it's almost morning, and we'll scarce make it there before the muffin man.'

The sky to the east had lightened even as they talked. The city stirred to life, with dustmen and street hawkers beginning to head for their chosen areas.

'About that kiss,' he said with some reluctance, 'I know I ought not to have done that, but I felt that whoever lingered in the hall would not enter the room were we so occupied.'

'A diversionary tactic, as it were,' Pamela said, hoping she sounded as prosaic as desired. 'I quite understand, Your Grace.'

'Were you not such a proper miss, you'd have known any number of kisses.' However, the duke admitted to himself that he rather liked the notion of being the first to kiss this amazing young woman. Her slim form slid over to the far side of the carriage as they turned the last corner. There, she remained. 'I meant no disrespect, you know.'

'Of course,' she replied, sounding muffled from within the depths of her hood. 'But there might be repercussions after all. Although my cloak is ordinary, your attire is distinctive. You may have to think of a woman with whom you might have been having a light dalliance following the ball.'

'You aren't supposed to know about things like that,' he scolded, yet sounding amused.

'I am aware of that, Your Grace,' she quietly replied. 'But then, I know a number of things I'm not supposed to know.'

When they stopped before Gresham House, the duke assisted Pamela to the ground. He studied her shadowed face for a moment, wondering what actually went on in her head.

'Good luck, Your Grace.' With those parting words, she hurried up the steps and into the house. He heard the click of the key in the lock before he moved off.

⋆ ⋆ ⋆

That morning Pamela rose far later than had been her custom. But then, she didn't make a habit of middle-of-the-night dashes after a would-be robber.

Upon entering the house, she'd made certain the jewels were safely tucked in the small vault in the library before retiring to her room. Now she glanced at her stays where they lay in a jumble with her splendid gown. One or two sequins dangled from the skirt, otherwise the dress seemed amazingly free of damage. The consideration of the duke for her apparel made her realize again the great difference between them. That he might think of such a thing while kissing her was somehow lowering.

'Roses for you, my dear,' Lady Gresham said when she bustled into the bedroom, her arms full of glorious pink roses the color of a country wild rose, but far more beautiful. 'His Grace sent you a tribute worthy of a duchess.'

'Mama, I told you not to allow your hopes to run away with you. We are good friends, nothing more.' Pamela might wish it were more, but wishing didn't make it so.

'Well, I appreciate the gentleman. He told me his mother's nostrum for the headache, and it worked like magic. I slept better than I have in ages. Dear man! I ought to send *him* roses!' The countess beamed a smile at Pamela, then perched on the side of her bed with a look of curiosity. 'You enjoyed the ball after I left?'

'I did, although we did not remain long, for Lady Anne also acquired a headache. She wondered if they were catching,' Pamela said in an attempt at humor.

'The room was a trifle stuffy, I suppose. And I admit I have known more than usual concern. I confess I did not expect you to take so well, my dear.' The countess studied her hands a moment, then looked at Pamela. 'I can only hope you will marry someone worthy of you,' she added unknowingly echoing the duke's sentiment.

'No one has asked for my hand, has he?' Pamela said with alarm.

'Your father has rejected one offer as beneath your regard. With the duke at your side so often, your standing has risen a good deal. In spite of those magnificent roses, I truly do not expect him to offer for you, but perhaps a gentleman of polish and rank will emerge from that court that gathers about you at every ball and party you attend. Do you favor anyone in particular?'

'It is difficult to say, Mama,' Pamela hedged. She could barely sort out names, for the duke tended to overshadow all others. 'Mr Thynne is nice, and he is the heir to Lord Lyndon.'

'You would retain your style as an earl's daughter, of course,' her mother mused, staring off into space as though she might see a wedding before her. 'Lord and Lady Pamela Lyndon sounds lovely, and your son would inherit the barony from his father. It is awkward when a woman outranks her husband, but I feel sure you would cope graciously with the matter.'

'Well,' Pamela said, her practical nature asserting itself, 'he hasn't asked me as yet, nor has he shown a marked partiality for my company. He is always with the duke and so asks me to dance. But the Season is not over, and there is time for other things to happen.' She carefully omitted to mention that the duke hovered at her side far more often than any other man, and as for those kisses — best to disregard them. She ought to resist them, and didn't.

Quickly dressing for a ride in the park, Pamela ate some toast and drank her tea with more haste than the grace her mother attributed to her. Adjusting her hat before the looking glass in the entry hall, she went out the front door to greet Timson with a calm smile. They set off toward the park at a discreet walk, with Pamela deep in reflection.

How naughty to give her mother the notion that poor Algernon might be interested in her. It was most unfair. But what else could she do? When Algie and the duke joined her in the park, she gave him a highly self-conscious look that brought a frown to the duke's brow.

'Good morning, gentlemen,' Pamela said without the faintest tremor in her voice as her gaze happened on the duke. It really was too bad of him to look so utterly dashing this morning, refreshed as though he had slept the entire night.

They fell in beside her, one to each side. She welcomed her guard, as it were.

'The roses are beautiful, Your Grace. Thank you. And Mama extends her appreciation for the treatment you recommended,' Pamela said earnestly. 'Her headache left shortly after she consumed the herbal potion, and she slept better than she has in ages. Please pay her a call so she may thank you in person. Those megrims are truly horrid,' Pamela concluded.

'I have my mother's assurance that it is a blessing, and I'm pleased if it helped the countess.' He studied her face that she was certain looked pallid and drawn from her lack of sleep. 'And you? I trust no bad ogres haunted your sleep?'

She smiled at this bit of foolery. 'No, I was far too tired for that. I confess that I will be happy when the true owner of the necklace is found and I can be free of its responsibility.'

'Should have had a guard with you,' Algie said with a dark look at his friend. 'Stands to reason with the ransom in jewels that you've had on display around your neck at every ball and party in town that someone might try to steal them. Not well done, Wexford.'

'Cut line, Thynne,' the duke replied more formally than in the past. 'What happened was totally unexpected. Why didn't the thief attack the Gresham town coach? Because he knew Lady Gresham had gone home *alone*. As well, Lady Anne and Sir Cecil were not accosted, and she wore a very fine necklace of emeralds last evening. How did the chap know Pamela was with *me*? He had to be watching the house mighty well — or have an accomplice on the inside who knew what was going on.'

Pamela gave them each a dismayed look, hoping they did not part enemies because of her. 'Gentlemen,' she began.

'There ought to be a better way,' Algie argued, ignoring Pamela's soft objection. 'Ain't fair to subject this lovely lady to such hazards.'

Pamela thought of the mad dash to the country inn on the outskirts of London and the body they'd found. Unable to prevent a shudder, she had to listen to Algie when he scolded the duke again. 'Even now she trembles at the thought of what she endured.'

That was worse, because her mind flew to that breathtaking kiss that even now set her on fire. She could feel the heat rising in her cheeks; she must resemble a cooked beetroot at this point. Rather than have them remark on her high color, she nudged her mare to a canter, calling gaily, 'Come, let us work out our fidgets. You can quibble later.'

They met Sir Cecil along the Row. He informed them that Lady Anne was better this morning, but inclined to take things easy. 'She would like to see you this afternoon, if you would be so kind as to call on her,' he said with a bow to Pamela.

'Of course, I shall,' she replied warmly. 'I trust Lady Anne will feel more the thing by then.'

Algie and the duke remained at her side throughout the ride, dismounting when they returned to Gresham House.

'Perhaps you would come in? I know my mother would be most pleased to see you,' Pamela said before she recalled what she had implied regarding Algernon Thynne an hour or so ago. Only after they joined her in the hall, leaving the capable Timson to handle the horses, did her words return to mind. Mercy!

The countess received both gentlemen with supreme grace and charm, praising Algernon and extending profuse thanks to the duke for his thoughtfulness.

Pamela felt pleased with the two men, who now sat at ease in the drawing room, effortlessly handling the social banalities required in society. There was much to be said for propriety; the world indeed ran better on good manners.

They sipped the finest of sherries with appreciation, admired the restrained elegance around them that bespoke wealth and taste, saw the respect and love shared between mother and daughter all too often absent in families, and could not help but be impressed.

At the proper time, the men rose, bowed

low over Lady Gresham's hand, then turned to Pamela.

'I shall see you this evening at Almack's?' Algernon asked with an encouraging smile.

'Of course, she will be there. Where else would she go?' the duke said irritably before Pamela might utter a word. 'Would you join us on our way down, my lady?' He gestured to the door.

'Naturally,' Pamela said after a glance at her mother. Heavens, dear Mama was eyeing Algernon Thynne with a highly speculative gaze as he left the room. When her mother turned that same consideration to the duke, Pamela rushed him out of the room and down the stairs.

'I have heard nothing regarding the situation that we discovered last evening,' the duke confided after Algernon had gone out of the front door. The duke paused near the entry. 'With any luck at all, we shall manage to scrape through this unscathed. But if there is trouble, I want you to know that I stand to do what is proper.'

'Please do not say it, Your Grace,' Pamela pleaded, holding her hand up as though to ward off his words. 'It is not what I wish.' The look he gave her seemed almost one of hurt, except that she was well aware he could have no desire to be saddled with her.

14

'I cannot believe all that happened last evening after we parted,' Lady Anne exclaimed, languidly curled upon her daybed and looking interestingly wan when Pamela was ushered to her room. She perked up upon hearing a carefully edited version of what occurred after the Chetwynd-Talbot ball. Placing dainty feet on the floor, she rang for her maid to bring tea to the private sitting room where she entertained Pamela.

'It was highly improper of me to command the duke to take after the would-be thief,' Pamela declared once the maid left. 'Only we so hoped to uncover his identity. If you ask me, he was a singularly inept robber. He missed the duke by a wide margin — thank goodness — and turned tail in an instant when one of the duke's bullets grazed his arm. I just wish he had not disappeared at that inn.' She bit her lip in vexation when she recalled the frustration of seeing the man vanish.

Pamela said nothing about finding the baron on the floor of the inn bedroom. The duke had suggested it would be as well were they to keep it a secret. As for that spectacular kiss, Pamela kept that in the recesses of her heart, to be dwelt on whenever she wished for a bit of romantic recollection. It was not likely that it would be repeated, at least by His Grace.

'How vexing for you, to be sure. I shan't repeat your story, believe me,' Lady Anne vowed. 'It would be considered improper, as you say. You realize your parents would be within their rights to demand that the duke marry you. Yet nothing would be more dreadful than to force a man to wed, especially because of circumstances as unusual as yours — the necklace, you know. I mean, you merely begged his help. It is not as though he came courting only to be discovered in a compromising situation you both found delightful.'

Pamela hadn't considered that haring off in the wee hours of the night could have led to a forced marriage. She resolved to consider a matter more carefully next time before acting with uncharacteristic impetuosity.

'Yes, well, that is certainly true,' she managed to say by way of agreement. While there was nothing she might desire more than marriage to the duke, she wanted no part of a situation that compelled them to wed. However, she decided this was a subject best ignored for the moment. 'How are you this morning? I trust your head is better?'

Lady Anne adopted a smug look, then grinned, her pretty eyes dancing with obvious delight. 'Cecil insists I rest and demands no more late nights. The doctor confirmed what I had suspected for a while — that I am in the family way at last. Cecil and I are in transports, for we want a family so dearly, and thought we might be denied this joy. It must be a boy, of course,' she confided, leaning against the pillows the maid had fluffed behind her after bringing the tray with tea and biscuits.

'I am so pleased for you, my lady,' Pamela said, clapping her hands with delight. 'You think you can order a boy, just like that? I do hope you are right.'

They visited longer than the usual afternoon call, for Lady Anne was not receiving today and Pamela had been declared beyond the realm of a caller, rather being deemed a friend — much to Pamela's added happiness. After mulling over a variety of names but reaching no decision, and speculating on the amount of infant clothing necessary for the heir to the Radcliffe title and fortune, Pamela left. She resolved to embroider a cap for the coming baby. She had seen a fetching pattern in a back copy of The Lady's Magazine and stopped at the linen drapers to purchase some fine linen and a length of lace for a decorative insertion.

★ ★ ★

At Almack's that Wednesday evening, the rooms were abuzz with the news of the baron's death. Murder was the word used. As to possible motive, everything from A to Z was offered, with the likelihood of a connection to his government activities — which of necessity involved spying — being high on the list.

Pamela thought of the man who had raced down the back stairs of the inn and the tryst Lady Vane had kept with the distinguished baron in that little village following her dinner; however she kept her opinion to herself. She had no doubt there was a connection between the two incidents, but to offer that knowledge was to open a Pandora's box of trouble for herself and the duke.

'What a blessing you had not formed a *tendre* for the baron,' Lady Gresham said quietly to Pamela after the news reached her. 'I cannot say I was particularly drawn to the gentleman,' she concluded, 'but he possessed admirable polish.'

'Nor I,' Pamela admitted. 'But one never knows what might happen, does one?' She made a point of listening to every account of the event that she managed to overhear, wondering if the presence of a couple in his room would be mentioned. At last it was.

'I heard,' Lady Jersey said with authority to an enthralled group, 'that there was a man and woman in his room shortly before his body was discovered. I also heard that they were in a most romantic embrace. How ghastly to be enfolded in a kiss with a dead man a few feet away,' she said with a moue of distaste. 'They think they know who the man is, but have no clue as to whom the woman might be. How clever to keep her anonymous. It offers such delicious speculation!' The countess looked around her with malicious glee. 'We do not have to look about us to guess who she might be. All we have to do is to ascertain who *he* is, then note to whom he pays court.'

Pamela shot a look across the room at the duke, wondering if he had truly been identified as being at the scene of the crime. And would she be targeted as the woman involved were she to allow him to continue to seek her out? Somehow she doubted it. Sensible creatures were simply not the target of that sort of speculation, were they?

Prince Radinski presented himself at that moment, narrowly beating the vicomte to her side. 'A dance, Lady Pamela, I beg of you,'

300

the prince declared with his usual flourish.

Knowing she had best accept as many partners as possible so that in the event the duke did seek her out she would not be conspicuous in the least, Pamela agreed.

'And when you return, I would take his place,' the vicomte said with a glare at the prince, who was again attired in white this evening and obviously looked far too princely to suit the vicomte.

'I shall be delighted to partner each of you in turn,' Pamela said with an impartial smile.

'I adore you, my lady,' the prince vowed, glaring at his rival. 'The vicomte cannot lay claim to such an emotion. To him, love is a game he plays rather well.' With that the prince led her through the steps of the cotillion, all the while assuring Pamela of his devotion.

She, in turn, suspected that the prince was far more attached to her jewels and dowry than her person.

Then she noted that Lady Jersey had sought out the duke, and she almost stopped breathing at the thought that the nosy woman might have figured out the truth and intended to challenge the duke. The pattern of the dance led them close to where the duke stood with Lady Jersey, and Pamela tried to listen without losing her place in the dance.

His deep voice rumbled through polite inanities, prompting Pamela to relax a trifle. He looked as though he had not a care in the world, much less had been involved with a murder in any way, shape, or form. That debonair air, the superior attitude that was quite a natural part of him, and his gracious attention to the countess, all gave lie to the notion he might have conspired to murder anyone. And why should he? There was no motive and who would dare accuse him? Pamela breathed a sigh of relief.

When the prince returned her to her mother's side, she accepted the hand of the vicomte with grace. There would be no scandal. All was well.

'You must be sorry to lose one of your court, my lady, particularly in such a dreadful manner,' the vicomte said while awaiting their turn in a country-dance.

'He was a very pleasant, if reserved, gentleman,' she replied politely. 'I should be sorry to see anyone murdered, particularly one with a knife grimly protruding from his chest. How truly frightful. As my papa says, what is the world coming to?'

'I had not heard he had a knife in his chest,' the vicomte said with a speculative look at Pamela.

Realizing she might have really landed

herself in the briars, she shrugged and said, 'I believe that is what Lady Jersey said. One hears so many stories in a place like this where gossip is the food of the evening — especially since the fare provided is so meager.'

That led the vicomte off on one of his favorite complaints — the inadequacy and poor quality of the food at such an elite establishment. '*Mais non!*' he exclaimed, 'I cannot see such a thing in France. Were we at liberty to offer such entertainments, the food would be superb!'

When he returned Pamela to Lady Gresham's side, the duke stood chatting with her ladyship, discussing the latest *on dit*. 'I am told that one of the people in question somewhat resembled me — at least the chap wore a coat similar to mine,' the duke concluded with a glance at the vicomte, who also wore a coat of much the same color and cut as the one the duke had worn the evening before. 'Astonishing how many men have similar taste.'

'But then, when one sets a fine example, others follow, my dear duke,' the vicomte shot back, not in the least perturbed. Apparently, he had a clear conscience and was not the least worried about being accused of murdering the baron. Moreover, he did seem to wish to butter up His Grace, which was not the least unusual.

'You look as though you might enjoy a glass of lemonade — even if it is tepid,' the duke said to Pamela, knowing her mother would not say nay to his escorting her anywhere he chose. Being a duke assured one of a great number of privileges.

'Indeed, it is warm here this evening, made more so by all the gossip flying about,' Pamela said as they wound their way through the clusters of gossiping females and not a few gentlemen exchanging views on the means of the baron's death. 'There is nothing liked so well as a breath of scandal.'

'How true,' he said, handing her a glass containing the despised lemonade, then guiding her along to a pair of chairs that had been placed close together.

'I almost put myself in a basket,' she confessed immediately. She related what she had said to the vicomte, then gave the duke an expectant look. 'Do you think I sufficiently diverted him, Your Grace?'

'Well, I think you are safe enough. It was clever of you to guide his thoughts in the direction of the food. Everyone has heard him complain about the dull offerings here. He is fortunate Lady Jersey dotes on him, or he'd likely be refused entrance.' The duke glanced back in the vicomte's direction a moment, then returned his gaze to Pamela.

'That is because he is a handsome gentleman, and I suspect every patroness has a soft spot in her heart for such,' Pamela suggested. 'Is it not said that there is no one more loved than a scoundrel?'

'Do you as well harbor a soft spot for such?' he asked with a curious expression on his face that Pamela couldn't begin to decipher.

'For a handsome gentleman? or the Vicomte Reynaud?' Pamela said with a twinkle in her blue eyes. 'Never say you believe I might harbor a *tendre* for a scoundrel!'

'I think you have become a minx, Lady Pamela.' A grin hovered on his lips a moment, then he grew serious. 'So far I believe we are going to escape unscathed. How fortunate I wore such an ordinary shade of blue last evening.'

'Somehow I cannot imagine anything to do with you might be considered ordinary in any way,' Pamela said impulsively. When he gave her an arrested look, she scolded herself for possibly revealing too much of her feelings for him. As one who had never been impulsive in her life, she had suddenly developed a penchant for doing the spontaneous. Such behavior could plunge her into a bumble broth, for certain.

'Most kind of you,' he said, polite as always, but with a gleam in his gray eyes that caught her notice.

'Yes, well,' she blurted out in a rash confession that was most unlike her former reserved self, 'when one is inclined to be deemed ordinary, one becomes most sensitive to the state.'

'Never say that anyone had the temerity and bad taste to consider you in anything but a highly favorable light!' he said with a charming smile that turned Pamela's insides into mush. 'You are a very lovely girl.'

'I was most improper to go haring off with you in the hours before dawn. We would have truly been in the soup had anyone seen us,' she reminded him, although she was certain he was all too aware of that by now. One tended to develop second thoughts about situations given a bit of time. The remark about her being lovely she stored away for future consideration.

'We do not actually know if we escaped detection, you know,' he replied casually, picking off a speck of lint from his rich coat of fine mulberry velvet that he wore with superb grace over a pair of white satin breeches. 'You may yet find yourself suddenly betrothed to me.' He crossed one knee, then idly swung his patent slippered foot quite as though he hadn't uttered such shocking words. He ignored Pamela's gasp, causing her to wonder what his motive might be in pointing out the possibility.

'I think not, Your Grace,' she said promptly, determined to scotch any notion he might have that she sought to ensnare him. 'If we keep our heads, we ought to manage well enough. As you said, your blue coat might have belonged to another and my cloak is a most ordinary color.' She gave him a thoughtful look before adding what she decided might be a telling bit of reasoning. 'Besides, I am well aware of what the duchess considers your due, for I have heard her tell my mama at least twice what she expects in a future duchess of your choosing. Do you think she would permit an alliance between us? I give leave to doubt it. And, as I told Lady Anne, a compelled marriage would be of all things most repugnant to me.'

'How much did you reveal to Lady Anne?' He did not comment on Pamela's remarks, to her disquiet. Nor did he deny his mother's possible reaction to news that he had been found in a compromising situation with Lady Pamela Taylor. Never mind that Pamela was the daughter of an earl. She suspected she did not have the position of a *sans pareil* to satisfy the duchess as a future daughter-in-law.

'Just the part about chasing after that singularly inept robber. Do you know,' Pamela said with a considering tilt to her head, 'the more I think about the matter, the more I'm inclined to believe that fellow was a novice. He ought to have had a better aim — not that I'd wish you dead, you may be sure. But to use single-barrel pistols? I would expect a robber to have two double-barreled pistols at the very least, if not triple! There is something that strikes me as rather odd about the whole incident.'

'Now that you mention it, I agree,' the duke replied, not for the first time thinking that the pretty Lady Pamela had a sound head on her shoulders.

'And I also think it most peculiar that we should have been led to the very inn where the baron had been stabbed. Confess,' she begged, placing a hand gently over his, 'do you not agree there is a definite connection? And that Lady Vane is somehow involved? Although in what manner is beyond me at the moment.'

'True,' he agreed, thinking she had graceful hands and a very gentle touch. They went nicely with her well-bred voice and manners.

Yet, in spite of her propriety this evening,

he could not forget how she had felt wrapped within his arms. Her submission to his kiss had rapidly turned into a warm response that had thrilled him to his core. Had it not been for the necessity that they exit the inn as quickly as possible, who knows where that kiss might have led? Her carnation scent drifted over to tease his senses, enhancing his memory of that most audacious of kisses. She had stirred him as no woman had done for a long time, if ever. And this was incredible, for by her own admission she was such a well-bred and proper little dab of a thing. He frowned while he considered this seeming contradiction.

His thoughts flashed back to the inn. What if one of the men had demanded their identities? What if they had been seen and recognized? While it was dark out, a lantern had thrown flickering light on the inn yard, and thus, on them when they had dashed for the carriage. Had her hood sufficiently concealed her?

Which brought him back to the gently bred female sitting at his side. He'd no right to involve her in something so dangerous as last night. From now on, she would have to be guarded more carefully. And he really must mind his own manners. A gentleman simply did not go about enfolding a young unmarried lady of quality in his arms and kissing her nearly senseless. What had she thought? he wondered.

'You have recovered from the ordeal?' He rubbed his jaw while studying her face to see if her words reflected what he thought he detected in those cerulean eyes.

'Indeed,' she said in a subdued voice, her fingers tracing the pattern on the skirt of her gown. 'Although I must confess, I did not think it *all* an ordeal,' she said, meeting his gaze with a fearless honesty that revealed an emotion he knew was not antipathy. 'There was a part of it I found most enchanting, I must admit.'

He could think of nothing to say in reply. Never had he been spoken to in such a candid manner. He was about to make a polite observation, allowing her to believe he misunderstood what she'd said — for propriety's sake — when Algie strolled up to join them.

'If you two are intending to become the next item of gossip, you are a fair way to accomplishing your goal.' He gave the duke an admonishing look, then turned to his companion. 'Lady Pamela, may I relieve you of that glass, then beg the next dance?'

She rose at once, handing Algie the glass — which he placed on a nearby table — then walked at his side to the next room, never once glancing back at the duke.

It was just as well, for he was looking something like a thunder-cloud at the moment, cursing himself for being ten kinds of a fool. He had not said what he ought, given her delicate and hesitant declaration of admiration — or more. Instead, he had sought to hedge, using his usual caution when dealing with women, and lost all. Or had he?

'Your friend makes off with the prize of the evening,' the vicomte observed as he came up behind him. 'Small wonder you look furious.'

'The prize of the evening, you say?' the duke replied, intrigued.

'When a gentleman knows her better, he realizes Lady Pamela is indeed a prize beyond compare. I understand her dowry is excellent and the entire estate comes to her, you know. Or did you? She will be an extremely wealthy woman in her own right. She is also a delightful person.'

The lady in question dipped and twirled through the measures of a minuet with her head in a fog. It was a wonder she didn't make a total hash of the dance. She had implied much to the duke, and he in turn had said nothing. He had merely stared at her as though she was an alien creature whose language he did not comprehend.

What a fool she was. Never would she make that mistake again. Never would she intimate that her affections were engaged until the gentleman had declared himself. Never had she been so mortified.

True, that gleam had remained in his gray eyes, but what that might mean was beyond her. He retained that touch of aloofness, emphasizing a distance between them that she had best not forget again.

It was with profound relief that she greeted her mother's decision to leave the assembly early that evening. Without bidding anyone good night, Pamela slipped on her soft velvet cloak, joining her mother in the entry to await their carriage.

★　★　★

The following morning did not find Lady Pamela riding in the park, as the duke had hoped. He compressed his lips, then decided he would call on her that very afternoon no matter how it might look. Actually, he was past caring about what others might think. He must find a way to mend his fences. And why that was most important, he refused to consider at the moment.

* * *

Lady Pamela sat with her mother in the drawing room entertaining the callers during her mother's customary at-home afternoon. She chatted politely — if somewhat distantly — about whatever neutral topic came to mind. The weather was always a good subject, as London weather was usually dreadful, and if splendid, all the more a matter of amazement.

Lady Vane was ushered up shortly toward the close of the afternoon. Pamela admired the pretty print gown she wore that had full sleeves, gathered with pretty ribands above the elbow and wrist, and of the latest style. Pamela studied the lady, wondering how she managed to keep a calm mien, given the death of her lover. Somehow more must be learned about the situation.

After offering a stiff curtsy and a few words of general chitchat, Lady Vane softly requested of the countess, 'Do you suppose Lady Pamela might join me and a few of our friends for a picnic in Richmond Park two days hence? She is always such a charming addition to our company.'

Pamela exchanged looks with her mother, nodding slightly to indicate she would welcome the diversion.

'I believe she would enjoy such an outing. Is that right, my dear?' Lady Gresham beamed a smile on her dear daughter.

'Above all, yes. I adore picnics,' Pamela said politely, then wished her words unsaid as Lady Vane continued.

'Prince Radinski and Vicomte Reynaud will attend. How unfortunate the baron was killed, for he was always a welcome addition to your daughter's court.' She gave Pamela a speculative look.

Having steeled herself not to react in any way at the mention of that scandalous event, Pamela gazed blandly at her ladyship, giving no clue to her emotions other than a look of proper distress. She wondered how Lady Vane could appear so unfeeling. 'I never felt his attentions were beyond polite, you know,' Pamela said in a prosaic manner.

'La, Lady Pamela,' Lady Vane said with a light laugh, 'you are too modest. It is not every young woman who wears a ransom in jewels every evening and has a ring of beaux including an English duke, a German baron, a Russian prince, and a French vicomte clustered at her feet.'

'The jewelry is distinctive. I'd warrant that without it, I might fade to nonexistence,' Pamela replied with an equal lightness.

That bought denials and laughter, both of

which sounded slightly false to Pamela's sensitive ears. She suspected the picnic would turn out to be an ordeal rather than a delight. However, she had committed herself, and to cry off did not bear thinking. Her mother would demand to know why, and Pamela felt she could not offer a reasonable explanation.

Grimes announced the duke, and Pamela felt pure shock jolt through her at the sight of him. She'd not expected him to call. It was the outside of enough that he came to see her after her silly admission.

He bowed low over Lady Gresham's hand, then greeted Lady Vane before turning his gaze on Pamela. 'Fine weather, is it not?'

'I trust it is.' She did not meet his gaze, concentrating on her teacup as though she'd not seen it before.

'You did not ride this morning,' he said in a flat statement, letting Pamela know that he had looked for her and found her absent.

'No, I was a trifle fatigued.' Pamela still refused to look at the duke, fearful that her eyes would reveal her admiration for him — in spite of his behavior last evening.

'The news of the baron's death was most alarming. What is the world coming to, I ask you,' Lady Gresham said, echoing one of her husband's favorite sayings.

Lady Vane cleared her throat, then spoke. 'I

believe we must look to something more pleasant. To that end I am organizing a little picnic at Richmond Park. Do say you will join us, Your Grace. It will not be complete without you.'

'I shall be most happy to join you. I trust Lady Pamela will be there, too?' He turned his attention on her with its usual effect, for he'd caught her looking at him. Unseen by Lady Vane, he gave a significant lift of his brows, indicating he felt the occasion consequential.

'I shall,' Pamela said, feeling as though life had just become infinitely more complicated.

15

She faced the prospect of the picnic with stoic calm. There was no use repining, she'd accepted the invitation to this event, which would place her in a social situation with the duke. In spite of those stolen kisses, Pamela had to again remember that she'd contacted him solely to locate the true owner of the necklace and nothing more.

They had run into a blank wall, since Lord Chudleigh — whom the duke was convinced had purchased the jewels — refused to reveal to whom he had presented the necklace. No one would talk. Short of using force, she could not see how they were to compel his lordship — or the jeweler — to reveal the identity of the former mistress.

Sleuthing had produced nothing. Lord Chudleigh was not only closemouthed, he was prudent beyond belief. Not a gossipy soul knew who it was he had in keeping — which led to the belief that his paramour was on the fringe of society, passingly respectable, and possibly someone they had met and mingled with at the opera and other social occasions.

The woman must yearn for the necklace. The effect of possessing such magnificent gems had transformed Pamela's life; it certainly hadn't been dull of late.

Sir Cecil had deemed the picnic acceptable entertainment for his expectant wife. Naturally, Pamela had been invited to drive with them in their comfortable carriage. Now Lady Anne's soft voice pulled Pamela from her musings.

'Have you learned anything at all in regard to the necklace? That is, anything more than you knew last we spoke?' Lady Anne asked with a sympathetic look.

'No, worse luck,' Pamela admitted. 'Would you not think that whoever wants the necklace would make another effort to regain it, especially when that last attempt came so close to success? Had that man's aim been better, I'd have been quite helpless. The pistols were on the duke's side of the carriage. I'd have had my hands full trying to control the horse, let alone grope across his body for a pistol and try to fire it at someone. It was difficult enough to reload them.'

'Never say you would shoot!' Sir Cecil cried, aghast at such a display of intrepidity. He obviously never expected Lady Pamela to utter such shocking sentiments.

'I have come to realize that I would attempt

a great deal if it meant saving my life,' she replied simply, as she sat with a gloved hand resting on the cushioned arm of the open carriage and her fringed parasol daintily against her shoulder in the manner of a Gainsborough portrait.

Upon arrival at Richmond Park the picnic began much as Pamela had expected. The prince and the vicomte vied for her favors with silly flummery intended to turn her head. She almost wished the two would find another woman to use as a field of competition.

'Come now, Lady Pamela,' the vicomte teased, 'you must decide what color horses you would select for a team, and the sort of carriage you would choose once you set up an establishment. Your husband would naturally seek out your desires,' he concluded with that seductive voice he used when he wished to be persuasive. Had Pamela not preferred the duke's rich baritone, she might have tumbled for the vicomte because of his velvet voice alone.

'Gray, I think,' she said, more intent upon the color of a particular gentleman's eyes than that of a team of horses.

Across the glade the duke leisurely walked beneath the trees with the delectable Lady Smythe. Her delicate pink gown was composed of gauze panels over a pale pink slip and ought to have clashed with her deep red hair but didn't, worse luck. Her matching parasol became a flirtatious weapon in her hand as she deftly handled it with the confidence of a professional beauty.

The duke bent his head to listen to her conversation. Pamela turned away, unable to bear the sight of those two in such proximity. Not that she believed the duke would consider marrying Lady Smythe. Upon reflection, Pamela had realized the duchess would have a nervous palpitation or worse should her son lean in that direction. The notion that His Grace might simply take the seductive widow as his mistress seemed the most likely conclusion. Pamela was not certain what was involved in such a liaison, but she suspected it involved more intimacy than passionate kisses.

At any rate she would limit her contact with the duke to strict involvement with the necklace. It was sensible, and she was, if anything, practical-minded.

'Are you enjoying the outing, Lady Pamela?' Lord Raeburn inquired, offering his arm to her after joining the trio.

Since the prince and the vicomte still debated the best sort of carriage horses Pamela ought to purchase, she nodded agreement. 'Please, I should like to stroll that way.' She gestured with her parasol in the opposite direction of the path taken by the duke and Lady Smythe.

'It has turned out to be a lovely day,' Lord Raeburn said, resorting to the neutral topic of the weather.

'Have you not noticed that bank of clouds rising in the distance? I would wager that we shall have a rainstorm before the day is over,' Pamela replied. She glanced at the kindly Raeburn, thinking him a true gentleman. Of course, he did seem to lean toward the sedate Lady Vane. Pamela wondered if he knew of her liaison with the baron. She recalled the duke's conclusion that the widow had parted with a number of paintings and other objets d'art in order to meet expenses. One did what one must. She deserved a gentleman to care for her, and perhaps Lord Raeburn wouldn't mind the widow's past.

'It would be a pity to have rain spoil our party, seeing all the effort that Lady Vane has expended for our delight.' He turned to look at the lady, who busily instructed a group of servants regarding the picnic repast.

'It is difficult to control the weather, sir,' Pamela said, feeling utterly insipid and dull. Could there not be something more interesting to chat about than the weather?

'You are looking exceptionally well this day,

Lady Pamela.' He spoke the words with courtly grace.

'You are too kind, sir,' she dutifully replied, uttering the proper young lady's response to a compliment.

'I am surprised to see the duke has deserted your side for that of Lady Smythe. Of late he has been seen deep in conversation with you quite often, it seems to me — particularly at the various balls you both attend.'

Startled by his keen observation regarding the duke's attentions, such as they were, Pamela gave him a guarded look, then cautiously said, 'I believe it amuses the duke to chat with me from time to time. You may be certain that there is nothing serious in his civilities. It is merely happenstance that we manage to attend the same balls. You and I do the same, yet I doubt that our names would be linked — if you follow my reasoning.'

'I shouldn't mind that linkage,' he said, beaming a smile on Pamela that bordered on flirtation.

'Why, Lord Raeburn, I do believe you are teasing me,' Pamela said, chuckling at his expression of injury at her reply.

'Teasing or flirting, my lady?' he said with a charming grin.

'Ah,' Pamela said glancing at his pleasant

face, 'that is hard to say. Shall we explore the matter while we continue to walk?' She smiled at him as she had at the duke, that radiant grin that had caught His Grace totally by surprise as it now did Raeburn.

His look of astonishment gratified her, to say the least. Intent, no doubt, on discovering precisely what she meant, he led her toward a pond on which busily swam a number of ducks.

On the far side of the park the duke paused in his perambulations with Lady Smythe to seek out the slender form he'd tried to keep in view since she'd come with the Radcliffes. Once they arrived, Cecil had concentrated all his attention on his wife, totally ignoring Pamela. Good heavens, the chit might tumble into a bumble broth as trusting as she was. Where had she gone now?

'Find her?' the dulcet voice at his side said, breaking into his worries.

'I beg your pardon?' he said with exquisite courtesy.

'I was not born yesterday, Your Grace. You have kept an eye on a particular young lady from the moment she came with the Radcliffes. Is there some problem? I beg leave to tell you that I am not accustomed to being so treated.' Her words might have been scolding, but instead were laced with humor, for the lady undoubtedly knew that her pursuit was fruitless.

'And I thought I was being so terribly clever,' the duke replied, grinning down at her.

'You did not answer my question, Your Grace,' Lady Smythe scolded.

'I feel responsible for her, you see. She is far too trusting, and those scoundrels seek only her fortune. Would they have a regard for the person that she is, I might feel differently.' He tossed a worried glance at his companion, then turned to again search the park for Pamela.

Relief swept over him when he spotted her slim form in the distance by the pond. She walked with Lord Raeburn. The duke couldn't decide if that was good or bad.

As did Lady Smythe, Pamela wore a simple gown with a matching parasol. Free of having to display the sapphires and diamonds on her splendid bosom, she now wore a gown of pale rose and possessed the grace of a swaying spring bloom in the breeze. In the light afternoon breeze her skirt swirled about her, clinging to the lovely form Robert knew was concealed beneath all that fabric. It was upon further acquaintance that one discovered the charming lady beneath the pretty face. Pretty? Well, there were a number of words he might use — like intrepid and sensible, daring and decorous, but above all surprisingly sensual.

'She is with Raeburn,' he said at last.

'I have heard nothing dubious about the gentleman,' Lady Smythe replied with a curious look at his lordship. 'It seems to me that he merely chats with your friend.' Lady Smythe wisely refrained from calling Lady Pamela anything more intimate. If the girl was not the duke's particular interest, far be it from Lady Smythe to put it into his mind. Like many widows, she never gave up hope until her goal was past praying for.

'Nor have I,' the duke murmured as he turned about and began to walk — rather purposefully, her ladyship thought — in the direction of the little pond with the ducks.

The duke and Lady Smythe strolled softly toward Lady Pamela and Lord Raeburn, where they stood watching the antics of the ducks. Poor Pamela almost landed in the water when the duke spoke, his obviously unexpected voice startling her.

'Goodness, do you always go creeping up on people?'

'You were deeply engrossed in something? The ducks, perchance?' He gave Raeburn a look that must have made the other chap believe his collar was too tight, for he eased a finger inside to stretch it a bit.

'They are quite cunning, are they not?' Pamela said with a defiant glare at the duke.

Lady Smythe drifted over to stand close to Lord Raeburn, then began to converse in a soft, seductive voice that made Pamela positively squirm.

Seeing Raeburn and Lady Smythe thus engaged, Robert took Pamela's hand and tucking it within his, ambled along the shore of the pond in silence. She observed that he had not said a word to Lady Smythe or Lord Raeburn upon their leaving. Was that good or bad?

'You might have asked for my permission to walk with me,' she said at last.

'True,' he agreed. 'Would you have come?'

'Not likely,' she said with a faint snap in her tone.

'What have I done to deserve your censure?' he said, pausing beneath a chestnut tree that stood on a rise overlooking the pond.

Usually honest, Pamela looked straight into the eyes of the duke, studying his noble features with a critical eye. 'It has something to do with what I said while at Almack's. Perhaps,' and she plunged into the realm of fabrication, 'you read something into my words that were not intended?'

'I trust not,' he replied as though unsure of what she meant.

She moistened her lips with her tongue, quite nervous, uncertain of what she ought to confess and what she must leave unsaid. 'I would not have you think that I . . . that is, we, er, our, that is, the friendship we share is nothing more than that — friendship.'

It was not surprising that this muddled explanation left the duke even more confused than he'd been before.

'Surely, we are closer than mere friends, after all we have shared together?' he said as smoothly as a pearl sliding down satin. 'Do not forget the inn. I know I have not, I could not, and that isn't because of the baron.' He placed his free hand atop hers, stroking her gloved hand in a way that sent shivers through her spine.

'You are improper,' she whispered, flashing him a gaze that revealed far more than she might have wished.

'I am?' He gave her a quizzical look that set her heart beating in triple time.

'I believe we are being summoned for the nuncheon Lady Vane intends to serve.' Pamela began backing away from the enticing figure that stood so close to her. She would have tripped and fallen had he not reached out to calmly steady her. Restoring her hand to his arm, the couple rejoined the alfresco party.

'You were right,' she mused aloud.

'What about?' His voice was silky and possessed an intimate tone that made her quiver for some reason.

'You always get your way,' she said, somewhat vexed. 'Someday, someone will give you a much deserved set-down, and then we shall see how you like it. You will join the rest of us mere mortals.'

'I certainly hope so,' he said with such a hint of laughter in his voice that Pamela longed to swat him.

She politely detached herself from the duke, aware of several speculative glances that had come her way on their return. Settling near Lady Anne in the shade of a glorious oak tree, Pamela allowed the prince to join her on the rug that had been placed on the grass to keep the moisture at bay.

Echoing through the wooded glen the women's high, fluting voices blended with the lower notes belonging to the gentlemen to create a pleasant chorus, a background against which nothing much else could be heard.

'You disappeared, my sweet,' the prince observed quietly. 'Can it be that you found more tantalizing matters to discuss than a probable carriage and two?'

'As a topic for discussion the weather

captivates all the English, you must know,' she replied with a demure smile. 'It is ever changing, never dependable, and only can be counted upon to do what you do not wish.'

'And you spoke of the weather,' he said as though digesting this remarkable circumstance. 'How quaint. When I am with a lovely young woman, I do not think the weather a suitable topic of conversation. Rather' — and he gazed at Pamela with soulful eyes — 'I believe it far more interesting to speak of warmer things — like beauty and love.'

'Fie, sir, you flirt with impropriety,' she scolded.

'And how does your Season go, my lady?' he asked suddenly, surprising Pamela greatly.

'My Season? Well enough. I must say, having that necklace from my great-uncle has added unexpected moments to what would be an otherwise ordinary come-out.' She watched his face, wondering if he would reveal any possible motive for wanting the necklace. She'd not forgotten his initials, and he persisted in pursuing her in spite of her lack of encouragement.

'The necklace is magnificent, you know.' He drained the glass of wine he'd held in his hands, then set the empty glass carefully on the rug before looking at her again. 'I would like to have a necklace like that.'

Pamela held her breath, wondering what he'd give as a reason, if any. 'Yes?'

'There is a woman in Russia.' He looked into the distance as though he could envision this creature of his mind. 'She is slim like a fairy and wears her long blond hair in a halo about her head. She would do those sapphires and diamonds great justice, you understand. I would impress her with such a gift.'

'And you love her quite passionately, do you not?' Pamela said in a soft, gentle, probing voice.

'Indeed,' he murmured, then realized what he had admitted almost at once. 'What have I said?' he muttered with a disgusted shake of his head.

'I am not surprised, you know. After all, you have far more in common with a Russian lady than with an English girl. It is only reasonable to surmise that you would have an inamorata in your homeland.'

'But,' he paused, then slowly continued, 'you are also lovely and to be admired.' For a moment he truly looked sincere, and for that she blessed him.

'Thank you. Perhaps you will find a way to attain your lady without a sapphire-and-diamond necklace?' Privately, Pamela thought a Russian lady might welcome the handsome prince even lacking such an inducement.

He stared longingly at her for a moment, then sighed. 'Since it is not logical that you would bestow a jewel on me, I must look elsewhere.'

'You thought I might give you my great-uncle's jewels?' Pamela didn't know whether to laugh or ridicule the prince. Could he really be that foolish?

'Many women bestow jewels on me as a compensation for favors given,' he said without a trace of embarrassment.

'That might be. However, you have given me no favors.' She was truly amazed at his ingenuous impropriety.

'I would, were it permissible,' he said in the same silky manner Lord Raeburn had used not too long ago.

Pamela laughed, knowing the prince might be offended, but unable to hold in her mirth at the ridiculous notion he presented her. 'Your Highness, I am an unmarried lady, the daughter of an earl reared to be of highest propriety.' She ignored the niggling admonition that she had been highly improper with the duke on any number of occasions. 'It is inconceivable that I might consider such behavior.'

The prince nodded sadly and sat with her awhile longer before he rose, bowed over her hand, then sauntered off toward a very wealthy young woman who had an insipid face, an abundance of freckles, and a large ruby pendant.

Lady Vane flinched when a servant brushed against her arm. When the lady saw Pamela's sympathetic look, she joined the little group beneath the oak tree.

'Are you enjoying your outing, Lady Pamela? I hope your company has proven entertaining?'

Wondering if the lady referred to Lord Raeburn and was jealous of his attentions to Pamela, she said, 'It has been lovely, truly it has. Everyone has been so kind. I trust you did not injure yourself while arranging our picnic?' she said with a gesture toward Lady Vane's arm. There was the faintest of bulges under the long, loose sleeve of her gown, most probably concealing a bandage.

'It is a mere bruise, nothing more. I tripped on a hall rug and fell against that dreadful statue my late husband kept in the hall. Fortunately, it will be there no longer, for it tumbled and broke,' her ladyship said with a light laugh. 'Nothing is so bad, but what it isn't good for something.'

'True,' Pamela said, thinking that it was unfortunate the statue had been destroyed, for she recalled the duke saying it was a prize example of antique sculpture.

The vicomte came over at that moment to join Pamela, bowing first to Lady Vane, with smooth compliments on the picnic, then to Lady Anne, with flattering words on her looks and liveliness, then to Pamela, with a request that he be allowed to join her.

'But of course,' Pamela replied, curious to see if the vicomte might be lured into revealing an interest in her necklace as had the prince. Since Vicomte Reynaud had not been in France — by his own admission — for many years, she doubted if he had a *bien-aimée* awaiting him there. So what attracted him to Pamela? With the vicomte, as with the prince, she was not so naive as to believe he merely sought her for her sparkling wit or her beauty.

'You do not eat enough to keep an *oiseau* alive,' the vicomte scolded when he saw her barely touched plate. 'Allow me to fetch you another glass of wine. That will encourage a *bon appétit.*'

'I am quite satisfied with what is on my plate, thank you. Relax and enjoy your own food.'

'Lady Vane does not have the French cook,' he complained in an aside to Pamela, leaning back against the tree and watching her with a speculative look on his handsome face.

'Perhaps not, but she tried to please us, and

I think it is lovely to eat out in the fresh air surrounded by country beauty.' Pamela nibbled at a piece of chicken to prove her point.

'You would like the south of France,' he said suddenly. 'The war is bound to be over before too long, and then you might travel there, to see the lovely countryside.'

His accent was more pronounced when he spoke of his homeland, and she wondered what he would find when, if ever, he returned there. He seemed like a fish out of water here. Although accepted by most of society, there always remained a hint of suspicion in people's minds, knowing he was French and the French were the enemy.

'I very much doubt if I shall see France. Most likely I will eventually marry and settle in the English countryside to rear a family. It is the accepted role for the daughter of a peer, and as the only daughter of an earl, I would wish for an heir.'

'Your husband would not be an earl, however?' He gave her an arrested look, almost considering.

'Not unless I marry an earl,' she agreed. 'But my parents are unlikely to allow me to marry outside the nobility so my children would still have titles of some kind or other.' An Englishman would have known all this, but she was curious why the vicomte would ask. By now he ought to be aware of English peerage styles.

'Ah, *chérie*, were we to wed, I could look forward to a restoration of prestige.'

'I am not your dearest, and we are not likely to marry,' she said without any anger. 'But why do you need prestige? Surely as Vicomte Reynaud, you have sufficient respect in society?'

'Never enough.' He frowned at her, then his gaze roved over her gown. It was not an insulting look, but rather one of taking stock of what he saw. Most curious, indeed, to Pamela.

'You have such lovely jewels,' he said at last.

The non sequitur threw her for a little, coming as it did following a reference to titles and marriage. 'Indeed, I do, at least for the time being.' She wondered how long it might be before she must hand it over to the true owner — if, indeed, he or she ever showed up.

'It must be returned? Soon?' he said, a note of alarm creeping into his voice. When he saw her expression, he added, 'It is only that you do sapphires and diamonds great credit.'

Since that was a lot of nonsense, Pamela turned to the contents of her plate and picked up a pastry. 'Do not think that I shall part with the necklace for any reason, unless my great-uncle should request its return,' she said before taking a bite of pastry.

'Your great-uncle may do this?'

'He is very old,' Pamela knew this for a fact, 'but he is still capable of doing a great many things, among which is to request that the necklace be returned to him at any time.'

'But you stand to inherit it, surely.'

She was fast becoming tired of the necklace, beautiful though it might be. To be sought after merely because she wore such magnificence became distressing after a time. 'I have no notion of what may be in his will.'

'I see,' he said, plunging deep into thought while Pamela proceeded to eat the excellent food.

Finishing her meal and thanking Lady Anne, Sir Cecil, and the vicomte for their company, she said, 'I believe I shall stroll about. There might be a few wildflowers begging to be picked.'

Absentmindedly, the pair murmured agreement, totally absorbed in one another, discussing plans for the future, while the vicomte sought more promising company.

Pamela had not gone far when she heard the swish of grass and the impatient snap of someone's fingers.

'How are you going along? Highly entertained by the gentlemen, no doubt?' the duke inquired with a tinge of annoyance in his voice.

'It has been illuminating,' she admitted, somehow unsurprised to see him here at her side again.

'How so?'

'The prince desires the necklace so he might make an impression on his adored Russian lady. The vicomte seeks a titled family — along with the wealth represented by the necklace — to restore his prestige. I am becoming tired of the type of man the necklace attracts. I would far prefer a modest swain who desired my company merely for me.'

'I can see that,' he agreed with a thoughtful frown settling on his brow.

'And I believe we must look elsewhere for the man we seek. Actually, I believe we must look for a couple. Do you not recall? The note was addressed to Lady Pamela from J. R., indicating they are a *pair*. If some mistress received the necklace from Lord Chudleigh — somehow it landed in the hands of a man who wanted this Lady Pamela to keep it safe for them. Oh, it all is so muddled and confusing.'

He touched her arm, wishing he might

draw her into his arms to comfort her, for he sensed she desired comfort. He wished for more, but wondered if she would be receptive, given her behavior earlier.

'I have a feeling it will all be over soon.'

16

Pamela mulled over the notion that the ordeal — if one might call it that — would be over on the way back to the city. Her silence was interrupted by Lady Anne.

'We have decided to give a grand ball,' her ladyship bubbled with a conscious look at her husband. 'A celebration.'

'Wonderful' Pamela said with delight, for it was enjoyable to see how happy these two were.

'You shall come, and of course, Wexford,' Lady Anne said, then enumerated other guests she intended to invite until the list was indeed a long one. 'Shall I include the prince and the vicomte?' she said with a mischievous glance at Pamela.

'Well, I will wear the necklace again. As the Season is drawing to a close, our chances of luring the culprit into the open will soon cease. The duke agrees with me that the prince and the vicomte are not likely suspects. For one thing, they flutter around opera dancers, but have no mistress in keeping,' Pamela concluded without regard for Lady Anne's possible sensibilities. 'And while they both want the necklace, I do not think they would steal it. It would be beneath them . . . at least I think so.'

'On the list they go, in any event. Young ladies never give up hope of snaring a title, and the prince is exceedingly romantic, particularly when he is attired all in white.'

'Another thing,' Pamela said, ignoring the bit about the prince, 'both of the gentlemen remained at the Chetwynd-Talbot ball. I checked later. They couldn't have shot at the duke.' She frowned, feeling that something she ought to see was eluding her. Was there someone who'd left the ball?

The carriage rattled to a halt before the Gresham home, and Pamela momentarily put aside the frustration of locating the true owner of the necklace and the identity of the person who sought to steal it. She had felt for some time that the thief who broke into her room and the would-be robber were one and the same, even had she not seen his face.

'Thank you for taking me along and for the invitation to your ball. I'm sure it will be utterly splendid. If there is any way I might help, do not hesitate . . .'

'Invitations,' Lady Anne interrupted. 'Do say you will help me write them. And the menu — your suggestions would assist me with that as well. I want everything to be special,' she concluded with a fond look at her husband and a smile when he squeezed her hand in response.

'I'd be delighted,' Pamela said, suppressing a grin. 'Tomorrow?'

'Sunday afternoon, I believe. I know you spend a quiet day, and your mother ought not object to your writing invitations.'

Pamela nodded, knowing her mother would be most agreeable to her plans.

★ ★ ★

The following Sunday afternoon she sat in the Radcliffe library, addressing invitations and occasionally allowing her thoughts to drift back to the days when she had been installed in this room with the duke for company. It took hours to inscribe the names and direction on each invitation, especially since Lady Anne kept placing additional names on the list.

'Your house will overflow,' Pamela protested with a rueful smile.

'Pooh bah,' Lady Anne said gaily. 'A number of them will possibly be occupied that night, I make no doubt. We will have the cream, and that is what counts. My friends would never let me down.'

How marvelous to have such confidence in friends, Pamela thought. And yet, how good and kind Lady Anne had been, and Sir Cecil as well. Even the duke, while revealing a propensity for stolen kisses, had stood by her in the search for the criminal. Pamela had never been allowed to form friendships at home, for there was no one of suitable rank for her to befriend. School had been different, but the girls had all married, now occupied in other pursuits.

She was nearing the last of the crisp white vellum sheets when Sir Cecil and the duke entered the room. 'Good afternoon,' she said politely.

'How comforting you are,' the duke said. 'One can always count on you to do the polite, no matter what.'

'Far better that than to be rude,' she retorted with a pointed glare. '*I* am comforted by your remark that this will all soon be over. I do not see how or when the thief will attack again. As you know he must, with the Season so near the end.'

'Perhaps at the coming ball?' the duke joked.

'I hope not,' Lady Anne cried. 'I'd not have our ball turned into a scandal or worse.'

'Maybe an *on-dit* for a few days,' the duke

amended when he received a look from Sir Cecil.

'What do you intend to wear?' Lady Anne inquired of Pamela. 'More blue and white?'

With a hasty glance at the duke, Pamela described the dress. 'I have a gown of white Florence satin trimmed with Mechlin lace. The neckline is properly low to display the necklace.'

'Improper, should you ask me,' the duke murmured — at least that's what Pamela thought he said.

'You will glitter, I am sure, and the dress sounds interesting. Tell me more,' Lady Anne begged. So the two women left the table to sit on the window seat and discuss their gowns, quickly absorbed in flounces and tucks.

'Do you really think that chap may make an attempt to steal the jewels at our ball?' Sir Cecil asked the duke, a worried look in his eyes.

'Time is growing short. So far there has been no question regarding the tale about the great-uncle. I almost believe it myself, I've told it so often.'

'What will you do?'

'I intend to keep a close watch on Pamela, and if that sends a few tongues wagging, it's too bad. I shall also keep a pistol handy in the house, with your permission. Pity that evening dress doesn't allow for a bulge of that sort,' he concluded with wry humor. 'However, it might be wise to have a Runner on hand, just in case.'

Confident that all could be accomplished in record time with Pamela to assist Lady Anne and willing servants to carry out her every whim, the ball was set for a week's time.

Acceptances poured in, covering the library table in no time at all.

'I think you will have a sad crush, dear Anne,' Pamela said, omitting the title as her friend now insisted. 'Even Lady Vane and Lord Raeburn have accepted.'

'I thought it proper to include them, although I do not know them well at all. The picnic, you see.'

And Pamela saw perfectly. One always repaid social obligations.

★ ★ ★

Wednesday night at Almack's was aflutter with the latest scandal. A baron's daughter had run off with her footman, taking some of the family jewels with her.

'You see,' the prince said when he conducted Pamela through a dance, 'there are women who will *use* jewelry to a good purpose.'

'I doubt her parents look at it that way,' she said.

'Bah! Scruples! That is well if you can afford them.'

Pamela was glad she did not care for the prince. She would not wish to be married to one who thought as he did.

The vicomte was little better in his view of the matter, thus disappointing Pamela, who'd thought more of him.

'I should find myself a little maid who would bring me the contents of her father's safe. Would you, *chérie*? Would you bring me that splendid necklace if we ran off together?' That richly seductive voice chilled Pamela when she considered what he said and implied. She was insulted that he would dare to ask.

'No,' Pamela replied, flashing a look of disdain at him. Was this it? Were his intentions to lure her away so he might snatch the jewelry?

Leaving the dance floor he failed to return Pamela to her mother, going to the refreshment room instead. After handing her a lemonade, he ambled at her side, brooding upon something.

'Is everything all right?' she finally asked.

'No, but I cannot involve you. Debts of honor, you understand. I have paid all I can; the fellow demands more. Perhaps I can find another lamb I will not mind fleecing.'

'Forgive me if I do not wish you well in your quest.' She understood only too well. Perhaps the money was owed to that man he'd given the packet the night she and the duke had trailed him? He needed money, and for some odd reason he was not to seek it through her. She supposed she was grateful in a way, but it stung to know that it was the necklace and her fortune that had brought him to her side.

She was not sorry to leave Almack's.

★ ★ ★

The following days were spent mostly with Lady Anne, urging her to rest while Pamela saw to dozens of details necessary to insure a successful party. Since Anne's gown was blue, blue and white flowers were ordered from the florist, little blue dishes for the foods to be served — all ordered from Gunter's. Blue bows decorated pillars, urns, and just about everything else. When queried on the bows, Anne had a simple answer.

'Well, I am going to provide dearest Cecil with his heir, and I think it a lovely idea.'

Put that way, the bows made perfect sense. And even had they not, Pamela wouldn't have said a word.

* * *

The evening of the ball found Pamela with her nerves on edge. That the duke was convinced the crook would make an attempt this evening did not give comfort. It made her wary and suspicious as she studied each man who entered the house to see if there might be something ominous about him.

'Reached any conclusion as yet?' the duke asked quietly at her side. At her startled look, he laughed and continued, 'I have learned how your mind works, and I guessed you would examine everyone for signs of impending thievery.'

Hoping he did not know all her thoughts, she merely nodded. 'Silly, I know, but it does make me uneasy.'

'Do you suspect even your friends?' he questioned softly as the prince entered with a flourish, wearing white again and looking spectacular. Behind him the vicomte entered the room with that wealthy young woman who had the fortune along with a bland face and freckles, not to mention the ruby pendant.

'I believe I have been supplanted,' Pamela said, not answering his query about her friends. She turned to greet Lady Vane.

'Lady Pamela,' Lady Vane said with a gentle smile, 'you look ravishing this evening. Each gown you select to display the jewels is more superb than the last, I vow.'

'Thank you, Lady Vane,' Pamela said absently, noting that the duke had left her side to greet Lady Smythe. The exquisite courtesy he displayed to that woman was enough to turn any young woman green, and Pamela in particular.

'It seems they are old friends,' Lord Raeburn said when he paused beside Pamela and noticed the direction in which she was looking. 'He seems to enjoy her company, as do a number of others, I might add.'

'She is quite beautiful,' Pamela said in a tight little voice.

'Indeed.' He looked at Pamela, then gazed about the large drawing room with speculative eyes. 'Everyone is here.' He sounded pleased.

Pamela was distracted by a request from one of the serving maids. She was needed to solve a minor crisis.

On the far side of the room, the duke listened to the social chitchat issuing from Lady Smythe while scanning the guests to take careful note of who had arrived and what they wore. Bearing in mind Pamela's description of a slender man above average height, he was able to cross off a considerable number of men, thus reducing the possible suspects. He admitted — to himself, only — that he was uneasy about the evening. It seemed so simple. Merely to keep tabs on slender, moderately tall men? He noted that Pamela walked over to join them. Lady Smythe discreetly drifted away.

'Well, what do you think?' Pamela asked quietly as the musicians struck up a waltz. Lady Anne had insisted that there be a great number of waltzes this evening. Since it was her celebration, who would argue?

'We shall talk while we waltz. You are exceptionally light on your feet and dance the waltz as though born to it.' He swept her into his embrace and began circling the room in perfect tempo.

Pamela remained silent a few moments to savor the feel of his arms about her, knowing full well that if they solved the mystery, this evening could likely be her last opportunity to dance with him. Others joined them — mostly those who had engaged in the morning waltzing parties. They made a lovely, colorful pattern on the floor, had Pamela bothered to look.

She couldn't, for her eyes remained focused on the duke's face, memorizing every line. Why had she never guessed the beauty that could be held in gray eyes? The rich depths, the warmth!

The duke watched the changing expression on Pamela's face. What her thoughts held he could only guess. She looked like a princess this evening, the low-cut gown revealing more of that splendid bosom than it really ought. The sapphires and diamonds sparkled against her soft skin. The tiny puffed sleeves trimmed in exquisite lace emphasized her slim, perfect arms, and the cut of her gown accented her breasts, her tiny waist, and nicely rounded hips as well. Pamela had once referred to herself as ordinary. Would that the world be blessed with more ordinary women, were that the case.

They were close to solving the case; he felt heightened tension in the air. Yet he had no intention of ending matters with Pamela. He had mentioned her name to his redoubtable mother the other day. That good lady hadn't blinked an eye but merely nodded, saying that Lady Pamela came from good stock, had a respectable dowry, and was a pretty behaved girl. High praise, indeed.

And . . . she was going to be all his! There was no way in the world that he would permit another man to know those enchanting kisses or the feel of Pamela trustingly snuggled up against him. Robert thought she would slip into the role of his duchess with perfect charm, just as she entered his arms with such impeccable grace.

Both of them were reluctant to part when the waltz ended. Pamela felt a trifle dizzy, but expected it came from being in the duke's arms and not just revolving about the room.

'Come with me, my dear,' the duke insisted quietly but firmly, 'we must go over our plans once again.'

Willingly going along with the duke — although she hadn't a foggy clue what plans he meant — she avoided eye contact with any gentlemen, lest she be compelled to accept another's hand for a dance when that was the last thing she wanted at the moment.

He led her straight to the small conservatory at the rear of the house. Closing the door behind him — most improperly, he knew — he drew Pamela into his arms and proceeded to kiss her as he had longed to do these many days. And nights. Oh, yes, indeed, the nights.

The delight of it all was that she did not resist him in the least, but yielded so sweetly to his caress and kiss. His hands slid over the satin, learning the curves and hollows of her, cherishing the reality of his dreams.

A sound in the hall brought them both to their senses.

'Forgive me, I seem to yield to impropriety far too often when tempted by you,' he said, holding her close for a moment, then releasing her.

'You do seem to like having your way, as I believe I said once before,' Pamela whispered with a smile when she drew away. 'You mentioned plans?'

'It was a ruse,' he admitted, 'but we shall talk more later. As to this evening, simply beware of everyone.'

'How dreadful, to suspect one and all.'

'Much as I'd rather remain here with you, my sweet, we had best return. Pause in the withdrawing room for a few moments so to draw away any comment from us.' As he spoke, he led a bemused Pamela along the hall, giving her a loving, gentle nudge when they reached the withdrawing room. 'I will await you in the ballroom.'

She stared at her flushed, starry-eyed face. Anne had placed a bowl of rice powder on the table with cotton-wool puffs to use. Pamela fluffed a bit of powder on her cheeks and nose, then patted her hair before turning to leave.

Lady Vane entered just as Pamela reached

for the doorknob. 'How lovely to see you here. My, you do look splendid, my dear girl. A special gentleman?'

Pamela merely smiled mysteriously and nodded.

'How nice,' the gentle lady replied with a soft smile. 'Is there a maid around? No? I wonder if you could help me with a flounce I seem to have torn. There, in the back.'

'There are pins on the table. I can try to pin it in place if you like,' Pamela offered, admiring the rich blue ballgown with its long sleeves and slender skirt. A single flounce decorated the gown and had been sadly ripped at the back hem. Pamela couldn't figure out how, because the gown didn't trail on the floor in the least. Well, there were extremely clumsy men — she had danced with a few.

'How sweet you are,' Lady Vane commented when Pamela knelt to pin the flounce in place, crushing her own gown slightly in the process.

'There you are, all done,' Pamela said, rising quickly to her feet and returning to the door again.

'I understand there is to be a splendid repast later. Did you help Lady Anne? I suppose so, for I've noticed you are very close. How nice for you, but then, things seem to come your way quite easily.'

Pamela frowned at the words, thinking they didn't sound quite right. 'Would you like to see the tables?'

'May I? That would be lovely.' Lady Vane slipped her hand around Pamela's arm, clasping it tightly. It was a contradiction to her softly spoken words that puzzled Pamela.

'Oh, is this the library?' Lady Vane paused in the hall, tossing Pamela an appealing look. 'Do you think I might have a look at it?' She pulled Pamela into the room without waiting for a reply. 'What a perfectly charming room. And the window!' she exclaimed, drawing Pamela over to stare out at the night. Nothing could be seen, but Lady Vane seemed enthralled. She turned to examine the rest of the room — the shelves of finely bound books, the magnificent desk and leather chairs, and a lovely globe that occupied a stand near the door.

The room held precious associations for Pamela. She studied the woman at her side, wondering what could possibly draw her to this place.

'Ah, there you are, Julius,' Lady Vane said in a softly satisfied way.

Pamela looked up to see Lord Raeburn framed in the doorway. He entered the room. Julius? That sounded overly familiar for Lady

Vane to say to a gentleman.

'Actually, he is Egbert Julius, but prefers Julius, as do I,' Lady Vane purred.

'Indeed, my Lady Pamela. You said you would do it, and you have.' He added to an obviously confused Pamela, 'Did you know you and Lady Vane share first names?'

Utterly bewildered, Pamela stared first at Lord Raeburn, then Lady Vane. Was she dreaming? 'Do what?' Pamela decided to ask, feeling more and more uneasy.

'Bring you here,' he replied with a sly smile.

Stunned, Pamela looked from one to the other, her mind spinning as she assimilated the information. He was Julius, Lord Raeburn, J.R. She was Pamela, Lady Vane — called Lady Pamela by Lord Raeburn. The pieces fell into place with startling clarity. Oddly enough, she remembered that Lady Vane lived not far away down a side street in Mayfair. A respectable address, and the number matched that of Gresham House.

Mounting fear possessed her. Pamela placed her hands protectively to her throat. 'What is going on here? Why are you both staring at me that way?'

'You must have guessed. We want the necklace, my dear Lady Pamela,' Lady Vane's caressing voice commanded. 'How fortunate you are that I am not a vindictive creature, else I'd pay you for that bump on the head and the graze on my arm.' She smiled sweetly at Pamela. Only it seemed to her that the smile had a deadly quality to it. There was no hint of meekness now.

'It was you?' Pamela cried, aware that it was unlikely that the guests would hear a sound from the paneled room so removed from the rest of the house.

'You never guessed, did you?' Lord Raeburn said, walking toward Pamela, his hands rising to remove the necklace from her throat.

'Why was the necklace delivered to me?' Pamela managed to say, frightened to death and wishing that someone would rescue her at once.

'A mistake,' Raeburn said. 'My entrusted man confused the streets, although he had the correct number. Sheer ill luck that there was a Pamela at both numbers. You see,' he boasted, 'my lady had given me the necklace to have it appraised. I was returning it to her for safekeeping. We were astounded to see the necklace at your throat, learn of your supposed great-uncle. You wished to lure us, we wished to conceal our identity. Pity we could not.'

Pamela backed away from him, coming to a

halt against the sill of the window. There was nowhere else to turn. Lady Vane stood close by, her sweet smile looking slightly twisted now, and her eyes glittering with malice.

'Perhaps you might prefer to remove the necklace of your own accord,' she said in a low, dulcet tone that sent chills down Pamela's spine.

'How did you acquire the necklace in the first place?' she demanded of Raeburn, making a pretense of removing the necklace while praying she might find a way to prevent what she knew was to happen.

'Chudleigh came over quite handsomely,' Lady Vane said smugly. 'Julius thought it would make a splendid addition to our cache, and it will. The baron contributed matching earbobs, you know, as well as a number of other lovely pieces. It was a pity that he became so possessive. I truly hated to kill him. He'd been so useful.'

Lady Vane had killed the baron? Also been Chudleigh's mistress. Pamela darted a look at the woman, wondering how she could do such things. She had shown no remorse at the baron's death. What manner of woman was she? How could Lord Raeburn permit the woman he obviously cared for to place herself in another man's arms? Commit murder!

'It was you who climbed into my room,'

357

Pamela accused Lady Vane. 'And you also tried to steal the necklace, shooting at the duke. And you deliberately led us to where you had left the baron dead at the inn — or did you murder him while we hovered below on the stairs? I sensed something odd about the robber, but couldn't figure out what it was!' Pamela cried in vexation.

'The necklace,' Raeburn demanded. 'We do not have all night.'

Deliberately fumbling with the catch, Pamela murmured, 'This may take a few moments. Sometimes the catch is stubborn.' When Raeburn moved as though to assist, Pamela shook her head. 'Leave be. I'd as soon do it myself.'

'Independent miss, are you not? I thought you such a proper young lady,' Lady Vane sneered. Her soft voice had acquired a hard edge to it. 'Why, butter wouldn't melt in your mouth.'

'No words, my love,' Raeburn admonished, holding out his hand for the necklace.

Both Raeburn and Lady Vane took another step closer to her, facing her in a most menacing manner. Pamela prayed that someone would come.

At that moment she saw the door soundlessly inched open. The duke slipped inside, motioning Pamela to remain silent.

She gave no indication that she'd seen him, instead pretended to be intent upon removing the necklace. The pistol in his hand was trained on Lord Raeburn.

'I cannot imagine how you think you will get away from here with the jewels.' Pamela finally undid the clasp, knowing there was only so long she could stall.

'Quite simple. After you're bound, gagged, and hidden behind the desk, I pocket the necklace, and we walk out of here, down the hall, and out to our waiting carriage. We will drive to Dover and take a boat to Brussels. From there the world is at our feet. You see,' he boasted, 'this is the culmination of a highly successful Season. It has been so easy to take what we wanted — until you. We have a tidy fortune tucked away by now, and this necklace will cap it. It is time for us to leave.' He held out his hand.

Instead of handing the necklace over to Raeburn, Pamela slipped it down inside the neck of her gown, allowing the precious stones to nestle against her breasts, certain that her ample cleavage and snug fit of the dress would keep them there.

'You little fool,' Raeburn snarled, stepping forward to place a hand at the neckline of Pamela's gown as though to rip it open.

'That is quite enough, my lord,' the duke

said. 'Step away from her if you wish to remain alive.' His words were a sharp retort in the room.

Raeburn spun around, breathing in sharply when he saw the duke facing him, pistol in hand. 'You wouldn't shoot,' he scoffed. 'You might hit Lady Pamela.'

Lady Vane moved to Pamela's side in a trice, reaching toward her bodice to pull the jewelry from its hiding place.

'If you touch her, I will not hesitate to shoot. I'm accounted a dead aim and will have as little mercy for you as you did the baron. Forget the necklace,' the duke warned.

'No! I'll not leave it. I have worked hard for it, and it's mine!' Lady Vane ripped the bodice of Pamela's satin gown with fearsome ease, allowing the jewels to spill forth.

Her ladyship grabbed them while Pamela helplessly clutched at her gown, for the jewels weren't all that had spilled forth.

The shot was not as loud as one might expect, given the size of the room, but it hit its target with deadly aim. Lady Vane crumpled to the floor in a sigh.

Whipping a pistol from an inner pocket, Raeburn grabbed Pamela, thrusting her in front of him. 'I will take the necklace, and you'll not stop me,' he said in a cold, hard voice. 'Lady Pamela will be between us at all times. You'll not shoot her!'

'This is insane,' Pamela cried. She gave the duke a beseeching look, bending down when Raeburn tugged at her, then rising when he'd retrieved the necklace from the unconscious Lady Vane. Pamela kept her hands at the top of her gown, in part to hold it together and partly to calm her racing heart.

They edged toward the door, always with Pamela before him. The silence in the room was broken only by Lady Vane's faint moans and the soft scuffling sound of shoes sliding sideways on the wooden floor.

They had reached the table where Pamela had spent hours poring over the peerage to discover who the other Pamela might be. And now that other woman lay a few feet away. Angry past caution, Pamela wrenched her arm from Lord Raeburn's grasp, then dropped to the floor, scrabbling away from Raeburn, knowing that he couldn't have his pistol aimed at the duke and herself at once and praying it wasn't aimed at her now.

A shot rang out, and Pamela felt as though her heart might stop until she realized that the figure who slumped to the floor was behind her. Twisting around she saw Raeburn clutching his right arm, the pistol now dangling loosely from his fingers. Quick as may be, she grabbed the pistol from Raeburn and aimed it at him.

'Good girl,' the duke muttered as he stooped to check Raeburn, rising when he was satisfied that the wound was not mortal. 'You, sir, will stand trial. Although it will be at the House of the Lords and the outcome is dubious, for all that robbery is a hanging offense. But perhaps when your victims learn how numerous they are, they will demand satisfaction. Newgate is not a pretty place, I understand,' the duke concluded in a great understatement of the truth, 'especially when you do not have the funds to purchase a private room on the State side.'

The necklace tumbled to the floor, escaping from Raeburn's loosened clasp. Pamela grabbed it, then clutched her bodice again at the gleam she saw in the duke's eyes when he looked at her. She prudently rose to her feet, then backed toward the desk, unwilling to leave the duke alone. She didn't trust Raeburn in the least, even if he'd been shot.

A loud rap at the door announced the entry of a man in the garb of a Bow Street Runner. 'Sorry it took me so long, Your Grace. Was detained. 'Pears you done fine wi'out me.' He looked at one, then the other of the robbers and shook his head, before turning to arrange for transport.

Soon Lady Vane had been silently removed to another room. The physician in attendance determined she would live to stand trial. The bandaged Lord Raeburn was discreetly taken in hand by the Bow Street Runner. Finally, Robert was at last alone with Pamela.

Mercifully, the Radcliffes, absorbed in their ball, had been in blissful ignorance of all that had transpired. They would learn soon enough.

'At last we are free to settle our own affairs,' His Grace said, studying Pamela's face.

'We are?' she asked, her expression wary.

'Now, as to our future,' he said, enfolding her in his arms, where he'd wanted his brave darling this long and dangerous evening, resolving never to allow her far from him again. 'We shall be married in six weeks, I believe, if that meets with your approval,' he said, mindful of what she'd said about his always having his way. 'I find the thought of parting from you totally insupportable. You will have me, dearest Pamela?'

'Yes, I believe I shall,' she replied with a smile, satisfied at that hint of anxiousness she'd detected in his face.

'Precious girl,' he said with approval. 'Sensible, daring, generous-hearted, delightful. I could spend long minutes cataloging your many fine qualities, but I would far rather do this instead.' And 'this' turned out to be a most passionate and exquisite kiss, causing Pamela to melt quite shamelessly against him, wishing that the coming six weeks would whirl past as quickly as these last days had.

'We shall have to think of a way to settle the matter of the necklace, I suppose,' she murmured against the comfort of his chest within the clasp of his strong, protective arms. 'I am certain it is not proper for me to keep it, no matter that I adore it.'

The duke, thinking of the many charms of his dearly beloved girl and how he relished the sight of the sapphires and diamonds twinkling against her lovely skin replied, 'There are times when propriety can go hang, my love. Since Lord Chudleigh refused to acknowledge his purchase of the jewels, why you will simply inherit the gems from your great-uncle after all. And they do you exceedingly great credit,' he finished with his mouth against the tenderness of her throat. He leaned back a moment to glance down at the unmended gown and the treasure it no longer concealed, and dared to kiss the bare flesh that had recently cushioned the necklace.

'I believe you have a superfluity of

naughtiness, Your Grace,' she said with a twinkle in her eye. Then she slipped her arms about his neck, turned her face up to receive his kiss, and proved that he was right again.

Dashing, debonair, he always had his way.

We do hope that you have enjoyed reading this large print book.

Did you know that all of our titles are available for purchase?

We publish a wide range of high quality large print books including:
Romances, Mysteries, Classics
General Fiction
Non Fiction and Westerns

Special interest titles available in large print are:
The Little Oxford Dictionary
Music Book
Song Book
Hymn Book
Service Book

Also available from us courtesy of Oxford University Press:
Young Readers' Dictionary
(large print edition)
Young Readers' Thesaurus
(large print edition)

For further information or a free brochure, please contact us at:
Ulverscroft Large Print Books Ltd.,
The Green, Bradgate Road, Anstey,
Leicester, LE7 7FU, England.
Tel: (00 44) **0116 236 4325**
Fax: (00 44) **0116 234 0205**

Other titles published by
The House of Ulverscroft:

ALTHEA'S GRAND TOUR

Emily Hendrickson

Althea Ingram longs for a gentleman she can look up to, but, for the London dandies, it's her dowry that attracts, not her regally tall and lovely person. She flees to Europe and finds John Maitland, the Earl of Montmorcy. His towering physique and good looks are all she dreams of in a man. Unfortunately, the Earl finds that her delicate, beautiful companion, Cecily de Lisle, fits his idea about the weaker sex, not the fiercely independent Althea. Althea must take care not to fall in love with the Earl, though he presses her over the precipice of dangerous desire . . .

THE DASHING MISS FAIRCHILD

Emily Hendrickson

Rich and beautiful, Clare Fairchild decides to travel to Bath but, prior to her departure from a Marlborough inn, someone abandons an infant in her carriage. No parents or nanny can be discovered . . . Once in Bath, however, Richard Talbot, an old friend, offers to help solve the mystery. But after they confront the suspected villain, their lives are put in mortal danger. Clare discovers Richard's strength most comforting, whilst Richard, finding Clare ever more enchanting, longs to make her his own. Between the gossips of Bath and the danger of their quest, will they survive to make this possible?